·MOUNTAIN·
Freedom

·MOUNTAIN· Freedom

Johny Weber

Hildebrand Books
an imprint of W. Brand Publishing
NASHVILLE, TENNESSEE

Hildebrand Books an imprint of W. Brand Publishing
j.brand@wbrandpub.com
www.wbrandpub.com

Cover design by JuLee Brand | designchik

Mountain Freedom / Johny Weber — 1st Edition

Available in Paperback, Kindle, and eBook formats.
Paperback ISBN: 979-8-89503-006-6
eBook ISBN: 979-8-89503-007-3

Library of Congress Control Number: 2024924337

CONTENTS

To my "non-horse" friends, who walk with me through life...

Val, who was the first "reader" of my books and encouraged me to continue,

And to Jeanie, Patty, Heidi, Jayne, Kathy, Carol, and Gayle, who with their friendship always support me.

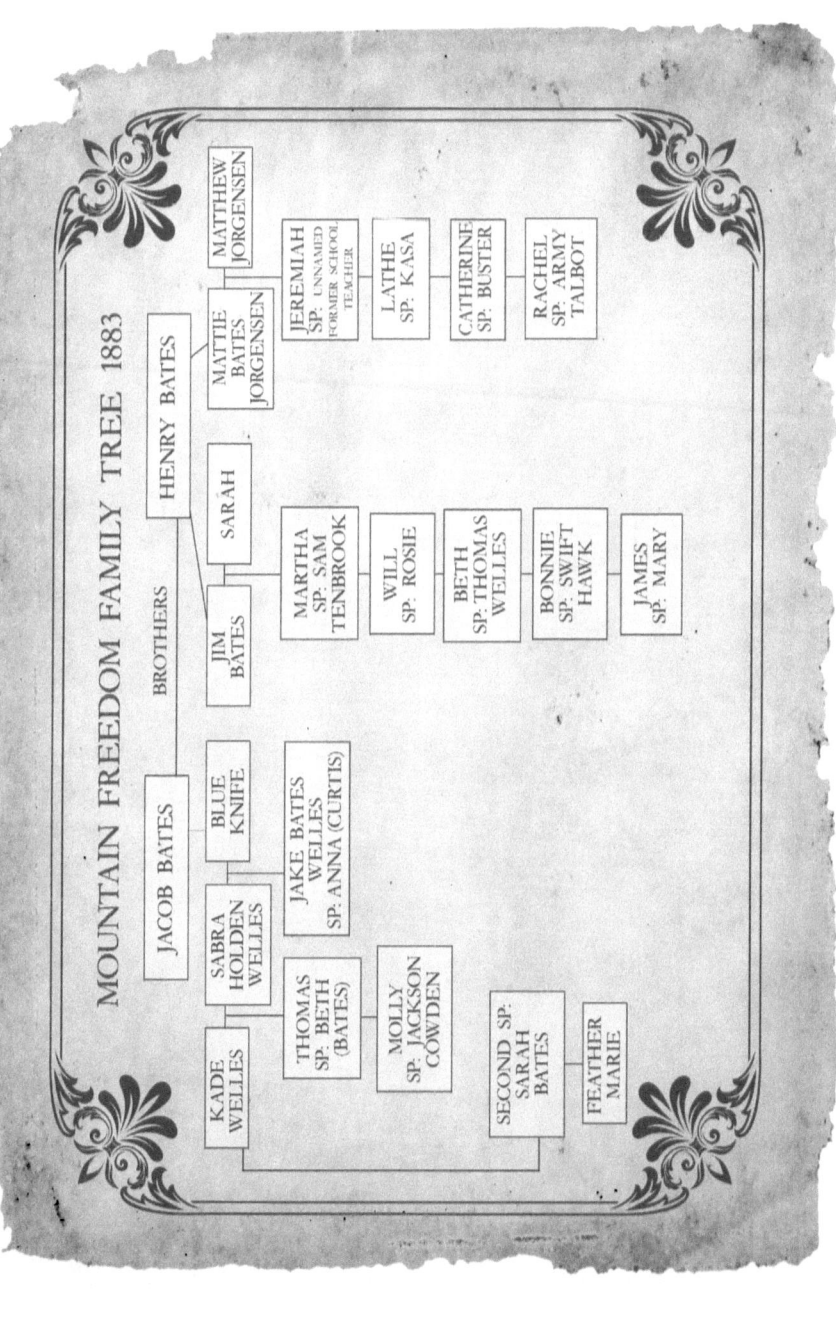

MOUNTAIN FREEDOM FAMILY TREE 1883

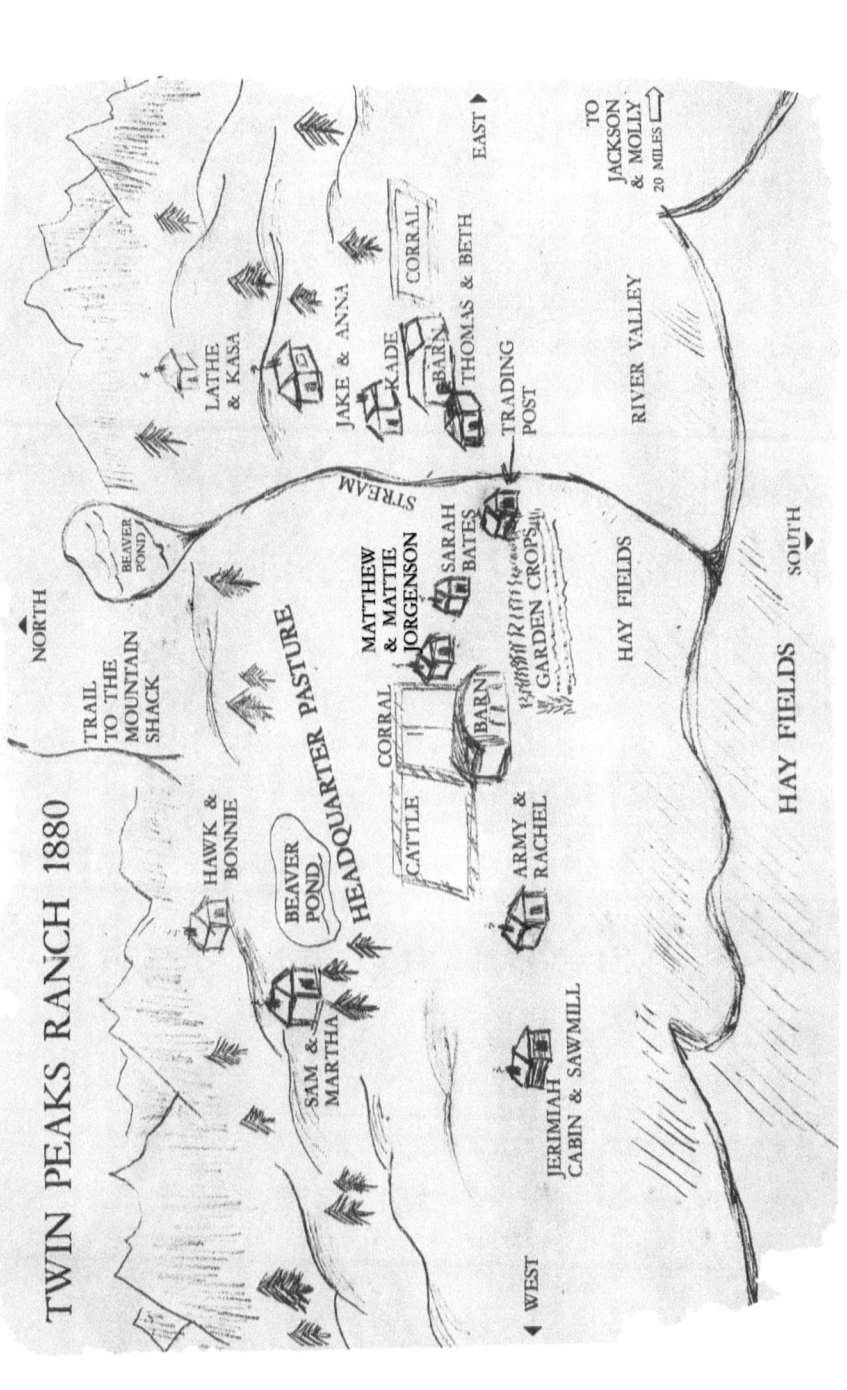

CHAPTER 1

Selling Horses – Late Summer 1883

"You aren't going to throw my clothes out and burn them, are you?" Jake asked Anna, softly nuzzling her neck.

They were standing in front of the cabin. Jake held the reins to his saddled horse and had gathered his "possibles," as his pa used to call supplies. Jake's packs and a bedroll were tied on the back of the saddle. Anna looked up at Jake and smiled, giving him a little push.

"I only wanted to do that once," she said. "But you better be good."

"Woman, I'm always good," Jake pulled her against him again. "You take care of the kids. Pa will look in on you, and Lathe will be back tonight too."

"How long will you be gone?"

"I think a week or ten days, but could be up to two weeks," Jake answered. "We will come back by the river. I want to stop and see Molly. I haven't seen her since she was home last Easter."

"Tell your sister hello from me," Anna replied. Then she smiled at her husband, "Just don't go everywhere Luke goes," Anna cautioned. "I know what bachelor men want, and you aren't a bachelor."

Jake laughed at her. A pretty twenty-six-year-old white woman, Anna was a slave in a band of Cheyenne when Jake bought her nine years earlier. Being raised by Indians allowed Anna to speak more easily about things a white woman usually didn't discuss. Native peoples were more comfortable with sexuality. "You are the only woman for me," Jake soothed. "If Luke wants to carouse, he will have to do it alone." Jake hesitated, thinking. "Anyway, what you are thinking about isn't a group activity. Quit your worrying."

Anna smiled at her husband. Only a little taller than she, Jake was her rock. His dark skin contrasted with her white, and she knew that when strangers came upon them, they looked curiously at the handsome part-Ute man with his white wife. But Anna was captured by Indians as a young child and raised in a tribe. Sometimes, she was more Indian than Jake, who was raised by his white family and only spent time during the summer with his Native relatives. Anna could be a jealous woman, and in the early years of their marriage, she became furious if he left her behind when he traveled. But she learned to trust him. In time, Anna knew he was good and was devoted to her. She loved him for it.

"Well, just be careful then," Anna cautioned.

"Beautiful Bird," Jake answered, using the Ute name he had given her. "I'm going to sell horses, not go to war."

"Rides the Wind," Anna answered solemnly, also using his Indian name, "whenever you go to white man country, you go to war. Come home to me."

Two hours before the sun heralded noon, Jake and his cousin, Lathe, pushed the small herd of horses into the mountain meadow. They could see the campfire outside the shack.

"Luke must still have coffee on," Lathe called. "He's a good man."

Jake grinned. "He better be, or we'd fire his ass," Jake returned.

They let the loose horses spread out onto the expansive meadow. They could graze or drink from the upland stream that ran through the meadow until the men were ready to push on. Lathe and Jake rode on to the cabin.

Luke had his string of saddle horses lounging in the corral, except for one saddled at the corral fence and one pack animal loaded and ready. He rose by the fire and taking the coffeepot from it, he filled two mugs.

"You made good time," Luke commented. "Set and grab a bite of meat before we head out."

"Left just at dawn," Lathe replied. "Easy pushing these horses up here. Most of them have been here before."

Lathe was a lean, blond-haired young cowboy with clear blue eyes and a ready laugh. Eight years younger than Jake, Lathe, now twenty-six, had followed Jake on his travels since he was eighteen. At twenty, Lathe had married Jake's niece, Kasa. Kasa, the name translated as Dressed in Furs, was a pretty part-Ute girl and daughter of Jake's late half-brother, Brown Otter. Through the mountain man, Jacob Bates, Kasa was also a very distant relative to Lathe. Old Jacob Bates was Jake's grandfather, Kasa's great-grandfather, and Lathe's great-uncle. Family ties wound their way through the men and women of Twin Peaks Ranch, both white and red.

Lathe and Jake dismounted, loosening the cinches on their horses. They hobbled the animals and took off the bridles before going to the fire. The horses could graze before they pushed on.

"Got some deer steaks and hotcakes ready to go," Luke said. "Reckon, you could eat before we head out."

"Good man," Lathe grinned. "Nothing like stopping where there is good hospitality. If you ever get laid up cowboying, you could be a camp cook."

Luke grinned but didn't reply. He liked cooking when he had to do it. He also had foodstuff in his cabin that needed to be eaten, or the mice would get it. A quiet, sandy-haired man, Luke had been with Twin Peaks as a hired hand for six years. He had hired on with the ranch when he was barely twenty, fresh from the Army. Clean-shaven, tall, and competent, he mainly worked with Thomas and the cattle, but he was a good horseman. When the young horses were ready to have a job on the ranch, Luke was one of the cowboys who was trusted to ride them the year before the animals were put up for sale.

"You did a lot of improvements here," Jake commented, looking around. "Added another room on the shack, I see."

"Well, I figured I better follow the letter of the law and improve the place. Don't suppose anyone would come poking their government noses around to see if I lived up to the Homestead Laws, but never hurts to do it right. That old log shack was in sore need of improvement anyway," Luke continued. "I added a second room and chinked the old walls again. Most of that old chinking was falling out." Luke looked at the two-room cabin. "I even grew a small garden and cut some hay. Wasn't much else to do other than riding the hills, watching the cattle, and doing a little hunting."

This upper meadow with its line shack was the Twin Peaks Ranch summer grazing headquarters. For twenty years, the cows, calves, and yearlings were pushed up into the high country to graze for the summer. Here, they grew fat on the mountain grasses, ranging for miles in all directions. All these years, the cattle pretty much fended for themselves. Men would rotate in and out all summer, checking on the herd. In the early days, the biggest threat was from predatory animals. Losses from mountain lions, wolves, or bears were intermittent. If there was evidence of kills by any of these prey animals, a hunting party went after the marauders. For the past two summers, though, the increase of rustlers on the plains brought a new threat.

"Seen any evidence of rustlers up here?" Lathe asked.

"No, but I have seen a campfire or two out at the edges of our range. Haven't seen any evidence that cattle have been driven off, and I make a circle every few days to check and throw any cattle back that wander too far. Been pretty quiet. Do you think there is a chance we will get rustlers way up here?" Luke inquired of Jake.

"We are pretty far out of the way up here, and most of the rustlers seem to stay hidden out on the plains," Jake answered, "but you know, there is going to come a time. We do business with a lot of ranchers, and they have many itinerant cowboys drift in and out. Those are the ones that often end up looking for an easier way to make a living than cowboying. Seems rustling is their next career choice. It isn't a secret that our cattle go to the mountains in the summer. I know the ranchers grazing the open range are having more and more trouble with cattle losses."

Luke nodded at that, and the three men hunkered down by the fire, finishing their meal and sipping on cups of steaming coffee.

"So, did you decide on your name?" Jake asked, changing the subject.

Luke grinned. "Thought I'd keep it simple. I'll use Brooks. That is pretty close to Brode so maybe I won't forget when people ask me my name."

Within the Twin Peaks community, it was well known that Luke had been part of a renegade calvary troop. He was a new recruit at the time and was just barely twenty. When Luke was the only member of the troop to survive an incident, he had no desire to stay in the Army. Technically, that made Luke a deserter. Now, he was filing on 160 acres of this mountain meadow. Luke was hesitant to use his real name in case someone stumbled upon it and put it together with one of the missing troopers from six years earlier.

Jake nodded and extended his hand to Luke, "Nice to meet you, Luke Brooks. Good name." Turning to Lathe, Jake said, "Maybe spread the word when you get home that Luke Brode is no more, it's Brooks now. Might as well just go with that name in all our business. Safer that way." Jake shook his cup out and stood. "Time we make tracks. We can get almost out of these mountains before dusk. Luke, you packed and ready?"

"I have a pack horse loaded with everything I want Lathe to bring back down to the ranch," he answered. "I'll take one saddle horse and send the rest back to the ranch with Lathe."

Lathe nodded. He would be back at the ranch by late afternoon with the horses and any supplies that wouldn't survive the rodents before the cabin was used next. It was a month before fall gather, and fresh supplies would be brought up then.

It took Jake and Luke three days to make the boundary of the Crow Creek Ranch northwest of Cheyenne. They were a day early, allowing Luke to go into the land office in Cheyenne and file on the 160 acres. Jake stayed out with the horses and set up camp near a small creek. Luke brought back supplies from Cheyenne to replenish what they had used, and the next day, driving the horses in front of them, they rode into the Crow Creek Ranch headquarters. Inquiring directions at the newly built ranch house, they rode on and found a camping spot.

The Crow Creek Ranch was only four years in existence. Jake had received a letter from the ranch foreman who had heard of the good horses coming from Twin Peaks Ranch. A big fall gathering was scheduled with several adjoining ranches, and there was a need for good horses. Jake was hoping to get a dozen horses sold.

Jake and Luke were up early the next morning, haltering their horses. The plains around the ranch headquarters were alive with activity as cowboys were holding cattle while others cut out cows, steers, bulls, and young stock to separate for the different owners. Some cattle needed to be branded or doctored, but most just needed to be sorted according to owners. There were several ranch crews there to help. Jake watched the activity and waited. He was there to sell horses, and the ranch owners knew that. Buyers would come.

Near midmorning, a young man shouted brusquely to Jake, his English accent unmistakable, "Hey, you there, bring me a horse to try."

Jake had noticed the young man for some time. He was a hard-riding, hard-handed rider, and harsh on his horses. He wasn't dressed in traditional cowboy clothes, dusty and well worn. This youth, who looked to be near twenty, was well-dressed in high-top boots, well-pressed trousers, and a shirt. In looks, the youth reminded Jake of his brother-in-law, Jackson, an Englishman who ran cattle on the southern Wyoming plains. Jackson was a good man, and Jake liked him, but Jackson was not a cowboy. He was the wealthy son of a landed English gentleman and would always dress and act like one. Married to Jake's half-sister, Molly, they made their home at the edge of the mountains about a half-day ride from Twin Peaks.

This young man that Jake watched was different from Jackson because he was belligerent and confrontational. When the cattle he tried to sort got away from him, he loudly blamed one of the turnback cowboys for the miss or blamed the horse he was riding. Jake watched him change horses several times by midmorning leaving panting, lathered horses standing with heads down. Jake could tell by the body language of several of the cowboys that this young man was disliked, but no one said anything to him. Now, the youth came striding toward Jake.

"I said get me a horse," the young man demanded.

Jake glanced at Luke, "You think he's talking to us?" Jake asked casually.

Luke just nodded, watching the young man approach.

"Hey, Indian, I said, get me a horse," the repugnant youth said, stopping twenty feet away.

Jake turned toward the man, studying him. "Sorry, these horses don't belong to you, and I'm not your groom. Find your own horse."

"They said these horses are here to sell," the youth ordered, "and my father is a buyer, so let me try one out."

"If you are the rider," Jake said slowly, "then these horses are not for sale."

The young man colored at that, Jake's refusal causing him to flush. "How dare you speak to me that way?" he said, almost choking with anger.

Cowboys on horseback and on foot started drifting toward them, seeing the quarrel. The attention of an audience only escalated the young man's anger. He was not wearing a holstered gun, but he reached down into his boot and jerked out a Sharps four-barrel Derringer. Jake had seen Jackson with a similar weapon. The young man pointed it at Jake.

"I said get me a horse," he ordered again.

"Don't reckon I will," Jake answered casually. "You aren't riding any of my horses."

"You're a breed," the young man said, voice dripping with venom, "and you think you can get away with insulting me? You think I won't use this?"

The crowd of people ringed nearby fell silent when the youth waved the gun. Jake just watched the young man, making no move.

"Not many men can pull a little gun like that and hit anything with it. You are a good twenty feet from me," Jake spoke conversationally. "You only have one shot to get me. You think you are that good?"

"Hell, I have four shots."

"But you won't get four shots off," Jake answered. "You want to gamble that you can hit me on the first shot? At this distance?"

The youth looked around, then blustered, "I have four shots. What do you mean I have to get you on the first shot? You aren't wearing a gun."

Jake looked around. A green-painted wagon parked nearby had bedrolls and extra supplies in it. It was about fifteen feet from the youth and farther from Jake. The wagon manufacturer's name, WEBER, was painted in gold lettering in the middle of the wagon's side.

"Tell you what," Jake said slowly, "I'll give you a chance to save your life. See that wagon. It is closer to you than you are to me. Let's say my heart is the top circle of the B in WEBER. Take a shot at that and see if you can hit it."

The young man looked aggressively at Jake and then at the faces ringing him. He saw the men near the wagon move back, wanting to be well out of the way of any wild gunshot. Taking the challenge, he sighted on the wagon and pulled the trigger. There was no answering thwack of a bullet hitting the wood.

"So, what does that prove?" he asked angrily. "I still have three more bullets."

"Try again, I'll give you a second chance and show you what it means," Jake said calmly.

Again, the youth sighted. This time when he pulled the trigger, it was followed by the sound of a bullet hitting wood. But only a half-second later, there was a sharp thunk, and the hilt of a knife stuck out of the wagon, perfectly centered in the upper circle of the B. The knife had appeared so suddenly that the crowd was taken by surprise.

"Now, where did that bullet end up?" Jake asked casually to no one in particular.

Several cowboys jumped toward the wagon, searching for the bullet hole in the green paint.

"Here it is," one lean, lanky man said, pointing to the rear of the wagon, above the back wheel. "He hit back here."

"Don't reckon if my heart was the B, you'd have gotten close to me with the second bullet either," Jake commented, walking forward to pull his knife out of the wagon. "And that is why you only have one chance. Because my knife doesn't miss."

The youth colored, looking around at the men around him. "You were just lucky," he protested.

Out of the crowd emerged two men. The first was definitely a gentleman dressed in a fine jacket and carrying a cane. The second was an old man, grizzled with age. The old man wore his hair in two braids. He wore homespun trousers and a beaded leather shirt. Belted at his waist was a knife in a sheath. These two men came forward to face Jake.

"I am Lord Henley," the gentleman said. "What is the problem here?"

"He insulted me, Father," the youth replied. "I was just teaching him a lesson."

"Reckon he taught you a lesson," a voice in the crowd shouted.

The youth colored again. "Father, fire that man."

"Manly, what did you do?"

"I just needed another horse to ride, and this breed wouldn't bring me one," Manly said defensively.

"And you are?" Lord Henley directed the question at Jake.

"Jacob Bates Welles."

"You brought the Twin Peaks horses?" Lord Henley asked. "You work for Twin Peaks Ranch?"

"I am one of the owners of Twin Peaks. I own these horses."

"And why won't you let my son ride one?" the words were asked calmly with no venom.

Jake looked toward the string of tied-up horses. "Every horse your son brought back was abused. He's a terrible rider, blaming his horse or another cowboy for his faults." Jake looked back at his own horses. "If the likes of him will be using my horses, then they aren't for sale. He would treat them poorly and then blame the horse for his own inability. My horses deserve better."

"See, Father!" Manly burst out. "He insults me."

"Ain't an insult iffin' it's true," spoke the old man, looking hard at the youth.

"Manly, go back to town and get ready. The train leaves this afternoon, and your mother is expecting you on it," Lord Henley said firmly. "You have gotten into enough trouble here."

"But, Father," the youth protested.

"Go," the word came out harsh. "Wendell will take you in with the buggy. I'll be in to see you off."

Manly stared hard at his father, then kicked the dirt. He turned and made his way to a waiting buggy. Lord Henley stared after him before letting out a sigh. Turning, he faced Jake.

"He spends most of his time with his mother in England. She spoils him," Lord Henley said apologetically. "It will be a relief for him to return there. This western life doesn't suit him."

It was the old man who regarded Jake quizzically. "I knew me a Jacob Bates once. Old mountain man done live with the Utes. He had a good reputation."

"My grandfather," Jake replied.

"Recollect old Jacob trapped many a year with a Welles from St. Louis," the old man went on. "Be that a coincidence that you carry the Welles name too?"

"My stepfather is Kade Welles. Both Kade and his father before him trapped with Jacob. When my father died, Kade married my mother and adopted me. I took his name."

"Then who would your blood father be?"

"My father was Jacob's Ute son, Blue Knife. My mother was a white woman who came out to the mountains with Jacob. Jacob was her protector and friend." Jake looked directly at the old man. "They are all gone now, except my stepfather, Kade. He is the founder of our ranch."

The old man stepped forward, extending his hand to Jake. "I rode one winter with your grandfather many years ago. He was as good a man as any I knowed. Proud to meet you, young man."

The old man looked at Lord Henley. "There weren't better men in the mountains than Bates and Welles. I'd say this young man's horses will be just as he says they are." Looking at Jake, the old man continued, "Glad I happened to wander in and meet you. Good to know what all happened to the good men I used to know."

For a day that started out so odious, it wasn't a bad day after all. Lord Henley turned out to be a significant investor in a neighboring ranch. After seeing Jake's horses work, he bought three of the fine animals. Six more were sold to the Crow Creek ranch, and the remaining three head were purchased individually by cowboys working at the gather. That night, Jake and Luke joined the campfire around one of the chuckwagons at the invitation of the ranch owner. Many around the fire knew the Twin Peaks' reputation for fine horses, and several cowboys had heard of Jake. The old mountain man who knew Jake's grandfather also joined the group, so it turned out to be a pleasant night of storytelling and visiting. It was well past dark when Jake and Luke made their way to their campsite. They only had their personal saddle horses left, hobbled out on the prairie grazing.

"You ever get tired of it?" Luke inquired as they spread out their bedrolls.

"Of what?"

"Of fighting for your name. Of being insulted?"

"That young man didn't insult me," Jake countered. "He didn't have enough respect from anyone to make his words mean anything."

"Still, he meant to insult you," Luke said. "And here's the thing. We were standing together, but he meant to insult you, not me. He targeted you. Why is that?"

"A man will target who he thinks is inferior to him," Jake answered. "That kid saw me as an Indian, and therefore, in his mind, I was inferior to him." Jake stopped talking, thinking through his answer. "That tells me that the man is inferior to me. He judged me without knowing me, just by the color of my skin. It doesn't happen as much as it used to."

"Hell, man, you almost got hanged once because you were judged by the color of your skin!" Luke exclaimed. "When will it quit? Will your children, or Lathe's, or Hawk's young 'uns have to fight their way through life?"

Jake sighed. "It weighs heavy on a man wondering what life will be like for his children," Jake said reflectively. "Lathe worries about it. But our children have security at Twin Peaks. They will have the support of everyone there. Being on our ranch is the freedom to be ourselves and know we are accepted and respected. Outside of the ranch," Jake smiled sadly, "our children may have to fight for respect. I think feelings are changing. That is the best we mixed bloods can hope for," Jake grinned at Luke. "And we have to be prepared to fight if it comes to that. And we have to win when we do."

"Surround yourselves with good friends," Luke suggested.

"I try to do that," Jake answered. "I try real hard."

CHAPTER 2

Lady of the Manor – Late Summer 1883

Molly paced the porch, watching the distant river bottom looking for Jake. She had looked for him for two days now. She was impatient, wanting to see him again. It had been more than five months since she had seen her half-brother, and she missed him. Jake, ten years her senior, had been her mainstay growing up. Her other brother, Thomas, four years Molly's senior, was closer in age and would tease her mercilessly when they were young. Jake was the one who was always there to help her. He was always willing to take her with him when he rode, teaching her the ways of his Indian relatives, and she missed those times with him.

Now that the three siblings were all married, it was sometimes months until she saw one of them. Thank goodness she had Catherine, her best friend from childhood, living next door, but even that wasn't enough. Catherine, married to Jackson's foreman, could go on with her life much as she had while growing up at Twin Peaks. Catherine and her family might live next door to Molly and Jackson, but that is where the similarity ended. Catherine was a wife and mother. Her husband, Buster, was the ranch foreman. Catherine had a garden, and no one worried that her hands got dirty. Catherine had her brood of children, and they ran wild in the river bottoms or got in the way of the ranch hands at the corrals.

Molly was the lady of the manor, as Jackson called her. Things had begun to change the year before. Jackson had come home with elaborate plans to build onto their ranch house. With two bedrooms, a parlor, and a separate kitchen, Molly already thought they had a big home. But Jackson said they needed more room.

"We will be getting visitors soon, Molly," Jackson had told her. "We have to have more room. When an investor comes here, we need to make them feel we are worthy of their money. We have to impress them."

Lumber, both from Jerimiah's lumber yard at Twin Peaks and exotic woods imported from the east, was hauled in. Workmen were hired from as far away as St. Louis, and two wings were added to the house. Molly was in awe at the size of the house when it was finished. There were two identical looking two-story wings on each side of the main ranch house, all connected with a covered porch in front. In the wing on the south side were two big bedrooms on the main floor with dressing rooms for each room. This turned out to be a bedroom for Jackson and a bedroom for herself. Molly was aghast at that.

"You and I are going to have separate bedrooms?" she asked, stunned.

"Honey," Jackson said patiently. "We are going to have many visitors, and they will expect us to be living in the standards of my upbringing. We have to show them we are proper. We will both sleep more comfortably if we have our own space. We'll be right next to each other. This isn't an unusual thing."

To Molly, it was unusual. She had watched her parents all her growing up years, and all she wanted was a marriage like theirs. There was never any doubt that Sabra and Kade Welles were anything but in love with one another. Molly couldn't imagine her parents in separate bedrooms. But Jackson was insistent. It was how he was raised.

The next surprise was the upstairs in their wing. There was a nursery, a second bedroom for growing children, and a room for the children's nurse.

"A nurse!" Molly exclaimed. "I don't need a nurse for little Jack! We only have him, and I can take care of him just fine."

"Honey," again Jackson spoke patiently, "little Jack will soon need some more guidance on how to be a gentleman. And he needs more routine."

"I can guide him," Molly protested.

"Darling, you are a wonderful mother," Jackson continued firmly, "but you will soon have more duties than just being a mother. It just isn't proper to take care of the children and the duties of a house at the same time. I will need your help entertaining our guests. You will be glad to have a nurse for Jack then. And we might be having more children, and then you will be very grateful for the help."

Molly held her tongue at that. She dearly wanted more children, but it had yet to happen. She had one miscarriage when Jack was three, and that was all. But she suspected another baby would be slow in coming if they shared separate bedrooms. Jackson had become so busy with the ranch. He often traveled to neighboring ranches, with his cowboys out to the plains, or to Laramie to talk to his solicitor. She and Jackson didn't have the close relationship they had when they were first married. Jackson had become distant in bed. When he did make love to her, it was stiff and emotionless. Where had the passion gone?

In the early years of their marriage, Jackson often liked Molly to ride out with him or travel to Laramie or Cheyenne. They went to some cattlemen balls in Cheyenne, and Jackson loved showing her off. But lately, he traveled alone or with his cowboys, using the excuse that she needed to stay with little Jack.

Little Jack was five this summer, and when Jackson was away, Molly would get her homemade ranch skirts on, as Jackson called the clothes that Molly sewed herself. Jack would get his work clothes on, also homemade by Molly. Then, she and little Jack would go to the river with Catherine and her children to fish or hike the nearby hills. Molly would don her split skirts and go out riding, both with Jack on his pony or by herself if Catherine would watch Jack for her.

But now, when Jackson was home, he liked Molly to dress in the late afternoon to dine together in the evening. He ordered her fine dresses with corsets and frilly underthings sent out from distant cities. Many of the dresses took a maid to help her dress. Jackson said that this was another reason to get a nurse. He hired Lydia, a middle-aged woman from England whom Jackson's mother had recommended. Lydia was little Jack's nurse and Molly's maid. While Molly liked Lydia immensely, she was uncomfortable having a maid. Being the lady of the manor took some getting used to.

The south wing was finished last summer, and this summer, the workmen were back to put the finishing touches on the north wing. The north wing had three bedrooms on the main floor.

"What on earth do we need with more bedrooms?" Molly asked, early in the spring when she saw the plans.

"Darling, we are going to get visitors," Jackson said patiently. "I expect Peter Handley later this summer, and he is talking about bringing out an accountant. We need separate bedrooms for them. It certainly isn't proper to expect them to sleep in the same room."

Molly didn't respond to that. Instead, she thought of her childhood when visitors wandered into her folks' ranch. Visitors were put up on blankets on the floor of the main room of the cabin, or Molly was moved out of her room and into the loft with the boys so visitors could use her room. Having three bedrooms in her home now for guests seemed a huge extravagance to Molly.

"So, what will be upstairs?" Molly was almost afraid to ask.

Jackson smiled broadly, "There will be some smaller bedrooms up there. They can be used for an overflow of guests, but mostly they will be used for the maids and manservants that may come with our guests. And, of course, there will be a bedroom and small sitting room for the couple I hired as our housekeeper and my butler."

"Your butler?" Molly couldn't believe she was hearing this. They lived in Wyoming territory, for goodness' sake! "And a housekeeper?"

"Yes, dear," Jackson told her. "My mother found a wonderful couple. She said they may be a bit rough around the edges for the aristocracy in England, but she felt they would be just perfect for us. Mother has been training them. Mrs. Burton is also being trained as a cook, so she will take over the cooking when she comes. And the best thing is that they are willing to come to America and work. They will be here by July first. Isn't that just wonderful?"

Molly didn't think it was wonderful, but what could she say? Jackson was building a cattle empire, and he expected many friends, acquaintances, and business associates to visit during the summer months. He had been hinting at that for the last couple of years, but Molly hadn't taken him that seriously until the workmen came to expand the ranch house. And even then, Molly didn't know what getting guests would entail and how her life would change.

So, here she was in this awful dress—beautiful, yes, but the most uncomfortable thing to wear on a warm day. Jackson picked it out this morning for her. He did that a lot, coming into her room before he left and going through her closet. He had the habit of picking out the clothes he wanted her to wear both during the day and when she dressed for dinner.

Today's dress was not one of her favorites, if she actually had any favorites of the fancy gowns Jackson brought her. With its high neck, long sleeves, and tight waist, she felt trussed up like a pig to slaughter. This was something else new. Now instead of wanting Molly to dress just for dinner, Jackson wanted Molly dressed up all day to impress their guests. Peter Hadley had indeed come and had brought an accountant with him. Hadley invested in the Anchor J, and Jackson hoped he would increase his investment. Hadley and his assistant had been at the Anchor J for almost a month. Jackson took them out to look at the cattle and the open range. The men went on hunting excursions and watched the cowboys at work.

And while Jackson and his guests had so much fun experiencing the great American West, Molly was trussed up in the most beautiful and uncomfortable dresses whenever the men might return during the daytime.

Jackson felt Molly must always be a proper lady when they had guests. Only when Jackson and his guests went off overnight to the plains did Molly put on her split skirts and frolic with Jack or ride her horse. This was not the way she expected married life to be. This was not the way she wanted to spend the summer. Oh, where was Jake?

Jake saw the new twin wings of Jackson and Molly's home from the distance as they came around the bend of the river. Kade had told him of the improvements to the Anchor J headquarters. Kade had visited his daughter earlier in the summer, but this was the first time Jake had seen the additions to the house. The two-story additions on each side of the main ranch house, with the long porch that stretched the entire length of the front of the house, were certainly impressive. Seeing the house reminded Jake of the stories his mother told of the mansions she remembered from her youth. Raised in a two-story brick mansion, it didn't seem likely that Sabra would have adjusted to life in a one-room log cabin when she first fled to the mountains. But she not only adjusted, she thrived and never wanted to go back to the life of her youth. Still, her stories captivated her children, when in their youth, they sat around the fire or sat together reading books set in distant cities. As Jake looked at this elaborate ranch house, he remembered his mother's stories.

"Holy," Luke said, riding up beside Jake. "I heard they added to the house, but that is one hell of an addition."

Jake nodded. "Yes, it is that."

He saw a figure on the porch. Dressed in a brilliant green, the figure flew down the front steps and ran across the yard. It was Molly. Jake spurred his horse forward and loped to meet her.

"My goodness, little sister," Jake said, dismounting as he reached her. "You look beautiful. Like a princess."

Molly didn't reply; she simply flew into his arms and hugged him. Jake felt her gasping for breath from her run. He held her until she caught her breath, then he held her away from him and smiled down at her.

"I was afraid I'd get you dirty," Jake smiled.

"I'd love to get dirty," Molly laughed. "But I guess this isn't the outfit I should wear for that."

"You remember Luke?" Jake asked, turning toward Luke, who also dismounted.

"You have been with Twin Peaks for several years, if I remember right," Molly replied, turning to Luke. "But I think I only met you once, several years ago. You have always been away from the ranch when I was there."

"I've spent the last several summers up in the mountains at the line shack," Luke replied, taking off his hat respectfully.

"Luke filed on the mountain meadow," Jake explained. "He went to the land office in Cheyenne a few days ago and made it legal."

"Our fall gathering headquarters?" Molly was surprised. "What did Pa have to say about that? Where will you hold the fall gather now?"

"Oh, we will still be up there. Luke and Pa have a deal. The ranch will buy the land from Luke," Jake answered.

"You won't be a landowner very long then?" Molly asked inquisitively.

"Well," Luke answered, "I have been a hired hand for too long. Kade is buying my land, but instead of getting paid for it, I will become a shareholder of the ranch." He couldn't hide his grin. "I'll be part of Twin Peaks."

Molly smiled widely at Luke, extending her hand in a congratulatory shake. "Congratulations. I can't think of a better place to be part of."

Jake took Molly's arm and began walking toward the barn. "Walk with us to the corrals so we can put the horses up," he said.

Molly pulled away from him. "No, ah, Jackson doesn't want me to go out to the corrals," she said, looking away. "He doesn't like me around the hired hands. He doesn't think it is proper. You go, and I'll have some cool drinks ready for you on the porch when you get back." She smiled tentatively at Jake.

Jake gave her a puzzled look, but didn't say more. Kissing his sister on her forehead, he and Luke walked their horses toward the corrals. *Something is wrong here*, Jake thought. This was his little sister, but this wasn't the Molly he was used to.

The afternoon was the most pleasant that Molly had spent in months. She had fresh lemonade ready when Jake and Luke returned, each glass with a big ice chip. She had sent Mr. Burton to the icehouse to get the ice. On a table in the shade of the porch, Molly had a plate of cookies waiting when the men joined her.

The icehouse was another of Jackson's improvements. Dug into a hillside with a front wall insulated with a thick layer of hay, they had ice all summer. It gave the hands that Jackson kept on for the winter something to do, chopping out ice from a beaver pond and hauling it in to fill the icehouse. The cowboys grumbled some that they didn't hire on to chop ice, but Jackson just shrugged and told them they could move on then. There were always out-of-work cowboys traveling the grub line in the winter. Jackson was one of the few ranchers who kept most of his hands on after the season turned cold. So, they might grumble, but they stayed.

"I've never had lemonade," Luke remarked when they were all seated on the porch.

"Jackson orders fresh lemons when he goes to town," Molly replied. "He especially wanted some for our guests. So, we have plenty, and Mrs. Burton just squeezed a fresh pitcher."

 The afternoon passed quickly as Jake filled Molly in on his summer in the high mountains and news from Twin Peaks. For just a little while, Molly felt that all was good in her world, except for the abominable tight corset and dress.

"How long can you stay?" Molly inquired when the conversation lagged.

"We will head out in the morning," Jake said. "I promised Anna I wouldn't be gone very long, and I know she will be watching for me."

"I wish you could stay longer," Molly said wistfully. "I have a bedroom in the north wing that is ready for you, or if you want, I can put one of you up in an upstairs bedroom, although the workmen haven't finished those rooms yet."

"I can go out to the bunkhouse," Luke replied, clearly overwhelmed with the house. "You don't have to put me up."

"Nonsense," Molly said, "You are a landowner now and from Twin Peaks. Of course, I will put you up. We will eat about eight tonight, and I expect both of you to be there."

"Molly," Jake said softly, "I know you have some influential guests at the moment. Neither Luke nor I have any formal clothes or even clean clothes, for that matter. I'm not sure Jackson wants his Native brother-in-law ruining his image as a big cattle rancher."

Molly scowled at that. "Jackson has always liked you. You know that. And I don't give a whit about what those pompous men think about my favorite brother. You will eat with us." She studied Luke and Jake. "I will send you each a clean shirt of Jackson's. I think that will do." She smiled at the two. "You are shorter than Jackson," she told Jake, "and Luke is taller, but the shirts will fit. I insist you both eat with us. I've asked Catherine and Buster to join us too. So, you can't disappoint me."

Dinner was excellent, and the conversation centered around ranching for a good portion of the meal. Along with Luke and Jake, Jackson's two guests from England were there. The only other couple was Buster and Catherine. Catherine was a distant cousin of Jake's and the daughter of Mattie and Matthew Jorgensen from Twin Peaks. Mattie had been Molly's mother's best friend, and Catherine was Molly's closest friend. Now married to Jackson's foreman, Buster, they lived next door to the new mansion in a sturdy, but modest, foreman's home.

The men carried most of the conversation as they discussed the cattle market and the differing ranching methods. There was quite a bit of discussion about the free range that Jackson and all the big ranches used for their cattle. There was also some talk about the sodbusters moving into the region. But, finally, the subject of cattle began to wear thin.

"So, you work for Twin Peaks?" Peter Hadley asked Luke when the conversation lagged.

Luke looked at Jake for help before responding, "Well, yes, but I have become part owner of the ranch now."

"What he means," Jake clarified, "is that he owns shares in the ranch, making him a landowner now. Luke is too important to our ranch to lose him. If he is a shareholder, we have him tied to us," Jake smiled at Luke.

"So, how did you meet?" Hadley inquired.

Luke again looked to Jake, and Jake answered smoothly, "I was out pushing some cows home, and Luke rode up. When Kade met him later, he offered Luke a job. Been with us ever since."

"Pretty lucky for you, I'd say," Hadley said, smiling at Luke, "and here you are now, a shareholder in the ranch."

"Pretty lucky for both of us," Jake smiled, meeting Luke's gaze. "We both came out of that pretty good."

"So, do you ever see your Indian relatives?" Hadley asked Jake. "Do you even know any of them?"

"My Native relatives are Ute," Jake answered easily. "I spend my summers in the high mountains at my grandfather's cabin. Old Jacob, my grandfather, was a white trapper and had a Ute wife. She would be my grandmother, but she died long before I was born. My father, Blue Knife, was Jacob's son by that union. Both my grandfather and my father died before I was born. I never knew either of them. But I had a half-brother, Brown Otter. I used to spend a lot of my summers with Otter in the mountains. Otter was twelve years my senior, so he was more like a father than a brother. We were close. Otter taught me the Ute ways and language. He was killed at the Battle of Milk Creek four years ago," Jake hesitated there before going on. "The Utes were moved out after that, so I haven't seen my sister-in-law since they left. However, I have a niece and nephew, Otter's son and daughter, who live on our ranch. I am also distantly related to the Jorgensen and Bates offspring. So, there are a lot of family ties on the ranch."

"Jake's nephew, Swift Hawk, is married to my cousin, Bonnie," Catherine added. "They have been married for almost four years. And my brother, Lathe, has been married to Jake's niece for even longer. We find ourselves intertwined in many ways."

The Englishmen found the relationships between the whites and those of Native blood interesting. Mixed marriages were often looked down upon, but at Twin Peaks Ranch, it was just part of the community. If Peter Hadley and his accountant found that unusual, they didn't voice their thoughts.

It was at the end of the evening when Molly asked Jake when he thought he would leave in the morning. Jake knew Molly was reluctant to say goodbye, so he smiled at his little sister.

"How about having breakfast with you in the morning before we push off? I wouldn't mind seeing little Jack again before leaving."

Molly was relieved. She feared that Jake would leave before dawn. She was loathe to say goodbye in the gloom before dawn.

"I'll ride out with you, then," she said excitedly. "Jack will be having his lessons with Mr. Burton." Molly didn't meet Jackson's eyes. She hoped he wouldn't contradict her plans to ride a few miles with Jake.

Jake smiled at Molly and touched her arm gently. "Count on it, then."

Jackson came into Molly's bedroom shortly after Molly retired.

"Honey," Jackson began, "I'll have Burton bring your horse up for you in the morning." Jackson went to Molly's dressing room. "I think this will look nice tomorrow then," he said, emerging with a dark brown riding habit. He turned and hung it from a peg on the wall.

"Oh, Jackson, I don't want to ride the sidesaddle," Molly replied. "I want to ride out with Jake like I always do!"

"Molly," Jackson said firmly, "we have guests. Riding astride is just not proper. They expect my wife to act like a lady."

"Oh, for goodness' sake!" Molly protested. "I hate the sidesaddle, and what difference would it make if Mr. Hadley sees me ride astride?"

"Hadley will take all his opinions home with him and talk to many people who may be interested in investing with us," Jackson answered. "His word goes a long way, and so far, he has been very impressed with the ranch and with you, I might add. Old English money is much easier to acquire if it goes to businesses owned by the same social class. If we want investors, we must play that game. And anyway," Jackson said softly, running his hands through Molly's hair, "I like to see you ride sidesaddle and wear such pretty clothes."

Molly's protests withered with Jackson's touch. "Stay with me tonight," she whispered.

"Oh, honey, I wish I could," Jackson said, giving her a gentle kiss on the forehead before turning away. "But I'll be up early tomorrow. I have a big day planned. Soon, dear, our guests will depart."

And with that, Jackson went through the adjoining door into his own room, leaving Molly staring after him. *What had happened to them?* Molly thought. How long had it been since he had shared her bed? Definitely, since before the English guests arrived. Molly missed the Jackson she married. She missed the young man with dreams of becoming a big cattle rancher, but who still had time to be a husband and friend. Where had that young man gone in the six short years they had been married? When had things changed, and why?

Burton had Molly's horse tied to the hitching rail when Jake was ready to ride. If Jake thought the sidesaddle and the riding habit was unusual dress for his sister, he did not mention it. Instead, he and Luke patiently waited, while Burton helped Molly into the saddle.

"Jackson doesn't want our guests to see me riding astride," Molly explained as they rode away. "He wants me to act like a high-class English lady when they are here. I am supposed to show that we are all civilized, like in England. They will leave soon, so it is the least I can do. It is not a big deal," Molly finished, but she would not meet Jake's eyes.

He knew it was a lie. Molly was like his late mother, Sabra. Sabra lived to ride her horses. The faster and farther she could ride, the better. Molly's wings were being clipped, whether she knew it or not.

The morning was beautiful, though, and the three miles Molly rode with her brother and Luke went too fast. As they rounded a curve in the river, Molly pulled up.

"I better not go any farther," she said sadly. "Jackson doesn't like me riding too far when I am alone."

Jake didn't mention that she wouldn't be alone. He had sighted the butler, Burton, riding in the distance. Apparently, Jackson worried about his wife riding alone.

He wondered if Molly knew they were being tracked. He didn't have to wonder long.

"Well, I'm actually not alone," Molly said. "I see Burton lurking in the distance."

"Jackson afraid you will lose your way?" Jake asked dryly. He didn't much care for the changes in his sister.

"Oh, we have talked and talked about this," Molly answered. "But Jackson says our hired hands aren't like at Twin Peaks, where we all grew up together." Molly stopped and looked over at Luke then. "Well, except for you, but you weren't at Twin Peaks when I lived there." Molly turned back to Jake. "Jackson hires a lot of the cowboys that come up the trail from Texas. He says we can't assume that they are all nice men. He doesn't want me out alone. I think he is being unreasonable, but he worries about me."

"Honey, are you all right with these changes?" Jake asked Molly softly.

"Of course," Molly said brightly, then turned her horse toward home to hide the tears that came to her eyes. "A lot of this will end when the guests go home. I'm fine." Blinking her eyes to hide her tears, she turned back and gave Jake a brilliant smile. "Just don't stay away so long. I miss you. Tell the rest at Twin Peaks to come and visit too. It's always good to hear from home."

Jake pivoted his horse around and went to Molly, sidepassing his horse close to her. He leaned over and gave his sister a hug. She clung to him fiercely, and then, letting go, she turned away. This time, she couldn't stop her tears. Spurring her horse, she began to lope away.

"Goodbye, Luke!" she called as she rode away, waving her hand. Jake and Luke just watched her riding away before turning their horses for home.

When Molly was out of hearing range, Luke looked at Jake. "You have the most beautiful sister I have ever seen," he said admiringly.

"She is that," Jake looked over his back to see his sister in the distance. She had pulled up and sat on her horse, watching the two men ride away. "But I've never seen her so sad," Jake turned to Luke. "And there is nothing I can do about that."

CHAPTER 3

Early Fall 1883 – Unusual Appetite

It had been almost a month since Jackson, his English guests, and all the cowboys except old Punch had ridden off to the fall roundup. The ranch was a ghost town with just the women and old Punch left behind. Even Burton had left to experience his first roundup and to afford some comfort for the Englishmen. Molly had the best three-and-a-half weeks of summer riding every day alone or with Jack and riding astride too. If evening temperatures were any indication, fall had arrived, and winter would soon come. She wanted to ride as much as she could before winter kept her inside.

The roundup could last weeks or even a month, depending on how things went. Jackson's guests planned to experience the roundup for two weeks, and then Jackson would take them north to a stage line bound for Cheyenne. In Cheyenne, they would board a train for the east. Before winter hit the plains, their English guests would be on a ship back to England.

On the other hand, Jackson would send over half his crew with Buster to Laramie to market the cattle this fall. Jackson wanted to sort off a hundred of the best cows and trail them home. He had commissioned Peter Hadley to buy five purebred bulls to send out in the spring. Jackson wanted to breed the best cows to these new bulls to test the offspring they would get from this match. It was well known that Twin Peaks had superior cattle to most cattle ranches. Jackson wanted to see if he could raise a few of these superior cattle himself.

Twin Peaks cattle were products of cattle raised in the east and brought out with settlers along the Oregon Trail. After years of trading with the wagon trains, the ranch had begun its own breeding program, keeping back extra cows and bulls and developing their herd. In addition, Twin Peaks put up winter feed for their cattle and brought them off the high mountains in the fall to the ranch, where they were fed hay all winter. Kade Welles knew those plains from years of trapping along the rivers and streams. He said the big ranchers would pay for letting those cattle fend for themselves over the winter someday. There will come a time when a winter is too hard, and dead cattle will be littering the ground. Most of the big ranchers, however, paid Kade no mind, grazing free land in the summer and winter and raking in the profits.

Several of the ranchers, Jackson included, just shook their heads at the work that Twin Peaks men put into their cattle, but it did pay off when the cattle were sold. Twin Peaks might have at most 800 head of cattle to sell, while the big ranches grazing the free range might have several thousand. Despite the smaller numbers, Twin Peaks cattle always brought top dollar when they went to market. The profits were sizable.

Molly expected Jackson and part of his crew to come riding in almost any day now. She both welcomed his return and dreaded it. While the ranch was so empty with all the cowhands gone, she had free rein. Old Punch took care of the chores that were left. An old cowpuncher with a bad hip, he hobbled around, got his work done, and didn't bother Molly. She could visit the corrals, work with some of the younger horses, and take Jack out whenever she wanted. With Lydia and Mrs. Burton still in the big house, Molly had few responsibilities. When Jack was tired of riding or needed a nap, Lydia was there to take care of him. Mrs. Burton kept the house in order and made the meals.

Molly hadn't dressed for dinner once since Jackson and the men left. Often, Catherine and her brood of children would join them, and they had a boisterous meal. Molly would catch the look of disapproval from Mrs. Burton at times, but not from Jack's nurse, Lydia. Lydia was an English farmgirl and although she was much older than Molly at middle age, she understood Molly better than any of the others. Lydia was adept at helping Molly escape the confines of Jackson's tight rein.

On this day, Molly had ridden with Jack in the morning. They had ridden to the river and splashed and played in the water so long that they both had to change to dry clothes upon return. After a noon meal, Molly left Jack with Lydia and went to saddle a young horse that Jake had left for her in the spring. This was a five-year-old that just needed many miles put on him. The colt had been left much of the summer standing with the remuda while Molly was expected to entertain the guests. Now Molly was trying to make up lost time, riding him every chance she could.

Molly rode out several miles, enjoying the afternoon sun. She urged the horse forward, and the animal broke into an easy lope. She liked this gelding. He was smooth and responsive, although still on the spooky side. She had to watch him, or he would whirl if he thought a monster was after him. Molly saw a tree ahead that had fallen. It was not much higher than a couple of feet, so she steered the horse toward it and urged him on. She felt his hesitation as he approached the fallen limb, but she leaned forward and spoke to him. Molly felt the horse gather himself and sail over the log. She laughed with the joy of it and sat up, ready to pull the horse up, when she saw the small herd of cattle coming down the valley toward her. Jackson was home.

Jackson saw Molly appear in the distance, her horse flying over a log. By the time she pulled up, Jackson had urged his horse forward and gone to meet her. Molly was riding astride, and he didn't like her around the cowhands that way. Molly had been a spirited girl when he met her, and she had intrigued him. But she was young then, too young to think of marriage. When he returned to America the following summer, Molly had matured, and by fall, Jackson had spoken for her hand. They married the next year when Molly was eighteen, and they went to England for their honeymoon, where Molly met his family. Jackson loved buying clothes that fit her new rank in life.

When they returned from England, he was a bit disconcerted that Molly went back to wearing her prairie dresses with split skirts so she could ride astride. As the ranch prospered, and Jackson had large herds of cattle brought north from Texas each year, he hired more of the Texas cowboys. Jackson didn't trust them. He didn't like the way they looked at his pretty young wife. It made Jackson uncomfortable when Molly went to the corrals to work with her horses. It helped when he hired the Burtons this spring. Against Molly's wishes, Jackson sent Burton to get Molly's horse when she wanted to ride.

With the addition of the servants, Jackson asked Molly to dress for dinner each day. He liked Molly in her formal clothes. She was a lady now, he reminded her. She needed to dress like one. With their summer guests this year, Jackson insisted that Molly wear what he considered proper gowns all day. If she was to ride while they had guests, she was to ride sidesaddle. Now, here she was, riding astride again, her hair out of its pins and streaming behind her like a common woman. Jackson didn't want her coming close to his cowboys. He rode to meet her instead.

"Jackson, you're back!" Molly exclaimed when Jackson got close. She smiled and rode close for a kiss.

"I would have been happier if I saw you out here riding with a proper saddle," Jackson replied grimly. He gave her a chaste peck on the cheek and wasn't smiling.

"Oh Jackson, you know I hate the sidesaddle, and this horse is so spooky. I'd never ride him with the sidesaddle."

"Molly," Jackson said irritably. "Let's send this horse back to Twin Peaks then. You are a lady now and a matron with a child. You have no business riding astride. It is just not proper. And especially when the men are around."

"Oh, my goodness," Molly protested. "Those men have seen women riding astride all their lives," she said. "It isn't anything new to them. This is the west. They aren't English snobs." Molly was getting angry now.

Jackson frowned. He didn't like what Molly was implying. "Those men look at you riding your horse, and they all want to be the horse," he said angrily.

Molly stared at Jackson, not understanding what he meant at first. Then her eyes widened, and she went ramrod straight. "How dare you," she said. Pivoting her horse away, she leaned forward, cued her horse, and loped toward home.

Molly was still mad when she got home, and she was aware that Jackson was following closely behind her. She didn't look back though. As they approached the front of the mansion, Jackson rode up beside her.

"I'll take your horse to the barn," he said tersely. "I want you to dress for dinner. The yellow silk looks so nice on you."

Molly turned rebellious eyes toward him, but she reined in and dismounted. She let the reins drop. If he wanted to take her horse, he could reach down and get the reins himself, she thought. Then she turned and stalked up the stairs to the porch and entered the house, letting the door slam behind her.

With Lydia's help, Molly got dressed for dinner. The yellow silk dress was tight and had a dozen small buttons down the back. But at least the corset she wore for this dress laced in the front. Lydia was an expert with hair, and Molly's hair was combed out and wound elegantly into a bun. As Lydia worked on the hair, Molly began to calm down. This wasn't how she wanted Jackson's homecoming to go. He was so unreasonable about her acting like a lady. This was Wyoming territory, after all. And truthfully, the allure of the fine clothes and the requirements of a lady was wearing quite thin on Molly. She dreaded dinner. She had no idea which Jackson would come to eat with her. She longed for the carefree young man she first married. But that side of Jackson hadn't come home lately.

Jackson was waiting for Molly when she entered the dining room. He smiled at her, holding out a glass of wine. "You look lovely, my dear," he said softly. There was no lingering anger from the afternoon.

Molly took the glass, but didn't reply. She was still angry. She would let him do the talking.

Jackson held a chair for her and helped her arrange her skirts as she took her seat.

"The roundup went very well," Jackson began as if nothing was wrong between them. "I think Hadley was very impressed with the cattle, and the profit should be quite good. The cattle we brought up from Texas in the early summer are fat and should do very well. Cattle prices are so good now." Jackson paused to take a sip of his wine. "By the time I get to Laramie, Buster should have the herd there. But I think these cattle will pay off our present investor and many of our debts. If Hadley can get more investors, I want to bring twice as many cattle north. I'll keep more back next fall and raise calves."

Molly's reserve began to melt. She liked to be included in the interests of the ranch, even if it was just Jackson talking about his plans. "What about the cost of this house?" Molly asked. "What do you owe on it?"

"Well, a house like this is expensive," Jackson answered, smiling. "But if we keep getting the profits like I think we will this year, we should get the house paid off in the next few years. And, of course, I am buying up some land here and there from homesteaders, but eventually, everything will be free and clear. However, to do that, we need to bring more cattle north."

"If you plan to keep more cattle on the range, will you have to put up winter feed for them?"

"I know your father's feelings about that," Jackson replied. "And I respect his opinion, but I think he is wrong. There might be some death loss in the winter, but there is ample grass on the plains, and it is all free. These cattle are tough. Most of them do just fine on prairie grass. We will put up a little hay, like we did this year, for the few head we keep close to the ranch, but the bulk of our cattle will be on free range."

The conversation turned to Jack then and what Molly and her son had been doing at the ranch while Jackson was gone. The evening was actually a pleasant one. Molly only wished that Jack was allowed to eat dinner with them, but that was a battle she fought and lost when Lydia was hired. Jackson insisted that Jack be fed early and taken to the nursery by Lydia so that the grownups could have time to themselves. In Molly's mind, families ate together. Some of her fondest memories were of her whole family eating together. But Jackson was firm on that. Little Jack was only five. He could see his parents during the day.

As the meal ended, Jackson pushed back his chair and stood up. "I have to run out to the bunkhouse," he announced. "I promised the hands that came home with these cows that I would treat them to a frolic. It won't be the same as hitting town and carousing, but I will break out some whiskey, and they can play cards."

"Will you be long?" Molly asked, disappointed that he wouldn't join her in the parlor.

"No, I will just bring out the whiskey and get them started," Jackson answered. "I won't be late."

Molly glanced at the clock. It was almost eleven and still Jackson wasn't back. Molly had moved to the parlor and read at first, waiting for Jackson's return. Lydia had come down to ask Molly if she needed help with the dress, but Molly had sent her off to bed.

"Jackson won't be late," Molly said. "I can get him to help me with the buttons. I want to read a little before I retire."

That might have been true. Molly loved to read. It passed a lot of time, especially on a long winter day. But tonight, Molly hoped her fight with Jackson might bring him to her bed. At dinner, he was obviously trying to make up for his ugly words this afternoon. It had been more than two months since he had made love to her, first because of their English guests and next because of the roundup. Molly desperately wanted more children, but at this rate, no more would come. But even more important, Molly wanted Jackson in her bed. She missed him and their nights together.

When Molly finally went to her bedroom, she lifted the window and listened. It was dark, but she could see a glisten of light coming from the bunkhouse. She heard raucous laughter burst forth, then followed by quiet. Then, laughter again. The men were telling stories, she knew. She longed to be out there with them. Jackson was evidently not coming in early.

Now Molly was getting angry again. She had sent Lydia off, and she couldn't get out of this blasted dress without help. She had to wait for Jackson's help, and it was getting late. With relief, she finally heard Jackson's boots on the porch. He was coming in the front door directly into the hallway in front of the bedrooms. Molly got up and went to the hall to meet him.

Jackson was shrugging off his coat when she opened her bedroom door. He wasn't aware of her at first. He reached up to hang his coat on a peg on the wall, then pulled off his boots. Molly saw him lose his balance as he struggled with the last boot. But he caught himself on the wall. She knew right away that he was drunk. Her heart sank. Maybe he was too drunk, she thought. Alcohol could affect a man that way, she knew.

"Jackson," she said quietly, "I need your help."

Turning toward Molly, a smile lit Jackson's face. "Darling, I am at your service." He walked toward her, and Molly was relieved he could walk a reasonably straight line.

"I can't get this dress off," she said, leading him into her bedroom. "I sent Lydia to bed earlier."

Molly turned away from him so he could see the buttons on her back. She felt him fumbling with the buttons, but slowly, one at a time, they came loose. Molly held her breath. Would Jackson take the bait? Then she felt his hands on her shoulders, pushing her dress off. She felt his lips on the back of her neck. She leaned into him.

When Jackson pushed her dress off her hips, Molly turned to him. She unbuttoned his shirt and pushed it off his shoulders. Then she unbuttoned his trousers. Jackson just stood, letting her push his pants to the floor. Molly reached to the laces of her corset, loosening, and then shrugging out of it. She stood before Jackson in her lacy pantaloons and a loose-fitting chemise. She started to push the chemise down off her shoulders, but Jackson stopped her. Taking the garment, he pulled it over her head. She raised her arms so Jackson could pull it off of her, but he did a surprising thing. Instead of freeing her arms, he twisted the flimsy material, drawing her wrists together, then wrapping the chemise around her arms and through her bound wrists. He effectively had Molly's wrists tied together with the chemise. Molly was surprised, wondering what he was up to, but she wasn't afraid.

Jackson lifted her arms, using the material as a leash, and pushed Molly to the bedroom wall. He kissed her, first gently and then more roughly. He held her arms up with one hand, and with the other, he kneaded her breasts.

"You were very naughty this afternoon," he whispered drunkenly. "You should be punished, you know."

Molly moaned softly, enjoying his touch. It had been so long since he had touched her like this. She wanted to put her arms around him and draw him to her, but Jackson held her arms pinned against the wall while he caressed her body. She felt him untie the string that held her pantaloons up. He slid them over her hips, and Molly felt them fall to the floor.

"You were very bad," Jackson whispered again. "I was very disappointed in you."

Molly didn't care what words Jackson uttered at that moment; she just wanted to keep feeling his attention. She tried to lean forward to brush his hair with her lips as his mouth touched her flesh.

Suddenly, Jackson pulled her arms down, twirling her away from the wall. He sank onto Molly's dressing chair, pulling her face down over his lap. Molly's bound hands were pulled to the floor, and Jackson used one foot to step on the material. Molly was so surprised that she could only gasp. But before she could protest, she felt Jackson's hands caressing her bare back, over her buttocks, and down her legs. It felt so good to be touched that despite the awkwardness of the position, she relaxed. This was something different.

That was when she felt the first slap. The sound of Jackson's hand on her rear startled her more than the slap. It didn't hurt. He hadn't hit her hard. But it surprised her, and she tried to get up, but Jackson held her tight to his lap with one hand and held her hands to the floor with his foot.

"Shh," he whispered to her, his lips on the back of her neck, "you have been naughty. You need to be punished."

Slap! Slap!

These were harder, and Molly jerked. "Jackson!" she began, but then she felt his hand gently stroke her back again, caressing, moving, exploring. Then, underneath her stomach, she felt him. Ever so slightly, she felt him growing hard beneath her.

Slap! Slap!

These were decidedly more intense. Her rounded rear was stinging from these spanks. Molly gasped but still held hard against Jackson's lap, she couldn't move. She felt him again against her. In her confusion, she had the thought that Jackson wasn't too drunk after all.

When Molly woke up in the morning, she was alone. She hadn't heard Jackson leave, and she missed him beside her. The night had been strange and passionate, yet more than that. Jackson had been rough. She had to think about that. How did she talk to him about the night? She wanted him to know she wanted his passion, but not the near violence.

She got up, put on a dressing gown, and began picking up the scattered clothes on the floor. She noticed that Jackson's clothes were gone. She thought vaguely that he must have picked them up when he left the room.

Jackson must have heard Molly moving around because the bedroom door opened, and he walked in. He was fully dressed in traveling clothes. His demeaner was solemn. Molly smiled at him, but he spoke before she could say anything.

"Molly," Jackson began seriously, "I am going to Laramie today. I should get there just about when the herd gets in."

"Do you have to go?" Molly asked. "So soon."

"I think it best, yes," Jackson said. He didn't approach any closer. "Molly, I have to apologize. I treated you terribly last night."

"But . . . "

"I promise you I won't ever do anything like that again," Jackson went on, cutting off her protest. "You are my wife. Last night was not proper. I am ashamed of myself."

"But . . ." Molly began again. She needed to talk to Jackson about this.

"No, I am sorry," Jackson cut her off again. "I was drunk. It won't happen again." And with that, he turned and left the room, closing the door firmly behind him.

Molly stared after him. What in the world has happened to them? If the night left her confused, the morning did not clear anything up. Her husband was turning into a stranger, and he was turning her into . . . what? What was she being turned into? If this was what being a lady was like, she didn't like it. She didn't like it one little bit.

Jackson rode alone the day and a half to Laramie. He had Buster and a crew there to ride back with him if he wished, and this part of the range was pretty safe these days. He reached the line shack and its utilitarian bed before dark. There were line shacks all along the way that afforded a traveler safety from the elements, and these were Anchor J line shacks. Jackson had them built not only for his cowboys who rode the range summer and winter, but also for him and his guests to stay in as they traveled to and from Laramie. Usually, he posted cowboys in them to ride the area and check on cattle. At the moment, all his hands were either in Laramie or at the ranch.

Jackson hoped that the miles would ease his disgust at himself. How could he have treated Molly like he did? Yes, he was drunk, but this was precisely what he had been fighting to contain in himself for years. When he married this spirited girl, he thought the excitement he felt with her would be enough. It had been in the beginning years. But now it wasn't. They hadn't been married even two years when he started having the urges again. His lovemaking with Molly became an effort to control his desires.

He was eighteen when he and his friends ventured into London to visit a house of prostitution. When he was nineteen, his cousin Rudolph took him to a different house in London. He didn't like his cousin very much, but Rudolph was visiting the manor, and he suggested taking the carriage to London for a few days of pleasure. Rudolph was older than Jackson by several years, and he told Jackson he knew of a special house. The Red House, Rudolph called it.

It was special. Jackson had no idea how special until he went there. Rudolph was apparently a regular because when they entered, Rudolph was met by a middle-aged woman.

"You were told the last time you were here that you were too rough. If you think you are coming back to rough up my girls, you'd better think again," the woman said severely to Rudolph. "I will station my man outside your door and if you are too rough, you are out of here forever."

Rudolph looked contrite. "I lost control," he said. "It won't happen again."

"So, who is this young man with you?" the woman asked, turning to Jackson.

Rudolph glanced over at Jackson. "He's my cousin. He's new. You will have to have a girl teach him."

The woman looked Jackson up and down. "There is only one rule here," she said to Jackson. "You can pretend, but if you hurt one of my girls, you are out."

Jackson could only nod. This was a strange whore house.

It got stranger. The woman that came for Jackson was at least ten years his senior, but she was shapely and good-looking. She led Jackson to a room, and they entered. The lighting inside was from two kerosene lamps, the globes tinted red, bathing the room in an ethereal shade. It wasn't the lighting that astonished Jackson. The bed had a headboard and footboard with rings on each side. Attached to the rings were leather cuffs. A narrow table padded in red leather tilted as if waiting for someone to recline on it. There were rings on the wall above the table and at the lower end. Along the walls were an assortment of whips, prods, blindfolds, soft ropes, and scarves. Jackson just stared.

"Do you know what to do with these?" the woman asked Jackson. All Jackson could do was shake his head.

"Then I will teach you," she said. "Whatever I do to you, you can do to me. Do you understand?" He didn't, but he nodded. He had a feeling he would find out soon enough.

That was the beginning. Again and again, Jackson returned to the house. He learned just how much discomfort he was allowed to impart before his partner called a stop to it. He learned the best ways to use the tools hanging on the wall. He learned what was preferred, both by his partner and himself. He learned to dominate, and he learned to be dominated. It wasn't long before normal sexual relations didn't hold the excitement that he felt when he was at the Red House. His sexual appetite was changed forever.

The cattle sold well, and Jackson was pleased with the profit. He allowed his men to stay a day in town, and then Buster rousted them all out and headed back to the ranch.

"I have to spend a few days with my solicitor and my banker," Jackson told Buster. "I might ride to the Bar S for a few days too. They imported some bulls, and I want to see them. It may be a week or two before I head home. Assign some men to the line shacks. You know what to do."

On the first night at the hotel, a scullery girl came into the room and lit the fire in the fireplace. She was a young woman, dressed in nothing more than rags. He had seen her in the kitchen washing dishes after the noon meal. Jackson guessed she took on other duties as well. He tossed her a coin, and she smiled and thanked him and left the room.

The next morning, Jackson left the hotel entrance and walked around the boardwalk toward the side street on his way to his solicitor's office. As he rounded the corner, he heard a man's voice raised in anger.

The scene before him was of a rough-looking man and the scullery girl. The man was middle-aged and burly. He towered over the girl, who cringed away from him. The girl, in a clean, but ragged dress was trying not to cry, but tears coursed her cheeks. As the man advanced on her, she stepped backward, again and again.

"Ye be three weeks late with the rent," the man raged at the girl. "I kin rent that room and get paid fer it, so I want ye out o' there, or I'll throw yer things out."

The girl was crying now. "I get paid next week. I'll pay you then," she pleaded.

"Hell, girl, you said that last week," the man growled. "Ye been late since that no 'count husband of yers took off. I ain't in business to give no charity."

"How much does she owe?" Jackson heard himself ask. He hadn't intended to get involved, but the girl looked so forlorn.

The man named a price, and Jackson pulled out some bills. He counted out the amount and handed the bills to the man.

"This gets ye to the end of the week then," the man said gruffly. "See you get me paid then. I ain't letting you get that far behind agin."

The girl nodded. When the gruff man had turned and walked away, she looked at Jackson gratefully. "Sir, I cain't pay you all of this, but I get paid next week. I kin pay part of it back then."

"Don't worry about it," Jackson said. He turned and walked down the street. He had other things to think about. His kindness to the girl was forgotten before he got a block down the street.

Later in the day, Jackson was strolling a side street of the town, thinking about the profits his cattle had brought that fall. His solicitor had given him a rundown of the ranch's finances. The cattle sale had paid down his investors and given Jackson enough to pay down part of his own building expenses. Jackson also had a roll of bills in his pocket and ready cash at the bank. Things were going well.

As Jackson reached the end of the street, he saw a nicely kept little cottage. There were vacant lots next to the small house on both sides and an abandoned building on the opposite side of the street. Outside the cottage, a man was nailing a sign to the neat white picket fence that encircled the yard. The sign said: For Sale. Jackson stopped and looked at the cottage, thinking.

"This your place?" Jackson asked.

The man turned toward him. "Reckon so," he said. "It were my mother's, but she passed. My wife and I ranch out of town, a half-day ride from here. We've no reason to keep this little house."

"Show it to me," Jackson said.

It was a two-room house. The front door, the door between the front room and the back room, and the back door were all in a row. A shotgun house, Jackson thought they called houses like this because you could shoot a shotgun right through the doors, and it would exit out the back door, never passing through a wall. The front room was a small parlor. There were two chairs, a small loveseat, and a tiny table with a lamp. Against the wall was a small bookcase with a few volumes on the shelves. Doilies and knick-knacks adorned the table and bookcase shelves as well.

The back room was a combination bedroom and kitchen. The bed was on the left of the door in the corner.

There was an open space with pegs on the wall to hang clothes. A small wardrobe was next, and then a dresser. In the far corner sat a small metal bathtub with a folding screen leaning against the wall. The kitchen was on the right side along the wall between the bedroom door and the back door. There was an icebox, a dry sink, a cookstove, a counter, and cupboards.

"My mother and father lived here when we took over the ranch," the man explained. "My father has been gone for years, but my mother has lived here alone for quite some time. My wife and I took what we wanted. Everything else sells with the house."

Jackson looked in the wardrobe and dresser. There was a set of sheets and some rags but nothing else. The icebox still had a chunk of ice, but there was no food.

"Where does the ice come from?" Jackson asked.

"There's a delivery in town. I was going to go there next and cancel our account."

Jackson took another look around before saying, "Let's go down the street. My solicitor is there. We can write up the papers. I'll take it."

Jackson waited behind the hotel for the girl to come out. It was still light, but dusk would soon follow. He had spent the afternoon getting ready. Now, he only needed to implement his plan.

When the girl came out, Jackson could see she was weary. Her shoulders slumped, and she sighed as the door closed behind her. Jackson imagined she began long before the light of day. Jobs for women were few and far between and paid little. Long hours and physical labor wore a young woman down long before her time.

When the girl looked up, she was surprised to see Jackson. He stood and politely touched his hat.

"Good evening, ma'am," he said. "Would you be so kind as to go for a walk with me?"

The girl looked at him warily. "Where to?"

"I'd like to show you an option for a room," Jackson said, "unless, of course, you like the boarding house so well you couldn't leave it?"

The girl smiled ruefully. "Don't reckon I like it that well."

Jackson took the girl's arm and led her down the street. "That man this morning said you are married," he said carefully. "Do you expect your husband back soon?"

The girl looked away. "Don't reckon so."

"I'm sorry to hear that," Jackson pursued. "Was he called away?"

The girl sighed. "He ain't really my husband. See, we'd been married a few months earlier by a preacher, and then we came out here. I was from Denver, but he was from Omaha. He was in Denver for business, he told me, and after a few days, he asked me to marry him. I thought being married would be easier than mostly starving like I were doin'. He got a letter a month ago. He was married before me, but he left that wife. I didn't know about her. I didn't know he were married before. The letter said she had a baby boy. Ralph said he wanted a son. Now he'd gotten one. He packed up his things and he left the next day. Turned out our marriage was fake, only I didn't know that."

"That is a shame," Jackson said sympathetically. "Do you miss him?"

"Reckon I miss his pay," the girl answered, "but not him. He turned out to be a mean bastard."

They had reached the little house. It was dark by now, and a kerosene lamp shone in the window. Jackson turned in and walked the girl up the stairs to the porch. Opening the door, he ushered her into the little parlor.

"My, this is a pretty place, ain't it?"

"It is nice," Jackson agreed.

"Is this yer place?" the girl asked.

"I get tired of staying in the hotel when I come to town on business," Jackson answered smoothly. "I just bought it."

They went to the second room. "Land sakes, there is an icebox!" the girl exclaimed. "Seen one in the hotel, but not in a house."

"I think they are the going thing," Jackson smiled good-naturedly. "There is a service that delivers ice each week."

The girl was all eyes. They went out the back door. There was a chicken house with chickens, a small barn, and a pump halfway between the house and the barn.

"Do you like chickens?" Jackson asked.

"Raised on a farm. I took care of chickens all my life 'ceptin lately," the girl replied, nodding.

"Well, I have a proposition for you," Jackson said. "Let's go in the house and talk about it."

They made their way back to the parlor. Jackson took one of the chairs, and the girl sat on the loveseat.

"First, what is your name?" Jackson asked.

"Ida," the girl answered. "Been going by Ida Baker as that were my husband's name, but now he ain't really my husband, I guess."

"Well, Ida Baker is just fine. Keep using that name, calling yourself Mrs. Baker. Not your fault your man lied to you," Jackson smiled at Ida. "You have a reputation to keep, so from now on, you stay Mrs. Baker."

Jackson hesitated then began speaking again gently. "So, Ida, I have this house, but I will not be here that much, so I need someone to keep it clean and neat, ready for me when I come to town. Do you think you could do that for me?"

"I reckon so," Ida replied, looking around the comfortable parlor.

"You could stay here, and I would give you a salary to take care of it. You can take care of the chickens and sell the extra eggs to the café on Main Street. You can keep whatever money you make. But always keep back enough eggs so that if I drop by, there will be some for breakfast. Do you think you can do that?" Jackson asked casually.

"Yes, sir. I could do that," Ida answered, looking again around the pleasant little room. Jackson could see her eying its comfort, weighing it against a bleak boarding house room. "You'd pay me to live here and keep it nice?" she clarified.

"Definitely," Jackson replied. "I would give you a salary and also credit at the general store so you could get the things you need to live. I live a couple of days from here, but I try to get to town once a month or so when the weather permits. I wouldn't be around that much, but I would want this house taken care of."

Ida looked around again, thinking. Jackson knew this seemed like a dream come true to her, but she wasn't dumb. He knew the question that would come eventually.

"When you come to town," Ida asked slowly, "where do I go?"

"Why, Ida," Jackson said smoothly, "you'd stay here of course. I would want someone to take care of me while I am here."

Ida cast her gaze around the room and to the door to the bedroom. "There only be one bed in that back room," she replied.

"That is true," Jackson answered. "But it is big enough for two people. Do you have a problem with that? You were married, at least you thought you were. I would expect you to tell people you are still married. To Mr. Baker. And let's pretend that Mr. Baker works in the mines and comes to visit when he can. Do you understand what I am asking?"

Ida again looked around the room. Jackson could see she was weighing her options. He could see her thinking of the comfort of this little house, the salary she would make to stay here, and what he was asking of her. Jackson knew she wanted the house, but how badly?

"I reckon I understand."

"Do you think you could work for me then? That way?" Jackson asked softly. "Both when I am not here and also when I am here?"

"Maybe," Ida whispered, her face growing red.

"Are you afraid of me?" Jackson asked gently.

"I don't think so."

"Are you afraid to stay here alone?"

"I don't reckon I would be."

"Are you afraid to share a bed with me when I am here?" Jackson asked gently.

Ida glanced around the pleasant room again before shrugging her shoulders.

"Ida," Jackson prodded, "would you feel better staying with me tonight? And in the morning, if you don't want to do this, I will pay a month's rent at the boarding house, and we will go our separate ways. Would that help?"

Ida thought about that before she cautiously nodded, not looking at Jackson.

"Well, let's just have a little trial," Jackson said. "You go into the other room, and there is warm water on the stove, a basin, and some rags to wash with. You go wash up from your day at the hotel. Then look in the wardrobe and see what is in there. It is for you. Put it on and let me know when you are ready. If you get scared, you can leave anytime."

Ida watched Jackson as he talked, and then she got up and went hesitantly to the other room. Jackson sat and waited. He heard her take the kettle off the stove. The water was not hot anymore. He had heated it earlier and turned off the stove, but it should still be warm. Faintly, he heard the splash of water and the wardrobe door open. It had a slight squeak.

"This here silky thing in the wardrobe is for me?" Ida called. "It be awful nice."

"If you want it," Jackson answered easily. "Do you like it?"

There was silence from the back room. Jackson heard the squeak of the wardrobe door closing, then nothing. He waited, but he didn't have to wait long.

"Oh, this be pretty," Ida spoke softly. She came to the door and peeked out at Jackson. "I ain't never had something so pretty."

Jackson smiled at her. "Maybe it is time you do," he said, rising and going to the lamp in the front room, he blew it out. "Maybe this is your lucky day, after all."

Jackson woke just as the sun was starting to peak over the horizon. The little back room was still in gloom, but it wouldn't last long. He gazed at the sleeping girl beside him. She was not Molly. She was taller than Molly and not as slim. Ida was heavy-breasted and wide-hipped, but she was not fat. Sturdy is how he would describe her. She was not a pretty girl, but she was pleasant looking in a plain way. She was shy at first, but he was gentle with her. She was fingering the silky-smooth nightdress he bought for her when he approached her. It was another carrot to dangle in front of her. The house, the pretty nightdress, the salary, and credit at the store. It must have seemed a dream come true. He just needed her to want all of that enough. So, this first night, he didn't take the nightdress off of her. He didn't need to. He could work around the soft fabric. He had time to break her in slowly until she didn't want to leave.

He felt Ida stir beside him. She rolled off the bed and looked for her clothes. She started to dress quietly.

"Where are you going?" Jackson asked her. Startled, Ida looked at him.

"I best get to the hotel. I'm already late," she said.

"Do you like working at the hotel?"

"No, but there ain't much work for a woman 'round here," she said.

"You don't need the job, if you want to stay here," Jackson told her. He paused. "Do you want to stay here? I am paying you, remember?" He sat up and swung his legs off the bed.

"I want to stay here," Ida said softly.

"Good, that's decided, then." Jackson paused and continued, "This is what I want you to do today. First, go to the hotel and tell them your husband sent you money, so you don't have to work. Then go to the boarding house and get your things and bring them here. Do you need help with that?"

Ida shook her head. "I don't have much there that I can't carry myself."

"Good," Jackson said. "Do you know the Fine Lady's Shoppe on Sixth Street?"

"I've seen it, but I ain't never been in there."

"Well, after you get your other things brought here, go to the Lady's Shoppe and tell them you are the new maid for Mr. Crowden's wife. They will expect you. You are to pick out two dress choices they show you. You might not be able to bring both dresses home if they need adjustment but be sure to bring one home. I have an engagement this evening, and I will be eating out. I will be back after dark, but I expect to see you in one of your new dresses when I get here," Jackson smiled at Ida. "I won't be late."

"I don't have money for dresses," Ida said doubtfully.

"The dresses will be paid for," Jackson told her. "Also, go to the general store and the meat market and get food for yourself and for me in case I want you to fix me something tomorrow. There will be credit at the store and at the butcher, so you pick out what you think you will need."

Ida just stood staring. This sounded almost too good to be true.

"Ida, there is one thing you have to remember," Jackson said, his tone becoming serious. "My solicitor will arrange the credit at the store. Your story is that your husband, Mr. Baker, had good luck in the mines and sent you money through the attorney. No one is to know anything else. That is the story that you tell everyone. Do you understand?"

Ida nodded.

"Good. The second thing is that I am Mr. Crowden if you meet me on the street. Do you understand?"

Ida nodded again. "But what do I call you here? When we are in this house?" she asked.

"You call me Mr. Crowden," Jackson said firmly. "That is always what you will call me. That way, there will be no slip if you see me by surprise in a public place."

Seven days later, Jackson gathered his horse from the livery and began the trek home. He felt immense relief. His week with Ida had gone well. She was a quick learner. She had been mistreated by her husband, so Jackson's little pretend games were nothing to her. She had two new dresses from the Fine Lady's Shoppe that were finer than anything she ever imagined having. The frocks were not the fine dresses he bought for Molly. After all, he didn't want Ida to be a lady, he just wanted to entice Ida to want to stay so that she would accept his ways. And she did. On the third night he brought her home a fine silk scarf. She was in awe of it.

"You can wear this to Sunday church," Jackson told her. "But I want to show you what else we can use it for." And he did, and she wasn't frightened at all.

On the fifth day, he made a soft whip out of scrap material, and they practiced with it. "It is all pretend," he told Ida, and in a way, it was. Yes, Jackson thought as he rode home, this will work out just fine. He left Ida with credit at the store, enough money to buy herself a new shawl, and instructions to keep the house clean. He would be back in a month. Most of all, he rode home, satiated by his conquest. He could return to Molly and treat her as a lady should be treated. His other desires were fulfilled, and he was content.

CHAPTER 4

Will – Spring 1885

Jake rode his gelding down to the ranch store and dismounted, tying to the hitching post. He would soon be heading to the mountains, and he wanted to talk to Kade. He would need supplies and one of the ranch wagons. But most of all, he trusted his stepfather's opinion and wanted to visit before he and his family headed out. Every summer, Jake, his cousin Lathe and Jake's nephew Swift Hawk, took their families to the high mountains to the cabin that had been old Jacob Bates', Jake's grandfather. They took young horses and trained them in the mountains.

As Jake started up the steps to the covered porch, he met his cousin, Will Bates, coming out.

"Hey, Will," Jake said, hesitating on the steps. "You getting ready to move the sheep to high country?"

Will, a tall gaunt man five years younger than Jake, was dressed in sturdy trousers, shirt, and vest. Will used to tag along with Jake and Thomas when they were young. Of all the Jorgensen, Bates, and Welles offspring, Will was the only one still not married. At thirty-one, Will didn't seem to have any inclination to marry. He had built a small cabin across the river valley several years before and lived there pretty much as a hermit.

"Yup," Will replied, stopping on the porch.

"Think the snows will be gone in the meadows up there?" Jake asked.

"Yeah, enough," Will said, looking down at his feet.

"I'm thinking of heading up toward the high mountains in a week or so," Jake commented. "I hope you are right."

Will didn't reply to that, just nodded.

"How's your leg doing?" Jake asked. "It holding up pretty well now?"

"Doin' good," Will answered.

"Well, you watch your back up there," Jake said, starting up the stairs. It was always an effort talking to Will. A person just ran out of questions, and Will offered nothing. Will just nodded, and carrying his sacks of goods, he went down the steps and to his waiting horse. Jake watched him a minute and then shrugged and went inside.

Kade was sitting at a round table by the front window, lazily playing solitaire. He looked up when Jake came in and smiled, tossing the deck onto the table.

"Having a conversation with Will?" Kade asked.

Jake grinned. "I think I got five or six words out of him," Jake answered. "You do better?"

"Let's see," Kade reflected, "I got 'flour, hardtack, sugar, coffee, and tinned peaches' out of him. But he did loosen up some an' thanked me for the newspapers. Oh, an' he did make a comment 'bout an article he read," Kade grinned. "That man is not generous with his words."

"So, what interested Will so much in the newspapers that got words out of him?" Jake chuckled.

Kade laughed at that, remembering his conversation with Will. "An obituary. He asked me if I noticed a particular obituary in one of the papers. I don't usually read obituaries of people I don't know, and since the papers come from Joe in St. Louis, I didn't see anyone I knew. I think Will reads every single word in those papers, even the ads!"

"After Will gets done with his day, I don't suppose he has much else to do. He lives alone, mostly works alone, and hardly speaks. But I know he has always read a lot so it wouldn't surprise me if he read every word in every newspaper you share with him," Jake laughed. "What interested Will in an obituary?"

"That was the crazy part. It was an obituary of a man who left behind a wife an' seven kids. But they listed the address of the man, an' then of his wife an' children, an' it was two different addresses, but they were next door to each other."

"You're pulling my leg."

"No, really. Will wondered how that would have happened," Kade looked reflective. "I have no idea why he was interested in talking about that. I mean who else would even question that? He's a hard man to figure."

"I remember when he and Thomas used to tag along with me as kids," Jake said, taking a seat with his father. "You could go all day and sometimes never hear a word come out of Will. But sometimes he talked. Asked questions, things like that, but as a grown man, you about have to pull the words out of him."

"He comes to visit Sarah or take a meal with us, an' it is almost painful. Sarah doesn't understand him at all, an' she is his mother," Kade laughed. "I told her to leave him alone. He is just solitary an' that's his way."

"I think he got worse after Jim was killed," Jake reflected. "Being under that wagon and under attack with his dead father lying next to him had to affect him some. He was always quiet, but after that, it is as if Will just shut down."

"You're right," Kade agreed. "I think he has worked through Jim's death, but I think he just got used to being silent, an' that stayed with him." Kade paused before adding, "He's got a good heart though. He's the first to go help where it is needed. When Bonnie was alone, he brought her a pup for company, chopped wood for her."

"He did the same for Anna when I had to be off. She'd hear chopping and he'd be outside getting her wood," Jake added. "Never stopped at the house and talked to her, just left full water buckets at the door when he left and disappeared."

"So, what did you and Will decide accounted for a man and wife having two different addresses?" Jake grinned.

"I have no idea, really. The only thing I came up with was maybe the two couldn't stand each other so they kept their own households. Reckon the husband trotted over for meals an' his bed when he felt the need." Kade smiled wickedly at his grown son. "I said maybe it was like them Mormons who kept more than one wife an' had a house for each. Jest kept working through them all as he wanted. Maybe he had a mistress somewhere else. Whatever, Will was interested."

The conversation about Will lagged then. Jake changed the subject.

"I'm thinking maybe next week if this spring weather holds, Lathe, Hawk, and I will load up the women and kids and head to the mountains. I'm just checking that you can outfit us with supplies." Jake looked at the shelves in the trading post. "I'd hate to have to stop at Steamboat and buy at the prices there."

"You know I have plenty, son," Kade answered. "And I think Luke will head to Laramie in a day or two an' get a wagon load of supplies for the summer. I put in orders last fall so those things should be waiting in Laramie. If some supplies are depleted, I will have the shelves filled again in a week or two. You don't have to worry about that."

"I'll sort off the horses early next week that we will take with us," Jake continued.

"You checked with Thomas in case he needs you?"

Jake grinned. "Thomas has his own crew, and they handle the cattle end pretty much without us. But I'll check for sure before we finalize our plans. See what seasoned horses he wants left back. What about you? You need me to do anything before I head out?"

"Hell, son," Kade smiled fondly at this dark-skinned man before him, "what do I do any more other than sit in this trading post or ride out with the kids? When you take Kestrel, I only have Feather hounding me to ride. I will have a summer of leisure."

After Kade's first wife, Jake's mother Sabra, passed away, Kade married his late partner and friend's widow, Sarah. Having more children in their advanced years wasn't anything they expected, so, it was quite a surprise when Sarah became pregnant. Feather Marie was born in St. Louis, where Kade and Sarah went to be close to a doctor. Small at birth, the couple named the little girl, Feather.

"You've earned your leisure," Jake replied. "You're the best grandpa our kids could have. I know you were the best husband to ma, and now to Sarah." Jake stood and headed for the door where he turned and hesitated before leaving. "You're the best pa too, to all of us," he said softly, then he turned and left the store.

The herders had the sheep lined out when Will got to his cabin. He had two Mexican sheepherders this year, a father and son. They rode the train up from Mexico to Laramie and were here when the snows began to melt. The father had been working for Will for several years, returning to Mexico and his family every winter. This year the son was old enough to help, and Will's flock was getting large enough that he wanted two men with the flock in the mountains. Will didn't stay in the mountains with the sheep. He had Twin Peak's hog operation at his place, so he wandered back and forth from the mountain slopes to his headquarters all summer. He could leave the hog operation completely to Noah now, but he resisted. Noah, the stepson of James, was seventeen this summer. Noah knew what had to be done with the hogs, so Will wasn't tied down. Will could leave the day-to-day hog operation to the young man and know everything would be cared for. Will liked to get away, but he also liked being home in his small cabin, so he made his monthly excursions into the higher slopes, leaving for a week and then returning.

Maybe, Will thought, *I have some of my great uncle Jacob in me. Old Jacob liked to ramble, hunting in the mountains alone. But I'm not like Jake, Hawk, and Lathe who want to get away to the high mountains every year for the summer months. I just want to ramble alone for a week or so, and then come back.*

Of course, for the last four years, he didn't ramble so much when he went off to the mountains alone. He had a destination, and it had become his routine. He would load up a pack mule with supplies every few weeks and haul them to his sheepherders. He would check with his herders, maybe staying a night with them. Then he would ride the half day farther to Rosie. There he would stay for several days before heading home, relaxed and content.

Rosie was a woman referred to as a "soiled dove." She wasn't in the trade anymore though. She was Will's woman. Will knew Rosie from her years working in a house of prostitution in Laramie called Miss Tillie's. Several years ago, Rosie had been a victim of a brawl in Miss Tillie's, and she had two ugly knife welts across one side of her face. The brawl was the incident that finally shut down Miss Tillie's establishment. The town council, egged on by a new minister, was threatening to oust the madam and her girls. Miss Tillie had a buyer for her building, money in the bank, and was ready to quit the trade anyway. She and her Black barman loaded up wagons with her fine things and left in the night, taking Rosie with them. They bought a mountain homestead and lived a quiet life there. Will had come upon them the next year, and he and Rosie renewed their interest in each other.

Will felt comfortable with Rosie. She was quiet and she never pushed him to talk. She had her own small cabin, no more than ten by twelve, but big enough for a bed, a chair, and a heating stove. Rosie took all her meals with Susan and Marcus, Miss Tillie's and Charlie's real names, so when Will was there, he ate at the bigger cabin as well. When Will visited, he always left some money for Rosie. Sometimes he brought her something from town or from Kade's trading post. She was his woman now, after all.

Will liked Susan and Marcus, who owned the homestead. They made out that Marcus had been Susan's barman and bodyguard at the brothel, and he was Susan's employee now. But there was more between these two than that. Marcus was a Black man and Susan was white.

In the South, a Black man could be hung for loving a white woman. This may not be the South, but Will knew that Marcus and Susan kept a secret between them. Will was sure it was a secret about their relationship. That didn't matter to him. He liked them both and kept his suspicions to himself. Their secret was safe with Will.

It was growing dusk when Will broke out of the trees and into the open meadow where Susan, Marcus and Rosie lived. There was smoke rising from both cabins, and a small black dog came barking from the porch as he rode in. Will had brought the dog to this place three years ago, and when it recognized him, it quit barking and started wagging its tail. The people in the cabins would be alerted now to his arrival, and they would know exactly who was coming by the dog's behavior.

Sure enough, Marcus came out from the big cabin, pulling on a coat. Will rode up to the barn and dismounted, reaching out a hand toward the older Black man. Marcus shook his hand, grinning.

"Been quite some time, young man," Marcus said genially. "We thought you might not remember the way."

"Not likely," Will replied, a smile pulling at his lips.

"We got your letter last fall," Marcus continued. "Your leg healed up good then."

"Almost," Will answered. "Slight limp."

Will stripped the saddle from his horse, handing extra supplies to Marcus. "Thought you could use 'em," he said.

"Always come in handy," Marcus said, smiling. "I'm going to have to head to town soon and get supplies, but we got enough for now."

"Closer to come to Twin Peaks," Will told him. "Kade's got a good supply. Prices are fair too."

"I just might have to do that," Marcus said. "But we'll keep our acquaintance to ourselves if I do."

Will smiled and nodded at that, turning toward the cabins. "Rosie good?"

"She's been waiting for you."

As the two men walked toward the cabins, Susan came out on the porch. Susan was a middle-aged woman, stout but with a shadow of her early beauty still in her features. When Will knew her as a madam of the most successful brothel in Laramie, she had been an immensely obese woman. After moving to the homestead in the mountains, she had lost a massive amount of weight. Now she wore conservative dresses and lived the quiet life, but her cabin sported the bright gold and red furniture and rugs from her house of ill repute. It gave a visitor quite a start to come into her log cabin to see the tufted settees and fine, but gaudy, floor coverings.

Susan had a towel-covered plate in her hand. As the men approached, she called out to Will. "Thought since it has been over five months since you were here, I'd just make you a plate of food and send it in with you. Don't reckon you will want to come over this evening." Susan's raucous laughter was the same as it had been as a madam.

Will just blushed and grinned. She knew he wasn't interested in food at the moment. He shrugged his saddle bags over his shoulder, switched his rifle to his left hand, took the plate, and nodding his thanks, he went on to Rosie's door. No, he wasn't interested in food.

Will never knocked when he went in Rosie's door. She would know he was here. Sometimes she'd hear him coming and she'd meet him inside, totally nude. Sometimes she'd just be in her dainties, or just a skirt. It was always an experience to have Rosie greet him. There was something special about a woman who was not shy about her body. His body was adrenaline-filled with expectation before he got the door open. With rifle in one hand and plate in another, he fumbled with the latch. He couldn't get in fast enough.

The cabin was overly warm, the fire going in the stove and a lamp on the small table. Will turned, his eyes adjusting to the dim light, searching for Rosie. When he found her, he stared in amazement, frozen in place. Rosie sat in a new chair, a rocking chair. She had her blouse open, both breasts exposed. But that is not what made Will freeze. To Rosie's one breast a baby nursed. A tiny baby. A very young tiny baby.

Will stood rooted to the ground, plate in one hand, rifle in the other and just stared. If words were hard for Will to get out, at that moment, it was impossible.

"You can put the rifle down," Rosie said curtly. "He don't bite."

Will stared. Then he turned and leaned the rifle against the wall. He shrugged the saddle bags off his shoulder and hung them on a peg. He turned back to Rosie, plate still in his hand.

"He?"

"It's a boy."

"Mine?"

"Reckon so, lessen you think I got with child like the Virgin Mary," Rosie retorted shortly.

"Thought you workin' girls knew how to keep that from happening," Will replied gravely.

Rosie gave Will a steady look at that statement, her face turning hard. "Reckon we do, but when your man comes once a month, if that, sometimes it's the wrong time. Guess I got careless. If you don't want to claim this child, you don't have to," she said grimly. "There's the door. But I ain't giving him up. You kin jest go on your way. I ain't holding you."

"I didn't say that," Will defended himself. He was getting hot. It was warm in the cabin. He walked a couple steps into the room and put the plate down on the small table. Then he turned and took off his coat, hanging it on a peg on the wall. He needed time to think, to process this new development. He walked slowly to the bed and sat on it, watching Rosie and the tiny bundle.

"A boy, you say?"

Rosie nodded.

"You give him a name?"

"I named him William after his father, but I call him Billy," Rosie looked down at the infant and her features softened.

"Kin I see him?" Will asked quietly.

Rosie folded back the blanket exposing the little one. Will leaned forward, and reached to touch a little hand, his fingers engulfing the baby's.

"When were he born?"

"He's three weeks old," Rosie answered.

"You must have known the last time I was here," Will said. "You could have told me."

"Wasn't sure how you'd take the news," Rosie said, her eyes not meeting Will's. "I was going to tell you when you came back, but then you got hurt and couldn't come. Didn't want Susan to tell you in a letter. Figured I'd see you this spring."

Will ran a finger over the child's peach fuzz hair, feeling the softness. As he watched, the baby's eyes began to droop, but he continued to nurse greedily.

"What do we do now?" Will asked, looking up at Rosie.

"Reckon that's up to you," the woman replied. "You don't want this baby you just walk out the door. You want to stay, you stay. Up to you." Rosie moved the blanket back, tucking it around the baby.

Will regarded her. "Don't reckon I need to go anywhere jest yet." He reached out, fondling Rosie's exposed breast. She smiled at him then, her scarred face almost pretty in her relief.

Will stayed for two more days. He plowed up the garden spot and helped Marcus fix some corrals. He got a good supply of wood chopped and stacked in the lean-to connecting the two cabins. He hunted up a deer and some rabbits for fresh meat. But between the activity, he sat and held his son, fascinated by the tiny being. Oh, he'd seen many tiny babies in his community. But he had mostly left them to others. But this little guy was his. He felt the swell of pride when he watched this baby. He also enjoyed naptime. Some things didn't change.

CHAPTER 5

Muddy Waters – Late August 1886

Molly sat on a blanket in the shade of aspen trees that bordered the front lawn of the Anchor J ranch headquarters. She played with two-year-old Grace and marveled at her love of the child. With light brown curls and a ready smile, little Grace could charm the gruffest cowpoke. She was the apple of her daddy's eye, but to Molly, Grace was her savior. With servants in her home and restrictions on her dress and riding habits, Molly spent as much time as possible with the toddler. But even that had rules. Lydia was hired as the children's nurse. Jackson insisted that the children follow the same routine he grew up with. The children's nurse would get them up, feed and clothe them, and bring them to their parents. Molly then had morning time with the children. The nurse gathered the children for the noon meal, taking them away. After eating, it was nap time for Grace and lessons for Jack with Burton. Later in the afternoon, Grace and Jack emerged again, and Molly would spend a couple of hours with the children until Lydia took them away for an evening meal and bedtime. Molly hated the schedule. She hated the routine. She hated all the requirements Jackson imposed upon her. But they had important guests again, so Jackson insisted on it all.

"Mother, do you think Uncle Jake will come and see me before I have to leave?" Jack called from the edge of the trees.

A pain stabbed at Molly at his words. She did not want Jack to leave, but that was another part of Jackson's upbringing that he insisted on. Jack was eight years old. It was time he went away to a fine school to mold him into a gentleman. That was the way Jackson put it. So, Jack was enrolled in a prestigious military school near St. Louis for the fall term. Molly had argued and cried, and argued some more, but Jackson was resolute. Jack must go away to school.

"I hope so, honey," Molly replied to Jack, trying to sound cheerful. She didn't want to let Jack know how upset she was about his leaving. It would do no good to worry the child more than he already was about going. "One of your father's men rode over to Grandpa Kade's trading post for supplies and left the message that you were going to school. I just hope Uncle Jake is home from the mountains."

Jack turned back toward the big old tree stump that he used as a target. He was practicing throwing a knife. Uncle Jake had been teaching him when he last visited. Jack adored his Uncle Jake and was fascinated with all the Indian skills that Jake possessed.

"Why do I have to go away to school?" Jack asked, throwing the knife again, hitting the tree.

"Your father thinks it is best," Molly answered. She didn't want to contradict Jackson's decision in front of Jack. It wouldn't help and could put more distance between her and her husband. And there was distance enough. Her marriage consisted of evening meals together and stiff, polite conversation. There was rarely any intimacy anymore.

"And Grandfather and Grandmother Crowden will take me to school?" Jack asked.

Molly just nodded. That was Jackson's plan. Jackson's father, mother, brother, and his brother's wife had been here since the beginning of July. In June, an accountant from an English investor had been here for two whole weeks. This had been the worst summer Molly had spent, trussed up in the finery that Jackson insisted she wear to impress their guests. The week before his parents arrived, he had gone to Molly's dressing room, gathered all her split skirt riding outfits, and taken them away. Molly had been livid when she found out, but Jackson was firm.

"You were out riding astride when Benson was here in June," Jackson told her. "He was quite shocked to see you riding like a common hussy. I had to think fast and tell him your sidesaddle needed repair. I think he bought my story, but I don't want a repeat of that when my family is here. Mother would be shocked to see her daughter-in-law riding like a peasant. I do not want to disappoint Mother."

Molly had been mutinous then, thinking Jackson didn't want to disappoint his mother, but he didn't mind taking all that Molly loved away from her. She was still angry about this, but anger didn't change anything. By the time Jackson's parents were fetched from the train in Laramie, Molly had her composure back and would play the high-class wife. She would sit placidly with her mother-in-law and sister-in-law, sewing, reading, or visiting. The inactivity was driving Molly crazy, but there was nothing she could do about that. Yes, it had been a long, dreary summer.

Molly was startled when the screen door on the porch opened, and Jackson came out. Seeing Molly and the children in the yard, he descended the stairs and came to join them.

"Why are you three out here alone?" Jackson asked, smiling. "Where is Mother and Evie?"

"Your mother said she didn't sleep well last night and went upstairs to rest until noon," Molly answered. "Evie wanted to read."

Jackson reached out and pulled Grace to his lap. "How's my angel today?"

Molly watched him with Grace. He was a good father. He loved his children, but social standing and business came first with Jackson.

"How are you doing with the knife throwing?" Jackson asked his son.

"I'm doing pretty good," Jack answered. "I just hope Uncle Jake comes before I leave, and I can show him."

"Your uncle will come if he is home," Jackson replied. "I sent a message to Twin Peaks. I'll watch you practice now, though."

When Jack walked back to the big tree, Jackson turned to Molly.

"I talked to my father this morning, and I think we will head to Laramie next week." Jackson lowered his voice so Jack couldn't hear. "I want Jack to get to school when the term begins, and Mother is ready to go back to England, so I will take both buggies and the Burtons to help, and we will leave on Wednesday."

"I'm going too," Molly said quickly. She wasn't sure by Jackson's words if he intended to include her on this trip.

"Now, darling, that is a long ride for Grace. It might be best to say goodbye here," Jackson said placatingly.

"Jackson, he's my son!" Molly tried to keep the panic out of her voice. "If you are going to send him away, I want to see him off at the train!"

"Sweetheart," Jackson said patiently, "I don't plan to stay in Laramie. I have business over that way and will not be coming directly home. I don't want to leave you alone in town. It just won't work out for you to go."

Molly sat up straight and lowered her voice, "Jackson, I am going with you. I can come home with the Burtons. But you will not leave me behind when you send my son away." She fairly hissed these last words angrily.

Jackson stared at her for a few moments and then nodded. "I guess if you want to come, I can get you a room in the hotel for a night. It might be nice for Mother and Evie to have you with them on the trip. Just be ready on Wednesday."

"Nice job, Jack!" Jackson called to his son. "Keep practicing."

Kissing Grace on the forehead, Jackson got up and strode across the lawn to the house. Molly gazed after him. What had happened to them, she thought for the hundredth time. Where is the young man she married? How did he become this stiff, pompous Englishman?

Molly glanced at Grace, playing with twigs. Darling Grace, the product of one night of strange, but passionate, sex with her husband two years earlier. Jackson had ridden off the next day and stayed away for two weeks. He came back to the ranch relaxed and courteous. He brought Molly a new dress from the Fine Lady Shoppe. He was considerate and charming, seeking her out to discuss his plans for the ranch. But he seldom visited her bed since then, and when he did, the passion was gone. Oh, dear God, Molly thought sadly, what has happened to them?

It was quiet in the parlor as the women worked on needlework. Molly could sew, but there was little need for sewing clothes for her and Grace since Jackson was continually coming home with more fine dresses, and he didn't want her to wear her homemade riding outfits. But Mother Crowden had brought something she called needlepoint with her and taught Molly the stitches needed to make colorful pictures on a mesh canvas. Molly would much rather be out riding but since that wasn't possible, at least working on a needlepoint project kept her hands busy and from going crazy with boredom. Both Molly's mother-in-law and her sister-in-law, Evie, were content to sit all day working on different sewing projects. For two months, Molly thought that the departure of their guests could not come fast enough. That is until Jackson told her Jack would leave when her in-laws left. Then suddenly, Molly didn't want anyone to leave.

All at once, the house's quiet was broken by Jack's shout and his feet pounding down the stairs from the room upstairs where he took his studies.

"Mother!" Jack shouted, bounding into the room.

Clearly startled, Grandmother Crowden looked up at the young boy, "Honestly, Jack," she said irritably, "must you shout and run in the house like a heathen? Goodness, what a ruckus you make!"

"Sorry, Grandmother," Jack panted, but turned to his mother.

"Riders coming from the west, and they have loose horses too! It must be riders from Twin Peaks!"

"How many riders did you see?" Molly set her needlework down quickly and rose, heading to the front door.

"Four."

"Oh goodness, let's go see," Molly exclaimed, excitement coursing through her. Riders from the west with extra horses sounded like Jake, heading to Laramie or a fort with horses to sell. Molly and Jack let the screen door slam as they went outside to look. They didn't hear the disapproving sigh that came from Jackson's mother.

The horses and riders were just small figures at first, but as they came closer, Molly and Jack began to recognize the riders.

"That is Uncle Jake in the lead," Molly said. "And I think that is Grandpa Kade off to the side."

"That is Uncle Thomas in the back, but who is the other man?" Jack asked.

"I am not sure yet, but I think it might be that Luke cowboy who has been at Twin Peaks for several years," Molly answered, squinting at the distant riders. "You met him a couple of years ago when he came through with Uncle Jake. Remember?"

Jack nodded, intent on the riders as they came closer.

"You are right, Mother," Jack agreed after a few minutes. "That is Luke. I'm going to run out and meet them as they turn in here."

Molly smiled at her son and nodded. If she weren't in this blasted fancy dress and shoes, she would run out there with him. She hadn't seen her family since last Easter.

Jake waved as he led the little band of loose horses past the house, heading for the barn and corrals. Thomas rode close to Jack and leaning over, he hoisted the boy up in the saddle with him and they followed the loose horses. Kade pulled up in the yard and stepped off his horse, handing the reins to Luke, who stopped with him.

Then Luke cued his horse and leading Kade's, he headed to the corral after the others.

"Pa!" Molly called, leaving the porch and going to her father. "I am so glad to see you." Molly threw her arms around her father, then lost her composure and began to weep.

"Hope you are crying because you are happy to see me, daughter," Kade said softly, awkwardly patting her back.

Molly just nodded against his chest, holding him tight. After a few moments, she got herself under control and pushed away from him.

"I was so afraid no one would come before Jack has to go away," Molly's voice quivered, and she struggled not to break down again. "Oh, gosh, I am being so silly."

"Honey," Kade said softly, "you aren't silly. You are a mother. I know sending Jack away is hard for you." Kade found it hard as a grandfather too. He disagreed with Jackson's belief that Jack should be sent away to school, but Jack was Kade's grandson, not his son. This wasn't his business. He couldn't interfere.

"How long can you stay?" Molly asked.

"Jake an' Luke will take the horses on in the morning. Thomas an' I will head back to the ranch after breakfast," Kade told Molly. "We're still haying and getting ready for fall gather next month. Lots to do."

"There is always lots to do," Molly said wistfully. "I'll find you places to stay tonight, then."

"Don't bother," Kade said. "We brought bedrolls an' will jest bunk out under the stars tonight. Gonna be a nice night."

"Oh, Pa, I can find you a place."

Kade looked at the big house. "Molly, you have your in-laws here, an' I'm thinkin' we might not fit the best in there."

Molly followed his gaze, thinking. "I know," she had a sudden thought, "let's have a fire tonight and show my in-laws a night like we used to have." Molly looked at her father and smiled. "We first met Jackson and his father out on the prairie, and we sat around the fire. Remember? Let's do that."

Kade grinned at his daughter and nodded. He hoped Jackson would like the idea. He and the boys would feel the most comfortable out under the stars.

Kade Welles was an old mountain man, wagon scout, and hunter. At fifteen, he had gone west from St. Louis with his father, a trapper, in the waning day of the beaver trade. Together, Kade and his father trapped with Jacob Bates and Tom Grissom. Kade's father quit the beaver trade when beaver became scarce, and the price for their furs dwindled. Jacob Bates, married to a Ute woman with children of his own, stayed in the mountains for years after the fur trade crashed. Kade and Tom partnered for several years, leading wagon trains across the Oregon Trail, hunting for remote forts, and even supplying gold seekers in California with wild meat.

Then, one winter after his wife died, Jacob Bates returned to the settlements to live with his brother and try farming. He didn't last even a year before he yearned for his wild mountains and returned. Only he didn't return alone; he brought with him a young girl who would later marry Jacob's mixed-blood Ute son and have a child. Later still, Sabra married Kade Welles. When Kade and

Sabra married, they moved out of the high mountains and closer to the Oregon Trail. Here, with two other families, they started Twin Peaks Ranch. For decades they met the westward-moving prairie schooners, trading fresh livestock for worn-out animals with the emigrants until they amassed their own herd, grazing on the free land of the river valley and the high mountain meadows. Kade might have become a successful rancher and now the owner of a trading post, but he always remained the former mountain man. Growing up, his children had spent as much time outside their modest cabin as inside. Supper beside a campfire was a family tradition. Kade knew that sitting around a campfire instead of eating inside the mansion of his son-in-law's house would be more comfortable for him and his sons. He had a suspicion that his daughter would feel better outside as well.

Jackson thought a night around a campfire was a marvelous idea. He got the cook started on a meal they could take outside. In the back of the house was a campfire ring that the cowboys used a lot in the summer, sitting in the cool night air rather than in the cookshack or bunkhouse. There were logs to sit on or lean against, and in deference to his mother and sister-in-law, Jackson had chairs and a table brought out for them to sit at and eat.

Molly helped the Burtons and the cook bring out the food and serve it, then taking a plate, she went to sit on the ground between her father and Jake. Thomas and Luke were on the far side of the fire. Jack sat on the other side of Jake, and little Grace had climbed into her Uncle Thomas' lap.

"Oh, Molly," her mother-in-law exclaimed, "You'll ruin your dress sitting on the ground!"

Molly looked at Mrs. Crowden and then glanced at Jackson. "I have other dresses," she said in defense of her actions. "I always sit on the ground at a campfire."

Mrs. Crowden turned shocked eyes to Jackson, but he just smiled. "I am sure Mrs. Burton can put the dress right, Mother," he said, smiling. "Molly is happy seeing her family."

Molly looked at her husband gratefully. She couldn't figure him out. He wanted her to act so properly, yet he was supporting her here. Maybe he knew that in this, she would have thrown caution to the wind and fought him right here in front of everyone, if he told her she couldn't sit with her pa.

"This is exactly how it was the first time we met," Jackson's father, Richard, said. "We came upon this family along the Oregon Trail and camped nearby. We sat out by the campfire then, all of us sitting on the ground."

"Jake was shot by pirates, and I was kicked by a mule," Thomas smiled, remembering. "And Molly rode a stud horse of Pa's and beat Rudolph's fancy thoroughbred in a race."

"That was a long time ago," Jackson said quickly when his mother looked shocked. "Molly wasn't even grown up then."

The evening went by much too fast for Molly, even though they sat around the fire for hours. The men told stories, with Kade entertaining them with tales of his trapper days. Thomas and Jackson had stories of round-ups and mishaps with the cattle that were commonplace to the ranchers, but not to the English guests. Jake recounted stories of horse-trading trips or breaking some of the ranker horses.

After a time, when the conversation lagged, Jackson's brother, Stuart, asked Jake, "So, Jake, do you find it hard to adapt to life with your white family?"

Jackson shot his brother a hard look and began to answer, "I explained to you . . . "

"It's alright, Jackson," Jake answered smoothly, "It's a fair question." He turned to Stuart. "I was born in the high mountains in my grandfather's cabin, but I moved with my white mother and Kade before I was a year old. I have always lived with them and my other white relatives. So, no, I had no problem adopting to white life."

"But you lived with the Indians too?" Stuart pressed.

"My parents felt I needed to know my roots, so as a young child, they took me to meet my brother and other relatives," Jake answered. "When I was old enough, I spent a good part of my summers with my half-brother, Brown Otter. Kade, having been a trapper," here Jake smiled at his stepfather, "was almost as much Indian as a white man in many ways. I never felt out of place with either my white relatives or my red."

"Which place do you prefer to live then?" Stuart asked.

"I have a lot of places I like to live, but Twin Peaks is my home. The long and short of it is this," Jake said, suddenly turning serious. "I am three-quarters white and look more Indian than that. I walk between two cultures. I like them both. But my heart always pulls me back to my family at the ranch. I like to wander some, but my feet, whether they wear moccasins or boots, always take me home."

Eventually, the two Mrs. Crowden's took their leave and went to bed. Grace moved to her father's lap and finally fell asleep, so Lydia took the little girl off to her bed. Jack begged to stay up, and Jackson let him until the little boy couldn't keep his eyes open.

Molly dreaded the evening's end, but it came eventually. The fire dwindled to embers, the moon came over the peaks, and the stars twinkled in the clear night sky when the party broke up. Kade and Thomas were heading back to the ranch in the morning, while Jake and Luke were taking horses off to sell. They all promised to stay for a quick breakfast before saying goodbye. Molly, at least, had that to look forward to as she made her way to bed. In a few days, she would also say goodbye to her son. She was starting to hate the word "goodbye."

Mrs. Burton had a buffet set up in the parlor for breakfast. Jake, Thomas, Luke, and Kade joined Molly and Jackson early while the English guests slept in. Jack came down, rubbing his eyes, but he wanted to see his grandpa and uncles before they left. They sat around the dining table, visiting quietly until Jake got up, nodding to Luke.

"We'd best go roust our horses and get moving," Jake said. "How about you walk out with us, Jack, before we go?" Jake looked at his nephew.

When they were outside, Jake stopped to let Jack show him how he had improved with his knife throwing. Then, kneeling before the young boy, Jake took out a small blade in a sheath.

"This is for you," Jake said, handing the knife to Jack. "It will fit inside your boot. Never hurts a man to have a knife handy, and they may not let you wear one in school. But this will be hidden in your boot, in case you need it. Practice throwing this one too."

"Thank you, Uncle Jake!" Jack was ecstatic. Then he got serious. "I sure don't want to go."

"I reckon you don't, little man," Jake answered. "But you write to us and tell us all about it. It is an adventure. Think of it like that."

The day of Jack's leaving came much too soon for Molly. She always enjoyed the day-and-a-half trip to Laramie, but not this time. Despite her stuffy mother- and sister-in-law and knowing her son was going away, Molly never wanted to reach town. Their little party reached Laramie by noon, and the train left town at five that afternoon. Molly went through the afternoon in a haze, trying to put on a good show while inside, she was weeping. Finally, everyone was loaded on the train, and Molly, Grace, and Jackson were standing on the side, waving their goodbyes as the train pulled out.

"Well, I hate to see my parents leave," Jackson said, "but it was good to have them here."

Molly didn't reply. It wasn't Jackson's parents that she would miss.

Jackson picked up Grace and took Molly by the arm, turning her back toward the hotel. "I'll get you settled in the hotel then and get on my way," he said.

Molly jerked back and stared at him. "You just sent our son away, and you are leaving me too?" she asked incredulously.

"Honey, I told you I had business to take care of," Jackson said patiently. "I didn't plan to stay in town."

"You just put our son on a train, and you are leaving me?" Molly repeated, voice lowering in anger.

Jackson contemplated her for a moment. "Okay, let's get Grace back to Lydia at the hotel, and then we can have dinner at the restaurant. After that, I'll leave. You,

Lydia, and the Burtons can drive one carriage home to-morrow, and I'll bring the other one later this month when I return."

Appeased, Molly followed Jackson back to the hotel, taking Grace to her suite and freshening up before joining Jackson in the dining room. But supper was not a healing occasion for Molly. They sat as strangers with little to talk about while waiting for their food. The ghost in the room was a little boy sitting on a train going far away from them. It was a relief when the meal was over. Together, they walked from the dining room to the hotel lobby.

"I don't know how long I will be gone," Jackson told her as they hesitated in the lobby. "I am riding out to the Bar S tonight. I want to look at some imported bulls they bought. I have a couple of other places I might stop and visit, and then I can meet Buster and the hands out at the round-up. That saves me a lot of riding. I'll be home after the round-up for sure."

Molly just nodded. Her heart was breaking. She had said goodbye to her son, and now her husband, distant as they had become, was leaving her too. Jackson gave her a chaste kiss on the forehead and turned to leave the hotel. Molly went to the stairs, but before going up, she turned for one last look at her retreating husband, hoping he might at least turn back and smile at her.

It was dark outside the hotel, the flickering lamps on the boardwalk casting shadows. Molly saw Jackson walk outside and stretch. Then he did a surprising thing. Instead of turning toward the livery stable and his horse, he turned the other way. Molly stared. He was going in the wrong direction.

Molly's curiosity was aroused. Since she knew she would not sleep for quite some time, she went to the hotel's front door and went out. She looked in the direction that Jackson went and did not see him. She hurried to the corner of the hotel and looked down the side street. It was dark on the side street, but the end of the hotel had lamps burning, and she could see Jackson just before he moved into the shadows. He was going down the street away from the hotel and not in the direction of the livery. Picking up her skirts, Molly made her way silently behind him.

Molly followed Jackson, staying in the distance. Once off Main Street, only dim lights came from residences and a crescent moon in the sky to offer meager light. The street was dark, but Molly's eyes adjusted enough to see the shadowy figure of her husband in the distance in front of her. If he turned back, he might be able to see her, but she doubted if he would recognize who it was that followed him. Jackson was at the end of the street before he crossed over and went to the last little house before town turned into the country.

Molly watched Jackson as he went to the door. It was a hot night, and the front door stood open with only a screen. A lamp burned inside, lighting the window. Jackson didn't knock, but just went it. For a moment, he was lost to her sight, but as she moved in line with the front of the house, Molly saw a woman was inside with him. The woman went ahead of Jackson to the back room carrying the lamp. The front room went dark.

Who lived here? Molly thought. Is there a card game going on here? Was that what Jackson was going to do? Go play cards? On this night?

When Molly got directly in front of the little house, she saw that the front door, the door to the back room, and the back door were in line with each other. She could see into the back room, but any activity must be to the left of the door. She couldn't see that part of the house. If she were in the backyard, though, she might be able to see inside. Making her way in the dark, Molly stumbled past the picket fence and groped her way to the back of the house. She found a gate in the fence and went in. In the glow of the back door, she saw a pump in the yard. She went to that and knelt by it. It didn't hide her, but in the dark, she didn't think she would stick out. She could see inside the back room now. When her eyes adjusted to the dim light coming from the back room, she froze.

There was no card game going on. There was only Jackson and the woman. The lamp was sitting on a dresser. Jackson's shirt and vest were off and hanging on a chair. He was smiling at the woman who, her back to the door, was holding her two hands out to him. Jackson reached up to a peg on the wall and pulled down what looked to be a silky scarf. Twirling it to fashion a soft rope of sorts, Jackson wound it around the woman's two hands. Then, pulling her close to the wall, he raised her arms to loop her bound hands over a peg. The woman stood there, back to Jackson, as he pulled her flowing wrap away from her backside. Taking what looked like a whip, Jackson flogged the woman. It looked like a flimsy whip, but still, Molly watched in horror. Her mind barely took in what was happening.

But that shock wasn't the worst one. When Jackson reached up and lifted the woman's arms down, turning the woman toward him, Molly saw what she hadn't before. The woman was pregnant. Very pregnant. Molly almost quit breathing. She gripped the pump, holding herself rigid.

Exchanging places with the woman, Jackson leaned back against the wall. He drew her hands, still tied together at the wrists with the scarf, to his chest, smiling at her. Then he put his hands on her head, pushing down, and the woman went to her knees in front of him. She blocked Molly's view of Jackson from the waist down. The woman's hands, fingers splayed, slowly glided down Jackson's bare chest, falling out of sight. Molly couldn't see, but she guessed what was happening. When the woman's head tilted and she leaned into Jackson, Molly had enough. Pushing away from the pump, she ran, stumbling to the road. She ran toward the hotel, great sobs coming unheeded. Reaching an abandoned building, she made her way behind it. Sinking down to the ground, Molly cried, pulling the hem of her skirt to her face.

She didn't know how long she sat crying. She cried until she had no tears left, leaving her exhausted, leaning against the dirty old building. Finally, weak and weary, Molly got to her feet. It was late, and Lydia would be worried. Wiping her face, Molly hoped her red eyes would be taken as sadness at Jack's leaving. Now Molly knew what had become of her marriage. It was a sham. There was another woman who received Jackson's attention. There was another woman in his life, and this woman was going to have a child. Molly had no doubt it was Jackson's child. Tomorrow, Molly would go back to the Anchor J and have to find a way to face this horrible new knowledge.

Mr. Burton had the carriage at the hotel right after breakfast, and the women loaded their few things and left for the ranch. Molly had no desire to go anywhere in town. She only wanted to escape. She was silent on the ride.

Often, her eyes would fill, and she would fight tears. She wasn't even sure if she was crying for her lost child or her new knowledge about her husband. In any case, Molly was morose and quiet. If the Burtons or Lydia noticed, no one commented on it.

They camped at one of Jackson's line shacks that night. Jackson had built several line shacks for his cowboys, but he had placed two along the trail to Laramie. One was a day's journey from the ranch, and the other was a day's journey from town. Since Laramie was a day-and-a-half ride, there was shelter each way to spend the night no matter the direction one traveled.

Molly picked at the light supper that Mrs. Burton made and then cuddled Grace until the little girl fell asleep. Feeling restless, Molly put Grace down on a bed and went outside. A creek wound its way near the shack, and Molly walked to the edge of that. When they had traveled to Laramie, the creek had been almost dry, with only a faint stream of fresh water in it. Like so many prairie creeks, it took a good rain to fill them. There must have been rain to the north because, this night, the creek boiled with dirty rushing water. That happened a lot. A storm out of the area would fill the creeks a day later.

Molly watched the dirty water as it tumbled over tree branches and rocks. *Muddy water*, Molly thought. *Muddy water like my marriage. It was clear and bright when we said our vows, but now is just the muddy waters of deceit.*

CHAPTER 6

Home – September 1886

By the time Molly reached the Anchor J, she knew what she would not do. She would not sit at the ranch and wait for Jackson to come home. She was going home to Twin Peaks. She didn't say anything to the Burtons or Lydia. She spent the afternoon unpacking and playing with Grace. She walked the river with Grace and thought about what she would need. The next morning, she was ready for the battle she knew would come.

"Where are my riding clothes?" Molly asked Mr. Burton. "And my everyday dresses?"

Burton looked at Molly warily, not sure if he should answer. He was Jackson's butler, and his allegiance lay with the man of the house.

"Mr. Jackson packed them away," Burton finally answered.

"Where?"

Burton looked at his wife, who was serving coffee. "I am not sure."

Lydia came into the room then, carrying Grace. "He went up the attic stairs," she said. Burton gave her a scathing look, but did not speak.

Molly got up and headed toward the stairs. Before she got there, Burton spoke again. "The trunk is locked."

Molly slowly turned back toward the man. "Jackson locked my clothes up in a trunk in the attic?" she spoke slowly, enunciating every word.

Burton nodded warily.

"Where is the key?"

"Ma'am, Mr. Jackson has it," Burton replied slowly. "I don't know where he put it."

Molly stared at the man for a minute before turning to the kitchen. Purposefully, she went through the kitchen and out the back door. At the woodpile was an axe. Taking it, Molly strode back inside and up the stairs. The three servants stared. When she reached the attic, she saw the wooden trunk sitting in the center of the floor. She never hesitated as she held the axe and smashed into the wood by the lock. The wood splintered. Molly aimed and struck again and again until there was little left of the lock, and she could throw the trunk open. Inside were her homemade riding skirts and her everyday skirts and blouses. She gathered an armload and, taking the axe, descended the stairs. Going to the parlor, she dropped the axe in front of Burton.

"It is not locked anymore," she said shortly. "Now I want my horse saddled with my saddle. Saddle Grace's pony too. We are going to Twin Peaks."

"Ma'am," Burton said haltingly, "Your saddle is hanging up in the barn. I can't get it down."

"What?" Molly's anger almost got away from her.

"Mr. Jackson had the boys hoist it up under the roof," Burton explained. "He said mice wouldn't hurt it there."

Molly felt her anger rise. It wasn't mice Jackson worried about. He put her saddle where she couldn't get it by herself. And apparently, Burton wasn't going to try to help her. Before she could speak, Burton spoke again.

"Ma'am," he said tentatively, "does Mr. Jackson know you are going to Twin Peaks?"

"Mr. Jackson isn't here," Molly said shortly, "and I am going home if I have to walk there. So, get me a saddled horse with anything except the sidesaddle. Throw the sidesaddle down the well."

"Mrs. Crowden, I will drive you and Grace in the buggy," Burton suggested. "Then I can come for you when you want to come home."

Molly contemplated the man. Yes, that was a good idea. Grace would find it easier to travel that distance in the carriage. She knew Jackson told Burton to watch over his family whenever he was gone. Burton driving her would alleviate Burton of that responsibility once he got her to her family at Twin Peaks. Molly nodded.

"I will be ready in an hour," she said brusquely. "Bring the buggy to the house."

Molly said nothing to Burton on the half-day drive to Twin Peaks. She sat in the back seat of the buggy with Grace and allowed the little girl to play on the floor at her feet or play patty cakes on her lap. Molly had no desire for a conversation with Jackson's man. She just wanted to go home to Twin Peaks. Maybe being with family would soothe her soul.

The trading post dog alerted Kade to approaching visitors and he came out of the house, watching the buggy arrive. He recognized it as Jackson's. As it came closer, he saw Molly and his granddaughter sitting in the back and Jackson's man driving. He went down the steps to greet her as Sarah came out of the cabin behind him.

"Pa," Molly called, even before Burton had the horses pulled to a stop. "Can I stay for a while?"

Kade went to the buggy, holding up his arms for Grace to be handed to him. "You are always welcome here, daughter," he said, smiling, " for as long as you want."

"It's settled then," Molly returned, trying to look normal and smile back. Turning to Burton, she said to him, "Tell Jackson where I am. He can decide when I come home. And please bring my trunk in before you go." It was obvious that Molly didn't expect the manservant to stay.

Molly took Grace from her father and went to greet Sarah. Together they went in the cabin. Kade looked at Burton. "I'll help you carry this in," he said. As the two men untied Molly's trunk, Kade said softly to Burton. "She's not taking Jack's absence well, is she?"

"No, sir, she hasn't been herself," Burton replied. "Mr. Crowden had business, so he left her to come home with us. She's been pretty quiet."

"Being at home then is maybe what she needs," Kade said. "She can stay until Jackson sends for her."

Burton headed home after resting the horses for an hour and getting something to eat. Molly was glad to see him go. She wanted no reminders of her life at the Anchor J. When Grace needed her nap, Molly went into the bedroom and stayed with her the whole afternoon. She emerged before supper to help Sarah and let Grace and Feather play together, but she was a quiet shadow of herself. Kade and Sarah gave her space, not questioning her, but when they retired to bed that night, Kade turned to his wife.

"There is more wrong here than just a son being sent away to school," he said to Sarah. "I'd expect Molly to be sad, but there is a hard look to her. She's angry. And she's running from something she doesn't want to face."

"Well, she could just be angry at Jackson for sending Jack off to school without talking to her about it," Sarah suggested. "If it were me, I'd be angry that Jackson didn't stay with me to comfort me."

"You could be right," Kade said thoughtfully. "I hope so anyway. But I don't think Molly has been happy for quite some time. This isn't helping any."

"Then all we can do is try to help her find some happiness here while we have her with us," Sarah smiled. "You better go find a horse or two for her to ride. She's like her mother. The horses will heal her."

Kade was over at the trading post the next morning when Jake rode by on the first horse of the day. Jake usually stopped when he went by in the morning, checking with his father to see if he needed anything. Kade was sitting on the porch as Jake rode up.

"Going to be a good day today," Jake started. "I think this horse will be good to sell in the spring. He's a good one."

"He looks good," Kade said, eyeing the young animal. Then he stood up and moved toward the edge of the porch. "Yer sister an' Grace came to visit yesterday afternoon."

Jake was surprised. "Were you expecting her?"

"Nope."

"How's she doing?"

"Let's jest say she's a might down. Don't reckon I've seen her so low."

"How long will she stay?" Jake looked over at the cabin.

"She told Jackson's man that when Jackson wanted her back, to come back for her," Kade said. "Then she jest went into the cabin an' left him to return. She spent most of the afternoon in the bedroom an' she isn't up yet this morning."

"Did she say anything about the trip to Laramie?" Jake asked.

Kade gave a sour chuckle. "That girl was as bad as Will in the conversation area last night. Sarah asked her if Jack was scared of getting on the train. Molly's answer was, "Not bad." I asked her if Jackson was sad to see his family leave, an' Molly simply said, "Not really." Even a comment like Grace is sure growin' big only brought a nod. We got nothin' from her."

Jake thought about that. "Tell you what. I'll be done with this horse before noon, and then right after I eat, I'll come by with a horse for her and get her out to ride with me if you will watch Grace. I don't think a horse can keep her from missing Jack, but it will help her feel better to get outside."

Kade nodded. That was his thought too.

It was a testament to Molly's depressed state that she didn't jump at the chance to ride when Jake turned up with a spare horse. Her first reaction was hesitation, followed by her words, "Well, I should stay and help Sarah clean up and get Grace down for a nap."

But Sarah jumped in before Molly could take a breath. "You go," Sarah said sternly. "The girls are playing, and when they get tired, I'll put them down together. There is almost nothing left of the dinner dishes, so just go and let me have some quiet time." Sarah smiled to soften her words.

Molly looked at Jake then and said, "I don't have my saddle."

"The horse is saddled already," Jake answered. "Just change and come out."

So, Molly changed into a riding skirt and boots and joined Jake outside. She knew right away which horse Jake intended her to ride by the smaller saddle that was on the animal. She studied it for a minute and then turned to Jake.

"This is Mother's saddle," she said softly, her hands running over the worn leather.

Jake smiled fondly at his little sister. "Yes. It is yours if you want it. Otherwise, I have been keeping it oiled and ready for Kestrel when she begins to fit it."

"You keep it for Kestrel," Molly said softly. "I have the saddle that Ma and Pa gave me for my twelfth birthday. Jackson wouldn't dare throw it away." Her words were tinged with anger.

Jake wondered at that last statement, but didn't pursue it. He just nodded at Molly's reply and mounted his horse. They rode west along the river. Jake didn't try to engage Molly in conversation. She was definitely not herself, and he decided that trying to draw her out too soon would do more damage than good. They had ridden out a good two miles when Jake finally spoke.

"That gelding you are riding is one of our better six-year-olds. We almost sold him this summer, but I felt he was almost too quiet and gentle for the Army or ranch work. I got a letter from the foreman of the Three Pines Ranch. The ranch owner is from St. Louis and comes out with his family in the summer. When they are here next summer, the daughter wants to ride. She's about fourteen. The foreman has been instructed to get a good horse for the girl. Guess the youngster rides but isn't very experienced. I'd like your opinion on whether you think this horse will do." Jake watched Molly out of the corner of his eye. He wondered if having a reason to ride might draw her out of her self-imposed shell.

Molly didn't say anything, but she nodded.

"All this horse has been ridden by is men," Jake went on. "I think he's really gentle, but that might not be your opinion. I was going to put Kestrel on him, but he's a big gelding, and Kestrel is still pretty young. So, what I was thinking is this. Let's open these two up for a quarter mile or so, and then see how the gelding pulls down for you. I'd like to see if his reaction with you is the same as when I ride him. How's that sound?"

Jake saw the first spark of interest light in Molly's eyes. She nodded, looking ahead.

"How about we race to that bend in the river?" Molly asked, pointing ahead.

Jake nodded, and they put their heels to the horses. Jake's gelding was off like a shot, but with Molly's urging, her horse was not far behind. Jake didn't want to outdistance Molly, so he let his horse settle into a good hand gallop. It didn't take long before Molly pulled up beside him. Then he urged his horse forward, making Molly work her horse to keep up. By the time they came to the bend in the river, flying by it in tandem, Jake saw the smile of excitement on Molly's face. He sat up and pulled his horse down to a lope, then a trot and walk, while Molly did the same. Jake's gelding jigged a little, excited from the run, but Molly's horse dropped to a walk like the gentleman that Jake thought the animal was.

As Jake got off and loosened his cinch, he said nonchalantly, "Let's lead them and let them puff a few minutes."

Molly dismounted too, also loosening the cinch. Then she fell in beside Jake, who was walking slowly.

"So, do you think this horse will do for a young, inexperienced girl?" Jake asked.

Molly nodded, then said. "He was no problem to pull up. It was almost more of an effort to get going," she laughed softly. "But once he knew I meant to run, he did. I think this horse is more laid back than most of our horses. He has a wonderful mouth and is really responsive. I think he'd do well for a young girl."

"I'll maybe take him to Three Pines then," Jake answered. "The foreman can use him over the winter and know the horse inside out before the owner and his family get here in the spring."

They walked in silence for a while. Jake didn't want to let Molly withdraw again inside her shell, but for once, he wasn't sure what to say to his sister. Finally, he thought he had to try. The horses weren't puffing anymore, and soon, they would mount again.

"Sis, I know it has been a rough week for you sending Jack off for the school term," he started tentatively. "But he will come home again, you know."

Molly nodded but made no reply.

"Burton told Pa that Jackson left the night Jack left," Jake continued gently. "I'm sure that upset you too, but sometimes we don't know how things affect others. Maybe that was Jackson's way of dealing with Jack leaving too? Maybe he just needed to get busy himself."

Molly's eyes turned hard, and her mouth formed a grim line. "Oh yes, that definitely was Jackson's way to deal with this," she said bitterly. "He was definitely thinking of himself."

"Honey," Jake said soothingly. He was surprised at Molly's anger. "It will get better."

Molly's eyes filled with tears that she tried to hide from Jake. She turned toward her horse, going to the saddle, and tightening the cinch. Jake stared at her a moment and saw her shoulders shake.

"Molly," he said softly. "What is it?" He took her by the shoulders, turning her to him. Molly wouldn't look up at him, but when he pulled her toward him, she collapsed against him. He felt the wetness of her tears against his chest and heard her sobs. As he held her, he knew she had lost all control. Her sobs were gut-wrenching. It was quite some time before she quieted and pulled away.

"I'm just being silly," she said bravely. "I'm fine now."

But Jake knew that wasn't true. There was nothing fine about his little sister, and he had no idea why or how to change that.

If Molly wasn't fine, she was better. She returned from her ride with Jake, still quiet and withdrawn, but not distant. Over the days that followed, Molly began to smile again, play with Grace, and carry on conversations with those around her. Every day, Jake rode over after lunch with a horse for Molly to ride. He always had a reason why he wanted Molly to ride each particular horse. Her friends from the community visited almost daily, and she took to riding out and visiting those who lived farther out, like Bonnie and Martha. But if a conversation veered toward Jackson or of Molly's return to the Anchor J, she shut down. Her answer to how long she could stay was short and to the point. "Until I have to go back," she would say bluntly, ending the conversation.

Molly had been at Twin Peaks for almost three weeks when preparations were made to go to the high country for the fall gather. Jake and Thomas stopped one evening to discuss the gather with Kade.

"We were thinking if you could get by without Juba and Ezekiel for a week or so," Thomas said to Sarah, "we would have them come with us and do the cooking."

"Of course, I can get along without them," Sarah answered. "I only have Juba come a few days a week now anyway."

Ezekiel was James's brother-in-law, Mary's half-brother. Ezekiel and his wife Juba had come west with Kade and Sarah after Feather was born. A Black couple, they had few options in their prior home and jumped at the chance to go west. Now that Feather was four years old, the couple didn't live in Kade and Sarah's cabin and had staked a claim on 160 acres along the river. Ezekiel worked for the ranch, and Juba worked part-time for Sarah and Kade. Childless, Juba and Ezekiel yearned for the children they didn't seem able to have, and Juba was much sought after from many of the young mothers when they needed help with chores or childcare.

"Well, Juba is a right fine cook," Thomas smiled. "And Ezekiel is good just about everywhere. It would be a relief not to cook for ourselves up there. I still miss the gathers with Ma along."

"I want to go too," Molly interrupted, surprising the men with her words.

Jake looked at his sister. "What if Jackson comes for you when you are there?"

Molly's look turned hard. "I'm sure Pa can tell him where I am," she said tartly. "I want to go. I haven't been to the high country for ten years. If Juba can go, I can go and help her."

"You want to leave Grace here with Sarah and me then?" Kade inquired.

"No," Molly said shortly. "I want to take Grace with me like we used to do as a family. We all went on the fall gather for as long as I can remember. I loved fall gather, and I want Grace to have at least one to experience." Molly looked defiantly at her brothers and father.

Thomas and Jake looked to their father, who looked mildly at his three grown children. "She's a grown woman," he said to his sons. "If she wants to go with you, I'd say let her."

CHAPTER 7

Fall Gather – Late September 1886

Molly was ready the next day when the remuda was let out of the corral and headed toward the end of the valley where the trail led to the line shack high in the mountains. She rode a favorite horse of Jake's and had Grace riding with her. Juba and Ezekiel were driving a buckboard filled with supplies. When Grace tired of riding with her mother, she could ride in the wagon with Juba.

Kade stopped Molly as she left the cabin and handed her a rifle and saddle scabbard. "I don't reckon you have yer rifle with you," he said seriously. "This 'ere was yer ma's. Think you should take it with you. Never know when a rifle is needed. Don't want you goin' off without one."

Molly looked at the shiny piece. It was well cared for, although she doubted it had been used for many years. She smiled gratefully at her father. "I'll take good care of it, Pa," she said. "Been a while since I held a rifle, but this one feels awfully good to me."

The remuda moved faster than the wagon, and with Grace riding with her, Molly stayed behind the faster-moving cowboys and the spare horses. She rode in front of the wagon, occasionally catching sight of the remuda ahead of them. She knew the way and enjoyed the ride up the winding trail to the high slopes. About an hour into the ride, Jake returned to find her.

"Look the same to you?" he asked.

"Well, the mountains are the same, but this trail has been improved quite a lot," Molly said seriously. "When you said Juba and Ezekiel were taking the buckboard, I couldn't believe they would make it. The trail has been widened with trees cut down. This must have taken a lot of work."

Jake looked up the trail and then back at Molly. "How long since you have gone on fall gather?" he wondered.

"Not since the year before I was married," Molly replied. "That's been nine years."

"I think we began working on the trail about then. At first, it was just to get branches and smaller trees out of our way, but then, we decided to widen it. The last couple of years that Luke lived most of the summer up at the line shack, he has worked on the road quite a bit, getting it wide enough to get the buckboard through," Jake looked thoughtfully at Molly. "When we get up a bit farther, you will see the hardest part to widen was going over the rocks and boulders where the ravine we follow narrows. Luke spent days with a pickax breaking boulders and rolling them out of the way. Won't say it is smooth as silk," Jake laughed, "but it is passable."

"It is nice to be able to ride two abreast," Molly agreed. "It was a long trail before, especially following a slow herd.

"Well, now we can sometimes have three head of cows traveling abreast, but we have more cattle, so once we send the herd onto the trail, we don't see most of them until we get to the other end," Jake smiled. "Still, we can move along a bit faster and easier. It is a needed improvement."

They rode for a while, enjoying the quiet of the mountains. After an hour more, Jake's sharp eyes picked up a deer trail.

"How long since you put your rifle to your shoulder," Jake asked casually.

Molly was surprised at the question. "It isn't my rifle, it's Ma's," she told him. "Pa told me to take it with me, just in case. But, to answer your question, I don't think I've shot a rifle for three or four years. That's another thing I miss." She couldn't keep the bitterness out of her voice with the last statement.

"Then let's do something about that," Jake said. Turning, he gauged how far the buckboard was behind them. "See if Juba will keep Grace for a bit, and let's go get our supper."

After passing Grace to Juba, Jake led the way, following the deer trail. It was rough going for a while, dodging thick underbrush and climbing over rocks. The horses, sure-footed mountain horses, took it in stride. Jake motioned Molly to stop as they approached a bend in the trail. They both dismounted, tied the horses to trees, and took their rifles. Going forward slowly and quietly, they climbed a rise and looked down on a small clearing. Lying on their bellies, Jake surveyed the scene below them. His eyes caught movement at the far end, and he motioned to Molly. She, too, had seen the deer, a young stag, grazing at the edge of a thicket.

"Let it emerge just a bit more," Jake whispered to Molly. "Then see if you can take a shot."

"Jake, it's been years," Molly whispered back. "You better do it."

"I'll be ready," Jake said firmly. "But you can give it a try."

Molly sighted on the young stag, waiting for it to emerge from the brush. The animal didn't take long to graze its way out into the open. She heard Jake whisper, "Now," and she squeezed off her shot. The deer jumped once and fell. Jake looked over at Molly.

"Good girl," he said, getting to his feet. "Can you go for the horses? I'll go bleed it. I don't fancy carrying it over this hill."

If the improved trail up to the ranch's summer grazing surprised Molly, reaching the mountain shack surprised her even more. For as long as she could remember, the Welles family all went to fall gather, along with assorted members of the Bates and Jorgensen families. The shack was just a log structure thrown together twenty-odd years ago by Old Tom and Kade to keep bears out of their supplies. If the weather got bad, it gave the women a bit more protection than tents, but although stout, the logs were never properly chinked, and the floor was dirt.

As Molly and Jake rode out into the open in the upper mountain meadow, Molly could see the shack at the far end. Her eyes grew wide with surprise.

"Jake, is that the shack?" she asked, incredulous. "It's bigger and looks like all the logs are chinked."

Jake smiled at his little sister. "Luke said if he was going to live here and put a claim in, he would do the required improvements. He added another room, chinked the logs, fixed the roof, and even has a garden out back."

"So, this is Luke's now?"

"He filed his claim on it a couple of summers ago. Sold it to the ranch for a share," Jake told her. "Luke was more interested in being on the owners' list of the ranch than owning a quarter of land in the high mountains. But that gave the deed to the ranch. We are acquiring quite a bit of deeded land that way. Just about everyone has filed on the quarters of land we live on and then deed it or lease it back to the ranch. Someday, this country will fill up, and when it does, we will have the paper to prove this ranch is ours."

Molly digested that. "The cattlemen on the plains are angry about the homesteaders coming in and breaking up the land. You worry about that here?"

"I wouldn't say we worry about it," Jake said reflectively, "but we are taking steps that will assure us of always having our land. The big ranchers feel the land is theirs because they got there first. But that is going to change, Sis," Jake told her. "I hope Jackson is thinking toward the future. The Indians couldn't stop the whites from moving in, and I don't think the cattlemen will have much better luck."

Molly mulled this over. She had heard Jackson talking to other ranchers about the encroachment of homesteaders on the open range. She had never asked him about it. The way she felt about Jackson now, she knew she never would.

As they approached the shack, Molly saw Juba and Ezekiel unloading the wagon, and Luke had a fire going under a spit. He looked up and grinned at Jake and Molly as they approached.

"Figured you brought us supper," Luke said. "I heard the shot. Thought I'd get the fire going and the spit set up so we'd get it cooked by suppertime."

Jake grinned back. "Good man," he replied, dismounting and untying the deer from his horse. "But I didn't get our supper. Molly did."

"No kidding?" Luke said, giving Molly an appraising smile. "One shot?"

Jake nodded, smiling. "I taught her all she knows."

Molly colored but smiled at the praise. "I think we can give Pa some credit for my shooting," she said. "But I did tag along with you a lot growing up."

It didn't take Molly long to settle into a routine. She and Juba were up early, starting the fires and food for breakfast. The men rose as dawn broke and gathered horses, choosing their mounts for the day. Then they came in to eat a hearty breakfast before taking to the mountain slopes, searching for cattle. They wouldn't be back for the noon meal, so if they wanted any food on the trail, they had to pack it.

After the men left, Juba and Molly first cleaned up the breakfast dishes and cook pots before starting preparations for the evening meal. Juba at first wanted to defer to Molly as head cook, but Molly quickly put Juba right on that.

"Jake and Thomas wanted you to come and cook," Molly said firmly. "I just begged to come along. And any cooking skills I had have long rusted away. I will help you with whatever needs to be done, but you plan the meals. It is your decision what we make."

It took Juba some time to get comfortable giving Molly orders or suggestions, as Juba referred to them, but after the first day, Juba understood that Molly just wanted to help. It had been years since Molly had been allowed to plan a meal or clean up after a meal. It was the menial chores that Molly gloried in the most. She felt free as she hadn't felt in years, getting her hands dirty, working with fresh vegetables and getting her arms, up to her elbows, into dishwater.

After the preparations for the evening meal were completed as much as possible in the morning, the two women could have a few hours of relaxation while waiting for the men to return. During the afternoon then, Molly could catch up a horse and ride the mountain slopes. At first, she took Grace with her, letting the little girl ride double in front of Molly. But some days, Juba would ask for Grace to be left behind. Childless, Juba loved children and enjoyed having Grace underfoot. On those days, Molly could ride farther and faster, covering more ground.

On one such day when the women finished by mid-morning, Molly decided to ride to Crystal Lake. Named this by her mother, Crystal Lake was a beautiful little mountain lake a couple of hours from camp. Molly hadn't been to the lake in almost ten years, and she wanted to see it again. The trail to the lake went higher into the mountains, following a ravine. While wide at both ends with a gentle upward grade, it had one narrow section where the path was only wide enough for one horse to pass at a time, with a drop-off of about ten feet to the bottom of the gulch. When the cattle were driven down this trail, care had to be taken not to push them too hard so that they bunch up and push each other off the trail. While not necessarily a life-threatening fall, a cow or horse could easily break a leg if it went off the side.

Breaking out of the gully, Molly came out on a slope that led to a beautiful open grassy meadow. At the far end lay the lake, glistening in the sun, several cows grazed in the meadow, peaceful and content. Molly thought she heard Jake say the men were combing the hills beyond the lake today, and if so, they would be coming this way and gather these cows when returning to camp.

Molly went to the lake, remembering the years she came to the high slopes with her parents. The whole family came for fall gather, but they also came up several times in the summer to check on the cattle. Crystal Lake was a favorite destination of Sabra's, and Molly remembered how she and her mother would often come to the lake. There was good fishing here, and they usually brought home a good meal of trout.

As Molly let her horse drink from the banks of the lake, she heard the catcalls of the men rousting cattle in the distance. Soon, the animals began coming through the trees and flooding into the meadow. It wasn't long before the riders emerged. She recognized Jake and Thomas first, but behind them came Lathe and Luke. She smiled. It would be fun riding home with the men, pushing these cows to the grass by the cabin.

"Hey, Sis," Thomas called, teasing. "I hope this doesn't mean we won't have supper ready this evening."

"Smartie," Molly called back. "I slaved all morning over the preparations. But I knew you needed some expert help, so I came to help you with these cows."

Thomas and Jake grinned at Molly and came to ride by her. "It is good to see you up in the high country again," Jake commented as he pulled alongside. "It's been too long."

Molly nodded. "I didn't realize how much I missed this," she said softly. "I am so glad I came."

They gathered the cattle on the meadow, pushing them toward the gully trail. The men cut small bunches off, sending them down the trail with riders between them to keep the leaders moving. They didn't want the cattle to bunch up when the trail narrowed. It took a good hour to get all the cattle through the narrow ravine, but it was easy going after that. Many of the cows were used to the gathering and knew their destination. It was easy pushing them once they got on the trail. Then, all four men could drop back and ride with Molly, only occasionally having to ride off to move a dawdling cow or calf. Teasing and trading insults, the men kept Molly entertained the whole way back. The ride was over much too soon for Molly. Being free to ride with her brothers and the other Twin Peaks cowboys was a delight for Molly. She felt young and happy, but underneath her pleasure, she knew this wasn't her life anymore. This would end, and she dreaded when the time came for that to happen.

Molly sat leaning against Jake with Grace on her lap watching the flames of the campfire dance. She wished this evening could go on forever. She loved the campfires in the evening. The men were always relaxed, full of food, and winding down from the day. After supper, when dishes were washed, and food was stored in the cabin, Juba and Molly could relax too. At Twin Peaks, women had always been included in the fall gathering until Sabra died. Now, after two years without Sabra, the men were glad to see Juba and Molly join them. It was like old times. Stories and songs were shared around the fire, and Molly joining in reminded them of Sabra.

But this was the last night. The last of the cattle were grazing on the meadow. Almost every day, bunches of cattle were driven down the mountain to the ranch. The meadow in front of the line shack couldn't hold the number of cattle Twin Peaks owned, so when the meadow filled, the cattle already gathered were sent down. Tomorrow, the remaining cattle and the remuda would head down the mountain, followed by the wagon with any leftover supplies.

As much as Molly wanted to stay by the fire, making the evening last, she knew Grace was tired. It would be a busy morning getting packed up and heading to the ranch headquarters. She handed Grace to Jake and stood up. Leaning over, she picked up the toddler, nodded to the men, and made her way to the cabin.

It didn't take long to get Grace and herself in nightdresses, and then wrapping up in a quilt, Molly made her way to the privy. The privy was new and a much-appreciated improvement to Molly and Juba. There had been an old ramshackle one in Sabra's day, but it had fallen over in a windstorm. This new one was built on the far side of the cabin, away from the fire.

When Molly got back to the cabin door, she hesitated. Grace was already asleep on her shoulder, warm under the quilt. Loathe to give up the last night in the mountains, Molly walked into the woods a little distance from the cabin. Finding a fallen tree, she sank to the ground, leaning against it. Here she could still see the campfire and hear the low murmur of the men's voices. She could not hear their words, but she would smile when the men broke out into laughter. A peace settled into her as she sat, warm under the quilt with Grace cradled in her lap.

Molly closed her eyes, enjoying the quiet, the night sounds muted. She opened her eyes when she heard footsteps come into the woods. She saw a figure coming toward her. It was too noisy a person to be Jake, Hawk, or Sam. Those three walked on silent feet, trained by years in the mountains. Whoever was coming toward her was neither mountain man nor Indian. And there was only one reason why one of the men would go into the woods at this time of night. Most of the men seldom used the privy. Men had the luxury of using the woods or anyplace else they happened to be.

"Woman and child in front of you," Molly said suddenly.

"Good to know," came a quick answer and the figure turned away, rustling branches as he went.

Molly tried to place the voice. It wasn't Thomas or Lathe. Perhaps Will or James? Jerimiah wasn't here so it wasn't him. Maybe Army or Luke. More words needed to be spoken to know the voice. She didn't have to wonder long. She heard the man coming back; twigs breaking, branches pushed out of the way. No, it wasn't Jake, Hawk, or Sam.

"Thought you and Grace went to bed," the voice said. "You lost?"

The figure came closer and in the dim light, Molly recognized Luke. He was taller than her brothers and seemed to tower over her as she sat. Luke moved away and, finding a tree, sank to the ground, leaning against it.

"I just couldn't bring myself to go in tonight," Molly answered. "It's the last night, and I don't want this to end."

"I'd think you'd be getting anxious to get back to the luxuries you have at the Anchor J," Luke said amiably. "This little cabin of mine is a mite rough compared to your ranch house."

Molly contemplated Luke's comment. "I like your little cabin," she said. "I could stay here forever." She thought about that briefly before amending, "Well, at least until the snows fall. I think it gets pretty socked in with snow once winter sets in."

"It does at that," Luke agreed. "I stayed up here a couple of years ago late into fall and got caught in a snowstorm. Took me a couple of days to snowshoe out, leading my horse. Not sure who was more exhausted, me or the horse."

Silence settled between them as they sat. After a while, Molly spoke softly.

"I had forgotten how much I loved to come here. It was always a family outing to come to this mountain. Pa loved to camp up here, and we did that on and off all summer. Then, for fall gather, we always had help from the Bates and Jorgensens. We were like one big extended family."

"Did your ma like coming here too?"

"She was as bad as Pa. She was happiest if she could talk one of the other women to come when we gathered to do the cooking so Ma could ride out each day. When we came up as a family in the summer, we all pitched in to cook because Ma was not going to be left back to do the cooking," Molly laughed at that. "Pa can fry up some mean fish, and he did a lot of cooking too. We ate pretty sparse, sometimes just meat or fish, but there was plenty of it, and none of us cared. We just enjoyed being together. Pa would tell us stories about the old days of trapping in the mountains with Jacob and Tom. I miss those stories."

"It is nice to have good times with family growing up," Luke said. "I lived on a farm, and we never ventured farther than town once a month. But every now and then, there was a dance at a neighbor place, and we would all go together in our farm wagon. Good times to remember."

"You miss your family back there?" Molly asked.

"Have an older brother who stayed on the farm. Heard he got married after I left," Luke said. "But the folks died when I was sixteen. It was a damp, cold winter, and they both took sick within weeks of each other. I stuck around a couple years and then headed out. Tried the Army but didn't like it."

"How long were you in the Army?" Molly inquired.

"Not long," Luke's answer was brief. "I reckon I'd best leave you and head to my tent. Dawn comes early." He rose easily to his feet.

Molly nodded in the darkness. "Here, help me up so I don't have to throw Grace onto my shoulder," she said, holding up a hand.

Luke took her hand, pulling her up. He was reluctant to let her hand free. He stood awkwardly for a moment before dropping her hand. He still felt the warmth of her.

"Evening to you, Ma'am," he said softly. Turning abruptly, he moved away. Molly watched his shadow; then she headed toward the cabin and her own bed.

CHAPTER 8

A Reluctant Understanding – Fall 1886

The remuda was started down the mountain lane toward home first. The horses moved more quickly than cattle. Then, the men sorted off bunches of cattle that were pushed onto the trail. As they disappeared down the mountain, each group was followed by a cowboy who kept the animals pointing down. By the time the last group of cattle were goaded down the trail, the breakfast dishes were washed and packed away, the buckboard was loaded, and the mules were hitched to it. Molly had a saddle horse ready, and she and Grace started the descent to the ranch on her horse. Partway down, Grace asked for Juba, so Molly passed her to the woman in the wagon. It was an easy ride, following the last of the cattle. Just before they broke out of the mountain slopes onto the valley floor, Jake rode back to meet them.

"Thought I'd ride in with you," Jake smiled at Molly. "I've enjoyed having my little sis around."

"Well, I've enjoyed being here," Molly smiled back. "This week has brought back lots of memories. Good memories."

Molly collected Grace from Juba after breaking out onto the home pasture, and she and Jake rode ahead of the wagon. They rode to Jake's cabin, a comfortable silence between them at times or occasionally visiting easily about the week, the weather, and good memories from their past. At Jake's cabin, Molly hugged him, leaning over to him from her horse.

"I could ride you down to Pa's," Jake told her.

Molly shook her head. "You have three little ones waiting for you by the cabin door," she smiled, nodding toward his cabin. "They would be disappointed to see you ride off now. I know the way."

She cued her horse into a collected lope and waving to Anna and Jake's kids, she and Grace headed toward Kade and Sarah's. It was warmer in the valley, and the sun was bright. Molly and Grace waved to Thomas as he unsaddled at his barn. Looking across the meadow, she saw Sam at his cabin, also unsaddling. Smiling, she waved to him as well. She was filled with contentment. These people were all so dear to her. It was so good to spend time with them.

Molly pulled her horse down to a walk as she rode up to her father's store. The door was open, so she knew he was there. Kade must have heard her approaching because he walked out to the porch. Molly smiled, lifting her hand in greeting before another figure walked out behind him.

"Daddy, Daddy!" Grace screamed excitedly.

Molly's smile faded, and her hand, mid-wave, fell. She knew that Jackson would come for her eventually, but she had just forgotten that fact these last few days. Seeing him standing next to her father was almost a physical blow. She rode slowly to Kade's store, feeling her anger rising again within her.

"Molly, look at you," Jackson said sternly. "You look like you have been camping out. I hope you have something decent to wear for the ride home." He reached up and took Grace.

"Home?" Molly murmured. In her mind, she was home. "Today?"

"I'd like to get going right away," Jackson said brusquely. "I asked Sarah to pack you something to eat in case you are hungry, and she would get most of your things in your trunk. The buggy is tied up in front."

Molly made no reply to this. Instead, she looked at her father. "I'll put the horse in your corral, Pa."

"I'll take care of it for you, daughter," Kade said softly. He could see her reluctance and the change that had come over her when she saw Jackson. Whatever was wrong between these two, the month Molly had spent at Twin Peaks hadn't eased the strain.

Molly was silent as Jackson eased the team out of the yard and headed toward the Anchor J. As he drove, he tried to make conversation but found Molly silent and morose.

"Molly," he said finally in frustration, "for goodness' sake! I have a letter from Jack waiting at home. It came just before I left Laramie after we drove the herd in. He sounds like he is enjoying school."

"Not now," Molly said angrily, her voice low. "Wait until Grace falls asleep, and then we will talk."

"Oh, come now," Jackson said, "Grace is almost asleep. Talk to me."

"No." Molly hissed these words. "Not until Grace naps."

They rode two more miles, horses pulling steady at a trot before Molly felt Grace completely relax in her arms. Looking down, she saw the toddler's eyes were closed, and her breathing was slow. Looking around, Molly spotted a good place to tie up.

"Tie up the team there, and we can talk," Molly pointed at a stand of trees.

"Molly, the days are shorter now. I don't want to take a chance of getting caught in the dark," Jackson responded. "We can talk as we move."

Molly turned in the seat, facing Jackson. "Tie up these damn horses," she said, venom in her tone. "Or stop them, and I will walk with Grace back to Twin Peaks."

Jackson stared at her. He had never heard her swear. It startled him. He reined the horses to the trees. When he got off to secure the horses, Molly slid Grace onto the buggy seat and climbed down, stalking away from the sleeping child.

"Molly, what in the world are you so angry about?" Jackson strode quickly to follow her. "Sending our son to a good school is not unusual for our social class. You have to . . ."

"I saw you," Molly interrupted Jackson, her voice low and biting. "I saw you with her."

Jackson stared. "You saw me with," he hesitated, then finished slowly, "with who? When?"

Molly took a breath, trying to keep from screaming at him. She didn't want to wake Grace. "I saw you in Laramie. You turned the wrong way when you left the hotel. I followed you. I saw you whip her."

Jackson stood mute, watching her, gathering his thoughts. Like gladiators, they stared at each other. Finally, he spoke.

"It wasn't a real whip. It didn't hurt her."

"I'm supposed to care?" Molly asked, voice dripping with venom. "You were with a woman. You keep her, don't you?" Molly's tone was accusatory.

"Molly, listen to me," Jackson replied, keeping his voice steady. "I do that for you."

"You sleep with another woman for me?" Molly laughed bitterly. "I can't believe you said that."

"Molly, I like to do things with a woman that aren't proper to do with a lady, with my wife." Jackson tried to speak calmly. "That woman doesn't care. I can come home to you and treat you as you deserve to be treated."

"Treat me as I deserve?" Molly's voice rose shrilly. "You hardly touch me, and when you do, you treat me like I'll break!"

"Well, that is what I mean. When I do come to you, I can treat you like a lady."

"You think I'll allow you to touch me anymore?" Molly spat the words at Jackson.

"Molly, you are getting all worked up over this. The woman means nothing to me." Jackson spoke placatingly. "She just takes care of my . . ." Jackson stopped speaking abruptly, not sure what to call it.

"Why did you marry me?" Molly demanded. "If you wanted a different kind of woman, why marry me?"

"Darling, we were so young, and you were so wild and free," Jackson replied. "I hoped that I would be satisfied with you. And I am . . . was . . . except for some things. This woman takes those desires away. Helps me cope. She isn't important."

"And the child?" Molly asked, trying not to scream. "It's your child, isn't it?"

Jackson nodded. There was no use denying what Molly already knew. "He will not be part of our lives."

Molly looked at Jackson incredulously. This time, her voice rose to an almost hysterical pitch." Not part of our lives? You have a mistress and a child in Laramie, and they won't be part of our lives? God, Jackson, do you hear yourself?"

"Molly, look . . ." Jackson began.

"Take me back to Twin Peaks," Molly demanded, her voice again low and angry. "I hate you."

Jackson went silent for a moment then, assessing Molly. "Are you talking divorce?" he asked. "Are you going to put your family through the shame of that?"

Divorce. The word caught Molly by surprise. She hadn't thought about divorce, but when she heard the word, she knew she couldn't do that. Divorce was shameful. She stood staring at Jackson, with silent brooding eyes.

"Molly, you are my wife," Jackson said softly. "I want you to come home with me. If you want to return to Twin Peaks, I will take you back. But Grace will go home with me."

"No!"

"Yes, she will, and Jack will come home to me in the summer," Jackson's voice took on a threatening tone.

"I'm their mother!"

"No judge in the country will rule against me," Jackson said reasonably. "Furthermore, if your family tries to interfere, I will take the children to England. You will never see them again."

"You wouldn't do that," Molly said doubtfully, but the fear of it rose within her.

"Molly, I wouldn't want to do that, but if you force me, it will be your fault."

"I could run away with them. My family would help," Molly wasn't sure why she said this. She knew she couldn't ask her family for help any more than she could file for a divorce.

"Molly, you are my wife. If you want to leave, I release you. Despite everything, I do love you. But if you fight me about the children, if you try anything extreme, I could also do something extreme. I could have you institutionalized. I could do that."

The words made Molly go cold inside. There had been a wealthy man Jackson's father talked about who had sent his wife to an insane asylum. While the man claimed the wife had dementia, it was not proven. And from the story, the man just wanted to get rid of his wife. The claim didn't have to be proven. A man had complete control over a wife. No judge or jury would intervene.

"You wouldn't," Molly barely breathed.

"Darling, of course, I wouldn't," Jackson tried to calm her. "But then, I don't think you would go to such recklessness as trying to run off with our children."

Molly just stared at him. When it came to Jackson, she no longer knew what to believe. But the threat was there. He could take the children. He could send her away where no one could find her. He could send the children to England. She couldn't think of anything to say. She wanted to scream, but that would do no good either. The two of them faced each other, waiting. Finally, Jackson spoke again.

"Honey," he began softly, moving toward her a step. "I understand you are upset. I didn't want to hurt you. You shouldn't have followed me. But, since you did, we have to move on from here. We have to have an understanding."

Molly didn't reply, so Jackson continued.

"We will go home," Jackson continued firmly. We will work this out. You are still my wife and belong at the Anchor J." When Molly still did not reply, Jackson continued, his voice decisive and firm. "Get in the buggy, Molly. We are going to lose the light."

"I want my saddle again," Molly said. She wasn't sure why that came out of her mouth, but she knew she was beaten. She wouldn't leave her children and knew she could not fight Jackson about them. No courts in the country would rule against her wealthy, influential husband. "I want my riding clothes."

"Of course," Jackson said smoothly. "We won't have guests until next summer, so you can ride as you wish and wear what you wish. But I insist you dress for dinner when I am home, and when we have guests, you will act and dress as a proper lady."

Molly stood rigidly, watching her husband with smoldering eyes. Jackson gave her a minute, then stepped forward and took Molly's arm. She jerked away from him and turned, going ahead of him to the buggy. She climbed in without his help and gathered Grace into her lap. She had no way to win this battle. She had lost the war years ago, only she didn't know it then. And defeat was a bitter pill to swallow.

Surprisingly, the fall did not drag for Molly. She had her horses back, and to his credit, Jackson did not unduly stand in her way. He still insisted that Molly stay away from the corrals and cowboys. Burton fetched her horse when she wanted to ride, but Molly could accept that. Jackson did not argue with Molly when she began going to Grace in the morning and spending time in the nursery with Lydia and the child. Grace was too young for lessons, so Molly had more time with her daughter. However, with Lydia as Grace's nurse, Molly could leave and ride whenever she wanted. Without household chores, Molly spent most of her time that fall with her daughter or her horses. That Burton shadowed her as she rode was of no consequence to Molly. She rode where she wanted and often lost Burton as she jumped streams and logs and disappeared into the trees. If the man told Jackson he couldn't keep up with Molly, it was never brought up at dinner.

Dinners were a quiet affair. Molly, as requested, dressed for dinner every night. She was punctual, polite, and distant. She listened to Jackson's discussions about the ranch, the weather, or Jack's latest news. But she did little to contribute to the conversation. She replied to direct questions, but nothing else. If Jackson minded the one-sided conversations, he did not address it.

Many of Jackson's conversations were about the conditions on the range. It had been a hot, dry summer, and the cattle were not fat going into the winter. Jackson ordered Buster and the crew to gather the older steers and take them to market after the fall round-up. But cattle prices crashed that fall, dropping to half of what Jackson's cattle had sold for two years ago in 1884. Jackson hoped to bring the bulk of his herd through the winter, gambling on better prices in the spring of 1887. Molly knew that Jackson was worried about the condition of his remaining herd and, consequently, of finances, but she could not offer him comfort. Her heart was as cold as the temperatures were turning that fall.

Every two or three weeks, Jackson rode to Laramie. He always prefaced his leaving with going for supplies, or for meetings with his solicitor, or for getting letters from Jack. But Molly knew the real reason why Jackson went to Laramie. Between husband and wife, it was no secret that Jackson went to the other woman. The fact that Jackson always brought Molly home a present from town, a shawl, a scarf, or a pretty bauble of some sort did little to alleviate the fury that Molly kept in check within her. It sat right below the surface and kept her unspeaking, moody, and angry.

The snows came in early November, temperatures dropping drastically. Other than the cowboys rotating from the ranch to the line shacks to check on the cattle and opening water sources, all other traveling ceased. The cowboys at the ranch cut ice and filled the icehouse. They fed hay to the remuda, and the few cows kept near headquarters, but little else. Long, dreary days of winter kept everyone close to a fire.

Now, the days dragged for Molly. There was no riding anymore. It was simply too cold, and the snow became too deep. And because Jackson forbade her from going to the corrals, she couldn't even go to her horse to get outside. The snow also kept Jackson home. With each report from the crew coming in from the prairie, Jackson grew more concerned. By early December, dinner became a silent affair, as even Jackson was quiet and withdrawn.

To fill her time, Molly and Lydia spent hours knitting scarves and mittens for gifts for the hands. Every Christmas Eve, the cowboys at the ranch were treated to a Christmas Eve dinner at the ranch house. Catherine helped Molly with the evening festivities, the Burtons cooked a huge beef with all the trimmings, and every cowboy at the ranch was invited. It was the one time all the hands came into the headquarters at the same time, if only for one night.

Christmas Eve turned out to be an enjoyable evening. Molly and Catherine played the piano and sang Christmas carols they liked or ones requested by the cowboys. The food was plentiful, and the house was festive with a tree and decorations. Grace was allowed to make an appearance early in the evening, and many of the men teased or picked up the little girl. Watching them, Molly knew they were remembering families far away or long gone. It was a successful evening and one enjoyed by all. In a cold white winter, little else brightened the world of the men and women of the Anchor J this Christmas season.

CHAPTER 9

The Weight of Guilt – January 1887

With the holidays behind them, there was little to look forward to in the white, cold world of Wyoming territory as 1887 began. In early January, the weather turned bitterly cold. Half of the ranch hands had gone out to the line shacks after being home for Christmas. The story on the prairie was not good. The cattle were stressed trying to find grass under the snow that came in November and stayed. The drought during the summer didn't help. The grass going into winter had not been abundant. Molly could see that both Jackson and Buster were worried about the animals. Molly wondered if Jackson now might understand her father's insistence on putting up enough hay for the cattle. But Molly didn't ask. Her heart hurt for the poor animals facing this harsh winter, but she still had no forgiveness for Jackson. She kept her thoughts to herself.

As the first full week of January began, there was a little break in the temperature, and the men hoped this would bring about milder weather. Jackson wanted to see for himself the condition of his cattle on the range. He had enough hay at the ranch headquarters to feed a few more animals, so he and Buster discussed how many they could bring home.

Jackson left with his entire crew of cowboys on the first Thursday in January, bundled up against the cold. Molly hadn't asked Jackson how long they would be gone, but when visiting with Catherine later, Buster told Catherine they should be home by Monday or Tuesday if all went well. Catherine was worried seeing her husband and the men riding off into the cold white land. A winter blizzard was always a possibility and was not something to take lightly, especially on the open prairie.

The only men left behind were old Punch and Mr. Burton. Punch really wasn't that old of a man, but after a crippling fall from a horse, he was severely lame and could only ride horseback for short periods before finding himself in extreme pain. Jackson kept him on as a cook for the hands and for some of the menial tasks that needed to be done around the ranch. Punch had been with the ranch since shortly after Molly married Jackson and was one of the few cowboys that Jackson felt was safe to interact with Molly. There were times when Burton had been so busy that Punch was the man who brought Molly her horse. Left behind while the rest of the crew rode to the prairie, Burton was instructed to help the women and keep the fires going, while Punch would feed the left-behind saddle horses and the small herd of cattle at the headquarters.

The days passed slowly. Molly took Grace and visited Catherine, letting Grace play with Catherine and Buster's children. It was too cold to bundle up to go farther than the house next door. Even stopping outside to play in the snow was out of the question for Grace. Winter is a tedious time, Molly thought. And it doesn't get better when she feels like a prisoner in her own house.

⸎

Jackson and Buster sat at the little table in the line shack, faces drawn with fatigue. It had been hard getting to the shack, and the sight of the cattle they came upon did little to lighten their outlook. The cattle were extremely thin, just short of starvation, and it was only January. Now, two days later, after spending the days gathering and sorting cattle in the vicinity of two different line shacks, the men were near exhaustion.

Jackson had both cows and steers on the plains. Cattle were sold when they reached three years old, leaving the yearlings and two-year-old animals to mature. However, Jackson had moved into raising some of his own cattle following Twin Peak Ranch's example. He bought beefier bulls from the east and was mating them with the long-horn cows from Texas. Jackson believed these animals would survive the winters on free range. But this year, Jackson was seeing the fury of winter. He remembered Kade's warning that the cattle losses from winter kill on the unprotected prairie would be devastating one of these years. Jackson understood what Kade was talking about now. The young cattle were suffering but the older breeding cows and bulls were near starvation already.

"Boss," Buster drawled slowly, "I'm thinking maybe you and two men should take these cows we sorted off today back to the ranch. We have some hay there, and if we ration it off, I think we can get these cows through to spring. They won't be fat, but even short rations at home will be more than what they can find out here."

"I was thinking the same thing," Jackson replied wearily. "But I don't have to go back right away. Pick three men and send them back."

133

"If we ride on to the next line shack and find the cattle in as poor shape as here," Buster continued, "we will have even a farther drive to get them home." Buster looked at Jackson, concern in his eyes. "No offense, Boss, but you aren't used to this. You got sand, but I think I can work faster if you take these cattle back before the weather gets any worse."

Jackson looked at Buster resignedly. "You're probably correct. Pick out the two men you think should go back with me, and we will start at first light in the morning."

A man has lots of time to think while pushing slow-moving cattle ahead of him. Jackson watched the horizon, seeing clouds building in the west. But the day wasn't as bitter cold as it had been, and he was grateful for that. The cold seemed to go through him, despite his heavy winter coat and leather chaps. He would be glad to get home. He wasn't sure if he would ever feel warm again. It was a given that he wouldn't be curling up next to Molly to draw from her warmth tonight. She hadn't thawed a bit since he brought her back from Twin Peaks. He wasn't surprised, but it still displeased him. He'd give it more time. He wished the weather would break and he could ride into Laramie. Ida wouldn't give him the cold shoulder. But seeing her would have to wait until spring. There would be no going to Laramie any time soon.

By midday, the wind began to pick up. Jackson looked around, trying to get his bearings. The whole world was white. But he thought they might be only two or three hours from getting into the foothills where there was some protection from this godawful wind. Jackson looked at the two cowboys riding on the outside edges of the herd. They were hunched up against the wind, hats tied on with scarves. Jackson ducked his chin into his coat collar, pulling his neck scarf tight. Damn, it was cold. It was January ninth, he thought, and a hell of a way to spend a Sunday.

After helping Jackson with the small herd, Buster and one of his hands had gone northeast while two other men went northwest. They would assess the cattle they came upon and open up stock dams to water, finally angling toward the next line shack. The cattle congregated around water holes in the winter, knowing a line rider would come and chop the ice open. Cowhands staying in line shacks had a circle they rode each day, opening water holes. In between, the cattle licked at snow, but getting a good drink was vital to the animals during the winter.

It had been a long, dismal day of seeing more emaciated cattle and hearing their mournful bawls. Buster was looking forward to the line shack and hoped the other riders would reach there first and have a fire going. The clouds to the west had built up all day, and Buster nervously watched them, trying to gauge how far they had to go to shelter. He signaled to his cowhand, and they pushed their tired horses into a trot as the ground blizzard increased and the day darkened. It wasn't enough. The wind rose, and the snow hit like an angry wall of white. The whole world turned white. The ground, already covered in snow, was white, and it became impossible to see more than a few feet in front of them. The horses wanted to drift with the wind, but Buster held his mount steady into the wind, hoping he had his bearings right. If he missed the line shack, he and his cowboy were in great danger. It was with relief that they ran into the corral fence, which appeared only a yard in front of them. A few more feet east, and they would have missed the shack completely.

"Give me your horse and get inside and start a fire," Buster commanded his man. "I'm 'bout froze through."

Going to the lean-to built for the horses' protection and hay storage, Buster stripped off saddles and forked the horses some hay. The other men were not in yet, and Buster was worried. He was glad he had sent Jackson home, hoping his boss had made the foothills before this hit. It was with relief that he saw a horse and rider figure come out of the gloom.

"Glad you got here," Buster called, forking over more hay. "This is goin' to be some blizzard."

The cowhand, ice crusted, nodded as he moved into the protection of the lean-to and started to unsaddle.

"Where's Boxer?" Buster called over the howl of the wind, watching for the second rider to come in out of the weather.

The cowhand looked around. "Ain't he right behind me?" Both men went to the corner of the barn and peered out into the swirling snow.

"When'd ya see him last?" Buster asked, tension rising in him.

The man thought about that. "We were watching the clouds building and mentioned we needed to move faster. I put my horse into a trot, and Boxer was right behind me then. Maybe thirty minutes or so ago. Damn wind hurt, so I jest had my head tucked into my coat, never looked back. Figured he'd keep up or call out."

Buster nodded. That was the way of these men. All capable and strong, they figured they could look out for themselves. But he was worried about this. If Boxer didn't come in soon, he was lost, and there was no way anyone could go looking for him in this storm.

When the blizzard hit the ranch that Sunday afternoon, the winds rattled the windows, and the temperature inside the main house dropped drastically. Catherine and her children were visiting, and the women had had a prayer service of sorts. Even Punch had come from the barns that afternoon to visit. The wind was suddenly so strong, and the temperature dropped so drastically it was decided that everyone would stay in the main house for the night. With the dropping temperatures and the bitter wind, the guest wing was too hard to heat, so featherbeds were dragged into the parlor for Punch and Catherine's older boys while Catherine slept with Molly. The Burtons moved their mattresses to the kitchen floor while Lydia and the little children slept in the nursery upstairs above the kitchen, where the heat rose from the stove. Only three fires had to be maintained this way: the kitchen, Molly's room, and the parlor. Even then, it took a lot of work for Punch and Burton, ropes tied around their waists and anchored to the house, to bring in enough wood for the night. Catherine's house next door had vanished in the swirling snow. Finding the wood stored in the lean-to between the two homes was an effort. Everything was white, and the blowing, drifting snow obliterated all sight more than a couple of feet.

On Monday, the wind and snow continued. Punch and Burton found all the rope they could in the tool-shed and made their way to the back of the woodshed.

Securing the ropes there, they fought their way onto the fence line that led to the corrals. When they finally made the corrals, they used shovels to dig out the gates, allowing the horses and cattle to fight the drifts to get out to the hay lot. It was impossible to try to pitch hay in the fierce wind. By this time, the two men didn't have the strength left to break open water sources for the animals. For one day, the horses could eat snow. At least the animals would have feed. It was nearing dark when the two men returned to the ranch headquarters, exhausted and nearly frozen.

As it turned out, it wasn't one day the livestock had to eat snow. The blizzard raged all day Tuesday, and it was late Wednesday when it began to blow out. Catherine was almost frantic with worry for her husband, and Molly found herself pacing from window to window over and over again during the day. Lydia tried to keep the children busy, playing games with them and reading them stories.

When the blizzard finally blew itself out, the silence was almost as hard to bear as the wind. Punch reported that the drifts in some places went over the top of the fences and were so hard the animals could walk right up and over them. The cattle and horses were making a mess of the haystacks, but Punch didn't think he had a place to put the animals where they couldn't simply walk right out again over the drifts.

Now began the long wait. Catherine took her children back to their own home, partly because she just wanted to be home and partly because she could find things to work on there, which helped her as she worried about her husband. Burton replenished the wood for each house and helped Punch where he could, trying to dig out fences or build some temporary fences above the existing rails. By Saturday, they were able to get the remuda moved back into a corral. Still, there was no sign of Jackson, Buster, or the cowboys.

It was late Sunday afternoon when Molly saw riders a half mile up the river valley, riding slowly single file through the snow. As she watched, the lead horse struggled to get through the snows. Soon, the lead rider pulled off and let the rider behind him take the lead. This went on over and over again as the lead horses were worn down by breaking through the drifts. At one place, the lead rider had to dismount and clamber alongside his horse to get through a drift. It was almost dark before the men reached the buildings. Bundled up against the cold, Molly couldn't recognize the riders. But as they drew near the two homes, Molly saw Catherine come flying off her porch right into the snow, struggling waist-deep before throwing her arms around the lead cowboy. Buster was home.

Buster immediately came to the main house, sending his horse on to the barns with the other men. Other than hugging his wife and sending her back inside, he hadn't spoken to her. Now he stood, hat in hand, looking around the parlor.

"Is Jackson here?" he asked slowly.

"Isn't he with you?" Molly replied, confused at the question.

"He started home with some cows a week ago," Buster said. "I hoped he got out of the plains before this hit."

Molly shook her head. "How many men were with him?"

"He had two men with him. I lost two men who stayed back with me. One man we found not more than 30 feet from the line shack where he must have just sat down and froze," Buster said wearily. "I ain't never been in such a storm."

"You didn't come across Jackson or any of the cows on your way home?" Molly knew he didn't, or he would have said so. Sometimes, one asked the dumbest questions.

Buster rubbed his wind-raw face and shook his head. "I'll take some men and go out tomorrow. The wind may have pushed him east. They might have blown clear to the shack toward Laramie. They could've taken shelter there. We'll need fresh horses and grub before we fight this snow again."

"Buster, don't take any chances," Molly said, but she knew he would. "I'm sure Jackson would find shelter." But she didn't believe it. This blizzard came up fast, and it came up deadly. Jackson never gave this western land the respect it deserved. She turned away from Buster and went to her room. She needed to be alone.

Molly spent the next week pacing the ranch house. Lydia kept Grace away most of the day, occupying the child in the nursery. Molly ate little and spoke less. The servants gave her space. They would be there for her if she wanted anything, but otherwise they left her to her own thoughts.

Again, Molly saw the riders come back as she wandered from one window to the next. Buster had taken three men with him, and when Molly saw them return, she could see that only Buster and his men were returning. But they were leading three horses, and the three horses had bundles strapped to them. Big bundles. Bodies. Molly turned and went to her room. She didn't need to be told. She knew.

Buster sent two men to Twin Peaks with the news. It took them all day to make the half-day trip. But they had a trail brokcn through the drifts by the time they got there. They let their horses rest overnight before they tried the return trip, and Jake returned the next day with them. Buster sent the news of Jackson's death, but Buster was more worried about Molly now. She had taken to her room when Jackson's body was brought back. She barely talked, ate almost nothing, sat with the Bible in her lap, and from the looks of her, she wasn't sleeping very much. Catherine and Lydia tried to talk to Molly, but she just sat in her rocking chair and stared at the fire. Everyone was worried.

Jake wasn't sure what he would find when he got to the Anchor J. He knew that there had been something wrong between Molly and Jackson. His father had told him how Molly changed when Jackson walked out of the trading post behiud him after fall gather. There had been no greeting, no welcoming smile, no warmth between the two. Molly's face had gone hard, and she went as instructed to pack her things. There was too much anger in Molly than simply having her son sent away to school.

So, when the news was delivered that Jackson was found frozen on the plains and Molly was taking the death badly, both men wondered if Molly wasn't feeling guilt for the way the marriage was before his death. In any case, Jake knew Molly needed family now, and he was the closest to her. Kade wanted to make the trip, but Jake talked him out of that. Molly wouldn't open up to her father, but she might to Jake. He had been her confidant since childhood. Molly and Jake, ten years apart in age, had a special bond.

It was late afternoon when Jake rode into the Anchor J. Even with a trail broken through the snow, it was tough going. He was glad to see the ranch house come into sight. Buster met him as he rode into the yard and took Jake's horse, letting Jake go directly into the ranch house.

Lydia and the Burtons met Jake at the kitchen door, grief and worry etched onto their faces.

"The poor missus is taking this very hard," Lydia began. "We are so worried about her. She just sits in her room, won't eat, sits with the Bible, and I hear her walking during the night. We don't know what to do."

Jake nodded, shrugging off his coat. "Take me to her," he said.

"I don't need anything," came Molly's reply as Lydia knocked on the bedroom door.

Lydia cast a look at Jake, not knowing what to do.

"Let me," Jake whispered. He opened the door slowly before going inside and closing it behind him. Molly didn't immediately look up. She was sitting in her rocking chair, staring into the fire.

"Molly," Jake whispered.

Molly turned her head, seeing Jake. She stared, and then her face seemed to crumble; tears rose in her eyes and overflowed, and her lips trembled.

"Jake," was all Molly could whisper.

Jake crossed the room and gathered his sister into his arms, cradling her. Molly put her face to his shoulder and sobbed, clearly out of control. Jake backed up to the bed and sat, holding Molly tightly. It took Molly quite some time before her sobs quieted.

"Honey," Jake spoke softly, "I am so sorry for your loss. I'm sure it was a terrible shock when they brought back Jackson's body. I don't know how to help you through this."

Molly pushed back, looking Jake in the face. "No, you don't understand." Molly whimpered. "It wasn't a shock. I expected it. Oh, Jake," Molly wailed, "I am such a wicked woman! I know God is going to punish me."

"Molly, no!" Jake spoke firmly. "You can't be blamed for Jackson's death."

Molly's eyes grew wide, her face showing her panic. "Jake, God is going to punish me. 'For the wrath of God is revealed from heaven against all ungodliness.' It says that in Romans."

"You are not ungodly, Molly. That wasn't written for you," Jake tried to soothe her.

"You don't understand! You just don't understand!" Molly's voice rose. She stood, trying to turn away from Jake.

Jake stood up too, grasping her shoulders to keep her facing him. "Then explain it to me," he said softly. "Help me understand."

Tears welled up again in Molly's eyes. She stared at Jake momentarily before dropping her eyes to the floor. "When the storm came up, I prayed Jackson wouldn't come home." Her tone was low, almost a whisper before she looked up again. "I didn't say I wanted him dead, but Jake, the only way Jackson wouldn't come home is if he was dead. I know that. I didn't say dead in my mind, but I must have meant it in my heart. Oh, Jake, I am so wicked."

Jake knew there were problems between Molly and Jackson, but he never imagined Molly was this unhappy. This was unknown territory, and he had no idea how to talk to Molly about this. He stood silent, watching his little sister.

"See. I had evil thoughts. Terrible, evil thoughts. God will punish me!" Molly was earnest, almost panicked, as she spoke.

"Molly, no," Jake began, pulling her toward him.

"Yes!" Molly's voice rose again, and she pushed back against Jake's embrace. "'For behold, the day is coming, burning like a furnace; and all the arrogant and every evildoer will be chaff, and the day that is coming will set them ablaze.' That's in Malachi."

"Molly, you are not an evildoer. You were unhappy. That is all," Jake tried to sound firm.

"It says in Mark, 'If your hand causes you to stumble, cut it off; it is better for you to enter life crippled than having your two hands, to go into hell, into the unquenchable fire.'" Molly looked imploringly at her brother. "Jake, how do I cut off my mind? I can't cut out my mind!" Molly began to shake.

Jake had no answer. He pulled her to him and sat on the bed, holding her tightly to him. He did not argue. But he remembered when outlaws attacked Kasa and Anna, and he killed the men. He remembered how he and Hawk had taken the outlaws off to be buried, but before covering the bodies, he and Hawk had mutilated them the Indian way so that the men wouldn't go to the afterlife whole. When Anna miscarried their son later that night, Jake thought God was punishing him for mutilating the bodies. It was Matthew who had talked to Jake then. Matthew had the words and the knowledge of the Bible. Jake didn't know the words, but he suddenly knew what to do. He had to take Molly home. Molly needed Matthew now.

They reached Twin Peaks in the late afternoon the next day. Jake had taken the small cutter of Jackson's, pulled by a single horse. The horse could struggle through the drifts using the path Jake and the Twin Peaks cowboys made. The cutter went through or over the drifts, slowing the horse and making travel difficult, but it was lightweight. Jake tethered another horse behind the cutter. He could switch horses that way. It was tedious, but they made the trip.

Jake had gone to see Buster that night. Buster told Jake how he and his men had searched for Jackson and the other two men for days. They had gauged the direction of the wind and finally came upon the bodies of cattle, strung out in a line, their backs to the wind, laying where they fell in exhaustion. They found one horse, shot, and used as a shield against the biting wind and cold. One of the men was huddled and frozen to death beside the animal. They found Jackson's body curled underneath his saddle and blanket, sitting in the open. A snow drift had eventually curved around him, but he had long since frozen to death. The final man had made it to a dry creek bed. His horse had survived, standing head down in the snow, but the man sat with his back to the wind, snow sifting around him.

"Never seen a storm like this one," Buster said sadly. "It came up so fast, and the temperature dropped to where neither man nor beast could survive it. I shouldn't have sent the boss home. But I never expected anything like this."

Jake nodded. "Even in the mountains, with the shelter of trees and ridges, it was bad. You didn't expect this storm. It wasn't your fault."

Jake and Buster sat down and discussed what needed to be done at the Anchor J while Molly was at Twin Peaks.

"You know what to do," Jake told Buster. "For now, you are in charge. I will bring Molly back before spring thaw but until then, you are the boss. If any of the cowboys give you trouble, fire them. There aren't other jobs out there right now. They won't want to leave."

Buster nodded. He had been Jackson's foreman since the ranch began. The men would listen to him.

Jake also instructed the house servants. "I'm taking Molly home. She needs to get away from here right now. I'm sure we will be back in a month. Take care of the house," Jake looked at Mr. Burton. "You are in charge in here. You know what has to be done."

With hot stones tucked under a buffalo robe, Molly and Grace were loaded into the cutter, blankets and a buffalo robe wrapped over them. Molly took almost no notice. She obediently got in the cutter and held her arms out to Grace. Then Molly pulled the blankets up to her neck and lowered her head. She didn't cry or say goodbye. She closed her eyes and rested her forehead on Grace's hair, silent and morose.

With the sun sinking fast in the west, Jake was glad to see the smoke from Kade's cabin come into sight. The cold would creep in once the sun left the sky. He wanted Molly and Grace warm in front of a fire long before then. But the trip, though slow, had not been bad. He had watched the sky like a hawk. If there was any chance of a storm, he knew he might have to stop and make a shelter and a fire. He didn't want to do that. He disliked traveling in the winter, but hated to have his sister and niece out with him. He was relieved to see the buildings of Twin Peaks.

Kade heard footsteps on the porch before Jake got to the door. Throwing open the entrance, Kade stared out at Jake, half carrying and half supporting Molly, who carried Grace. Taking Grace, Kade backed into the cabin so Jake could bring in Molly.

Jake gave Kade a shake of his head. Kade needed no words to know that Molly was not herself. Kade could see the concern in Jake's face and the downcast eyes of his daughter. He knew that Molly was not handling Jackson's death well.

"Molly needs to get warmed up, maybe something to eat." Jake looked at his stepfather. "Grace, too."

"I'm fine, Jake," Molly said softly. "I think I just want to lie down." She didn't look at her father or Sarah, who came to help Molly out of her wraps.

"It must have been a long day," Sarah said. "Sit down, and I'll get something on the stove to warm up for you."

"No," Molly retorted shortly, "I just want to lie down." She looked imploringly at her father. "Can I just lie down in the spare room?"

A look passed between Jake, Kade, and Sarah. It was Jake who responded. "Yes, maybe lying down would be good."

Sarah wrapped her arm around Molly's waist and helped her to the bedroom, leaving Grace behind with her grandfather.

"Molly's not dealing with Jackson's death, is she?" Kade inquired when Molly and Sarah disappeared into the bedroom.

"No, not at all, but Molly is not dealing with grief. She's dealing with guilt," Jake said. The two men took Grace and went to sit by the fire. The little girl was getting drowsy in the warmth.

Jake told Kade how he had found Molly and Molly's thoughts at the time.

"I don't know how to help her," Jake told Kade. "I think only Matthew can help her now. I hated taking the chance to travel with them in this cold, but I had to try. Molly thinks she will be punished for her thoughts. She isn't eating and barely sleeping. I'm not sure if she's afraid of going to hell or if she thinks her punishment might come to her right here on earth. But she's terrified, and I can't reach her."

Kade nodded. "I'll get bundled up an' go to talk to Matthew," he said. "Let Molly rest now an' Matthew can come in the morning."

CHAPTER 10

Picking up the Pieces – Spring 1887

It took almost two weeks until Molly began to forgive herself. By then, she was rail thin, eyes sunken and brooding. At first, Jake and Kade spread the word that she was not up to visitors. By the end of the second week, Molly quit hiding in her room. She began to take some interest in Grace and help Sarah with the household chores. She never spoke of Jackson, and they never asked.

In the beginning, Matthew came twice a day, bringing Molly out of her bedroom and insisting she eat. She did eat, but not enough. Matthew had long private visits with Molly, Bible in hand. He had been the spiritual leader of the three families since they settled this land. Molly listened to him, but it took her a long time to believe what he told her. It took her a long time to forgive herself.

By the end of the third week, Matthew felt it might be good for Molly to have visitors. Matthew, Kade, and Jake discussed it among themselves and decided that no one but themselves needed to know the real reason for Molly's breakdown. Let the rest think it was grief for Jackson. They cautioned people to leave the subject of Jackson and his death alone. Be her friend, they told everyone, and let Molly heal.

On a few warm winter days, Jake would bring a saddled horse and cajole Molly into riding with him. Like her mother, Sabra, the horses were a healing force for Molly. One day, Jake arrived with Hawk in tow and two extra saddled horses.

"Pa, you and Molly have to ride out with Hawk and me," Jake said, barely able to keep the excitement from his voice. "I have something out there that you both need to see."

Neither Molly nor Kade questioned Jake, but obediently, they bundled up and went out to the waiting horses. They rode about a mile west along the river toward where the two- and three-year-old cattle were fed that winter. Some of these cattle would be sold in the spring; the rest would be driven farther west along the river for the summer to fatten. For now, they needed to be close enough for hay to be hauled on hay sleds to feed them daily.

Just as they rounded a bend and the cattle came in sight, Kade's keen eyes saw the surprise that Jake wanted to show them.

"Wal, I'll be damned," Kade whispered, almost reverently.

Hawk, too, spotted the unexpected sight and pointed. Molly's eyes searched before she saw what Hawk and Kade viewed. Two frightfully thin bison cows and one yearling were trying to eat what hay the cattle had left from the morning feeding. As the small party rode slowly forward, they could see the scrawny yearling was a bull.

"Pa," Molly said softly. "I haven't seen any buffalo for ten years."

"Honey, it's been almost that long for me too," Kade said. "I think the last buffalo I saw was maybe seven years or so ago, when I was out on the plains. I hear they are 'bout extinct. These look like they are well on their way to dyin' too."

"Buffalo are hardier than cattle when it comes to winter cold and snow," Jake said, "but even buffalo will starve to death if there isn't any grass under the snow. They must have wandered along this river looking for better feed than they got out on the plains despite the deeper snow we have here."

"They ain't worth killing," Hawk commented, looking at Jake.

"I don't want to kill them," Jake responded. "My children have never seen a buffalo. I want to try to save these three. Get some meat on their bones and keep them safe from hide hunters."

"I agree," Kade smiled. He thought for a few minutes while they all sat on their horses, watching the buffalo eat. "There's that narrow ravine about three miles west of here that cuts off to the east. If you ride up it a bit, it comes out on a nice big mountain meadow. I've ridden it many times, looking for strays. Makes a pretty nice hideout."

"I thought that too," Jake answered. "We'll toss out a bit of extra hay every day, and I think they will stay with the cattle. Come spring, we can mosey the cattle west and into that ravine, then cut the cattle back and leave the buffalo there."

"We can fence off the mouth of the ravine so they don't wander back out to the river during the summer," Kade suggested.

"Is it fair to the buffalo to take their freedom away from them?" Molly asked.

"We ain't really taking their freedom," Kade said. "They can keep going up that meadow an' disappear over the mountain iff'n they want, but I'm thinkin' they will stay put. Plenty of grass in there, fresh water from a stream, an' when winter comes, we kin open up the ravine an' they can come out to eat hay again with the cattle. Be nice to be able to come up an' look at 'em sometimes."

Kade looked over at Hawk and Jake and saw agreement in the young men's eyes. They all grew up eating buffalo meat and wearing warm buffalo robes in the winter. Hawk remembered when the Utes depended on the buffalo for almost everything they needed. The loss of the buffalo was as hard to bear for Hawk as the loss of the land. For all three men, losing the great herds of buffalo was a sad part of watching civilization come to the country. These bison needed to be saved. With luck, maybe in the coming years, these buffalo might raise calves, increasing their number. Time would tell, but for now, Twin Peaks Ranch would do all it could to save these three starving animals.

Jake looked over at his sister and smiled. Molly nodded in agreement. It would be good to save a part of their past from extinction.

By the first of March, Molly was almost herself again. She was not the lively woman full of smiles and warmth that she used to be. Instead, she was serious, thoughtful, and reserved. As the weather began to warm with some spring thaws, Molly told Jake she needed to get back to the Anchor J. Soon, she could make it safely to Laramie. She wanted to talk to Jackson's solicitor and go to St. Louis to bring Jack home. Jack didn't know about his father's death, and she didn't want him to be alone when he found out.

So, it was that on a calm day the first week of March, Jake hitched up the cutter and he took Molly and Grace home. It wasn't an easy trip even then, but it was warmer than in January. Molly visited with Jake and played with Grace along the way.

"Will you go to St. Louis with me when I get Jack?" Molly asked Jake when they were close to the Anchor J.

"You sure you don't want Pa or Thomas to go with you?" Jake asked. "I always seem to attract the wrong attention." He smiled at his sister.

"I don't want you to go if you are uncomfortable about it," Molly returned, "but I lean on you. You have always been there for me."

"Molly," Jake told her seriously, "I am not uncomfortable going anywhere. I'll be glad to go with you. When do you want to go?"

"Unless we get some late spring snows, I was thinking next month. I will leave Grace with Lydia. We should be able to get to Laramie with saddle horses, shouldn't we?"

Jake nodded. "I'll go home tomorrow, but I'll return in a month. We will go to Laramie then and catch a train to fetch Jack."

There was much to do and plan when Molly returned to the Anchor J. Buster reported that they were finding more and more dead cattle on the open range. It didn't look good for the ranch, even if prices increased by fall. The cattle that survived the great blizzard were thin to the point of starvation. It would take a long time for the ones who pulled through the winter to gain the weight needed to sell. The cattle Jackson and his two cowboys were driving home were never found, other than carcasses scattered by the wind, snow, and cold.

Molly met with the Burtons and Lydia next. She thanked them for their concern and help during these trying times and then began to discuss the future.

"I won't know anything for certain until I meet with Jackson's solicitor in Laramie," Molly began. "But regardless of the state of the ranch, I do not intend to keep it. I suspect it may have to be sold to pay off Jackson's investors, but even if a miracle happens and we have enough cattle to meet the bills, I will not keep this place. I intend to go home to Twin Peaks as soon as my affairs here are settled."

Molly looked at the three servants ringed around her and saw anxious faces. She knew they worried about their futures. They were foreigners in this country and a long way from their homeland.

"If you wish it, I will keep you here as long as I still own the Anchor J and have funds to pay you," Molly said. "But you have to tell me what you want to do. If you want to stay in America, I will help you find a position somewhere." Molly fixed her gaze on the Burtons. "For instance, two years ago, Jackson and I visited a ranch up north owned by an Englishman. He was envious of Jackson and me having help who were trained in England. I could write to them and see if they still wanted a couple to work for them. But you have to give me some idea what you want to do."

"I would appreciate you doing that," Burton said, glancing at his wife. "I think we would like to stay in America if we can find appropriate work."

"I will write a letter then and post it from Laramie when I go next month to bring Jack home. I may even get an answer before returning to the ranch."

Molly noticed that Lydia didn't say anything, but Molly didn't press. She wanted to speak to Lydia alone, without the Burtons present. It was later that night, when Lydia was putting Grace to bed, that Molly was able to talk to Lydia alone.

"When we spoke this afternoon," Molly began, "you didn't say what you prefer to do after I sell the ranch."

"Mrs. Crowden, I have been happy at the Anchor J with you and the children," Lydia replied. "I don't really want to leave you. You and the children are like a family to me now."

Molly smiled. "I was hoping you felt that way. I will warn you, though, I haven't worked out yet where I will live when I return to Twin Peaks or how much money I will have. A lot depends on what we find out on the range after the snows are all gone and what Jackson's lawyer tells me." Molly kissed Grace on the forehead, and she and Lydia walked out into the hall. "I would like you to stay with me. Grace loves you, and I know Jack does too."

"Mrs. Crowden, I don't need much for salary."

Molly smiled at that. "Well, let's just wait on that until we understand what our finances will be. But there is one condition you have to agree to if you are going to stay with me," Molly added sternly.

Lydia nodded slowly before asking, "What would that be?"

"Once the Burtons leave, you are not allowed to call me Mrs. Crowden ever again. I am just Molly. Understand?"

"I can do that," Lydia smiled, relieved. "I don't think I could abide the disapproving looks from the Burtons if

I did that now, but once they leave, I'd be pleased to call you Molly."

Jake and Molly rode into Laramie at the end of the second week of April. There was still snow on the prairie, but most of what was left was the remnants of drifts they could ride around. Everywhere they went, they saw the carcasses of dead cattle. If they rode close to a ravine, they might see piles of dead bodies. The few cattle they saw alive were scrawny, pathetic animals. It was a pitiful and distressing sight.

After getting rooms in the hotel, Molly and Jake set off to see Jackson's attorney. Mr. Raile had an office on Main Street two blocks from the hotel. He was glad to see Molly until she told him of Jackson's passing. Shocked, Mr. Raile sank into his chair, gesturing to Jake and Molly to also take a seat.

"The reports from the range coming in this spring have been dire," Mr. Raile stated when he regained his composure. "Is it as bad as they are saying?"

"Might be worse," Jake commented. "We saw dead livestock the whole way in."

"That is why we are here," Molly injected. "I need to know the state of affairs of the ranch, who Jackson's investors are, and how much Jackson owes. After spring round-up, I will have a better picture of what cattle are left, but if our trip here is any indication, it could be twenty-five to fifty percent of the cattle out there are dead."

The lawyer nodded his head glumly. Then, going to a drawer, he rummaged in it until he found a folder, bringing it back to his desk. He opened it and shuffled through some of the papers, reading parts of each.

"Jackson was in pretty deep, what with the cattle he brought up last summer from Texas. It didn't help when prices plummeted last fall. That was the first disaster. Well, maybe the second disaster. The drought was the first. Jackson kept extra head back last fall, hoping for a better market this year. And then he had the breeding cows and bulls he bought last spring." Raile ran his hand through his hair, not wanting to meet Molly's eyes. "He put up the ranch as collateral. He borrowed against the ranch. On a good cattle market, you would need to sell at least half of the cattle the ranch has on paper to pay off the interest and part of the principal. That is what Jackson planned to do. But in today's market, I don't know. I could write to the investors and see if you could pay part of the interest, depending on how much livestock is still alive," he finished doubtfully.

"Mr. Raile," Molly spoke softly, "I don't want to save the ranch. I am going home to Twin Peaks when everything is settled. I just need to know where I stand in this. I want to do what is right by Jackson's investors."

"Well, as Jackson's wife, you will hold whatever is left of the estate for young Jack," Raile looked up at her. "It all goes to the male child, but he isn't of age, so it would be up to you to make decisions."

Molly nodded, thinking. "If the ranch is collateral, how extensive is that? Is it just the land, or the ranch headquarters, or what?"

Raile shuffled through some of the papers. "According to these papers, the ranch consists of several quarters of land that Jackson bought out on the range from homesteaders. He bought that soddy and quarter of land from James Bates' wife, Mary. But Jackson also got a few other sodbusters to sell out to him. Then, he has about 640 acres of deeded land adjacent to your headquarters. I know he runs on free range on the prairie and the river valley too, but they are free range. The headquarters includes one four-room main home, one foreman's home, a cookshack, a bunkhouse, and a barn with corrals. Other than that, Jackson relied on free range, like most other ranchers out there."

Molly thought about that. "So, when Jackson built the additions onto the ranch house, he did not add them to the loan agreement? How did he pay for those?"

The solicitor nodded, "He used his profits from the last two years. Those were good years, and he did quite well. He has some money in the bank that he drew on when he needed cash."

"If the additions disappeared from the ranch house, would that affect the loan papers?" Molly asked.

"The additions are not on any of these papers. I don't think Jackson ever feared losing the ranch, and he used his own money for the additions," Raile replied.

"Can I withdraw some money from the bank, then?" Molly asked. "I will need to pay our hands when I return, and Jake and I are going to St. Louis to bring Jack home. He doesn't know about his father."

"Oh, yes," Raile answered. "I'll walk over to the bank straight off and make the arrangements. Jackson put quite a bit of money in the bank over the last two years to pay for expenses. That, of course, will be wiped out eventually when you settle affairs, but at present, you can withdraw whatever you need."

Molly nodded and looked at Jake before rising. "Thank you for your time," she said as she and Jake started toward the outside waiting area. "I will keep in touch when the spring round-up is complete." Molly had just gone through the office door when she turned around.

"I just thought of something," she said to Jake. "I'll just be a minute." She went back to the lawyer's desk.

"I forgot to ask," she said, lowering her voice, "about the little house at the end of Bleeker Street. Is that part of the collateral, or did Jackson buy it with his own money?"

The lawyer looked up, startled. "I . . . um, it. . . um," he coughed, and then, regaining his composure, he said, "Jackson bought that with his own money."

"So, does the occupant pay rent, or has Jackson hired her to take care of the place?" Molly spoke neutrally.

Raile cleared his throat, looking down at his papers as if in doubt. It was clear he was uncomfortable. "She gets a salary for taking care of the house," he finally mumbled.

"Thank you, Mr. Raile," Molly answered stiffly. "I will get back to you on our plans for that as well as the ranch."

Jake had not followed Molly back into the office but could hear the conversation. He was not aware that Jackson owned a house in town. That is a curious development, Jake thought. But he did not ask Molly about it. Instead, he walked out into the bright sunlight and waited for Molly to catch up.

"Jake, I was looking at the additions to my house. If a hotel building can be moved from town to town as one town dies and another springs up, one of my additions surely can be moved, can't it?" Molly asked.

"I would think so," Jake answered.

"Would you ask around to see if there is someone I could hire who could do that? I think it would take a lot of horsepower."

"Where are you thinking of moving it?" Jake asked.

"I thought I'd like my own home to live in. I could tear out some walls, make a parlor and kitchen downstairs, and still have enough room for one bedroom," Molly answered. It was apparent she had been thinking about this for some time. "I could pick out a spot upriver a distance from Pa's where I could have a pasture for my horses. I don't want to be dependent on Pa."

"I'll ask around," Jake told her. "See what I can find out."

"I have to look at a dress at the Fine Lady's Shoppe," Molly said, changing the subject. "That will give you time to ask around now. I can meet you back at the hotel for supper." Molly didn't look at Jake and he sensed her sudden discomfort. She was hiding something from him.

"I can do that. I'll see you later," Jake replied. He watched Molly turn and move away from him. She was up to something, he thought. She didn't need any clothes, that he knew. Jackson had made sure Molly had plenty of nice dresses. He watched as Molly walked down the street. When Molly reached the next block, she turned and headed away from Main Street. It was the wrong way to get to the Lady's Shoppe. He looked at the street name. Bleeker Street. Jake waited until Molly was out of sight, then he turned and followed her.

Molly walked with determination, fueled by the rising anger inside her. Jackson bought the house on Bleeker Street, kept a mistress there and had a child with her. He paid for the house; he paid the woman. He felt no remorse for this transgression against her, his wife. The woman was a harlot. Molly was going to confront her and throw her out of that house. The closer she got to the end of Bleeker Street, the angrier Molly became.

When Molly reached the door of the small cottage, she didn't hesitate. She knocked loudly and firmly on the door. She heard movement inside, and the door was pulled open. The woman stood there with the baby on her shoulder. Her smile of greeting faded when she saw Molly standing on the porch. She didn't speak.

"You know who I am," Molly said, voice tight with anger.

The woman nodded, wary. "I seen you at the hotel years ago when I worked there."

Molly recalled her previous trips to Laramie years before, searching her memory. She had seen this woman. She knew that when she saw the woman close up.

"You were the scullery girl," Molly said. "You started the fire at night."

The woman nodded.

"May I come in?" Molly asked. It was cold standing on the porch.

The woman backed up and opened the door. Molly stepped in and glanced around the room. It was a pleasant room with two chairs and a small table. There was a bookcase with a few volumes on the shelves, and beside one of the chairs was a basket of knitting yarn.

Molly walked to the door of the back room. It was as she remembered when she saw it that awful night. It was a combination bedroom and kitchen. Like the front room, it was spotlessly clean and neat. A wardrobe stood against the wall, and the kitchen had an ice box, which was quite a luxury for Laramie. The bed, Molly noted, was large enough for two. Next to the bed was a cradle, and by the back door stood a perambulator. When Grace was born, Jackson had brought home a pram just like it for Grace.

"So, this is where you entertained my husband," Molly said sarcastically, turning to face the woman. "I'm sure he insisted you keep clean sheets on the bed."

"I ain't a soiled dove," the woman spoke defensively. "This ain't a crib. I was married before or thought I was. Mr. Crowden helped me when things got bad fer me."

This was getting nowhere. "The baby is asleep on your shoulder," Molly said curtly. "Go lay him down. We have to talk."

The woman took the child into the bedroom and laid him gently in the cradle. Molly turned away and went to the farthest chair, taking a seat. She took deep breaths, trying to calm the anger in her. She wanted to scream at this woman. She wanted to fly at her and tear her hair out. Instead, she sat and waited.

The woman returned to the front room and seeing Molly seated, she took the other chair. Molly studied her. She was taller than Molly and plain. She was stout, but not fat. She had heavy breasts and wide hips. Her hair, a light brown color, was tied up in a bun on the back of her neck. She was younger than Molly, but not by much. She eyed Molly warily.

"What is your name?" Molly asked brusquely.

"Ida Baker. Er, that is what I go by."

"What do you call the baby? It's my husband's child, isn't it?"

Ida nodded slightly. "My boy is Dick Baker. Mr. Crowden insisted he go by my other man's name, but we named him Dick after Mr. Crowden's father. Mr. Crowden's pa's name was Richard." Ida seemed a little proud of that. Ida took a breath before asking, "Mr. Crowden told you about me? You came here to tell me to leave?"

Molly hesitated briefly. "I came to tell you Jackson is dead."

The change that came over Ida was instant. First disbelief, then grief. "No," Ida whispered. "No."

"Jackson went out on the range with the cowboys in January to check on the cattle. He got caught in the great blizzard. He froze to death," Molly spoke bluntly with no emotion.

Ida stared, eyes wide and filling with tears. Suddenly, she grasped the bottom of the apron she wore and covered her face with it. Molly could see her shoulders shake, and the sobs came, full of anguish. As Molly watched, she felt her resolve melt. This mistress of Jackson's mourned for him as she, Jackson's wife, never had. Molly sat quietly, waiting. It was several minutes before Ida cried herself out, wiping her face and sitting up.

"You want fer me to leave," Ida stated this as a fact, not a question.

"Tell me how you came to know my husband," the words startled Molly even as she said them. "How did you come to live here?"

Ida took a breath, thinking through her reply. Then she started at the beginning. She told Molly almost everything, from the first meeting when Jackson paid her boarding room fee until he showed her the cottage and offered her a job. She did not mention sharing Jackson's bed.

"If Mr. Crowden hadn't took me in, I had nowhere to go. I couldn't make enough money to support myself after Mr. Baker done left me," Ida told Molly, imploring her to understand. "I knew I was doing wrong what with Mr. Crowden being a married man an' all, but I was desperate, an' this was sech a nice house. I never in my life lived in sech a nice place nor had sech nice clothes. I never meant you no harm."

"I saw him whip you," Molly said, her voice neutral. "I followed him last fall from the hotel, and I saw you together. He tied you up and whipped you, and you were with child."

Ida blanched, her face turning white. "He never hurt me. It was jest play pretend. He jest liked things that way, but he never hurt me. It was jest pretend."

Molly rubbed her forehead with her hands. This was not going the way she imagined. She was starting to feel sorry for this woman instead of wanting to kill her.

"And you didn't mind being tied up? Being pretend whipped?"

"My husband, him who I thought was my husband, beat me. He broke my nose once. He was mean. What Mr. Crowden done to me was jest different, is all, but I weren't hurt. That was a little thing to put up with to live here," Ida confessed. "An' Mr. Crowden was good to me. He bought me pretties to wear an' let me keep the money I got from selling eggs. He bought a cow an' I milk it an' sell the extra milk. I ain't never had anyone take care of me like Mr. Crowden done."

Molly sat in silence, digesting the woman's words and thinking about the differences between them. On the one hand, Ida had been used by Jackson, just like Molly was used, simply for Jackson's desires. In Jackson's mind, Molly's purpose was to be the perfect, proper wife, and Ida's was to be the willing mistress. They both had been exploited, just in different ways. When Molly discovered Jackson's secret life, she was furious and unforgiving. But Ida knew his lies and accepted them. To Molly, Jackson had become a reprobate. To Ida, Jackson was her savior. Molly turned and looked out the window, thinking.

"You want me to leave?" Ida asked for the third time. Molly could hear the fear in her voice.

"How much did he give you a month to stay here and take care of him?"

"Mr. Crowden gave me five dollars a month for whatever I wanted," Ida answered. "But there were credit at the general store an' at the butcher for anything I needed. I don't know how much. I never used more'n what was needed for food an' sech. Mr. Crowden brung me pretty things an' dresses so I didn't need anything like that. I weren't goin' to lose this house by spending a lot. Mr. Crowden paid for the other bills, like the ice that was delivered. I don't even know what that cost. An' I could sell the eggs an' milk. I had money to put away each month."

"Did he buy the pram?"

Ida nodded.

"The cradle?"

Again, Ida nodded. "An' he bought me books an' wanted me to read them. I kin read some. He wanted me to practice. If I wanted sewing material, I could get it on the credit at the store. I kin sew tolerable well."

"You keep calling him Mr. Crowden," Molly said softly. "What did you call him when you were alone?"

"I always called him Mr. Crowden," Ida explained. "He made me do that even when we were alone here. He didn't want me to call him by his Christian name by mistake an' said if I always called him one name, I wouldn't make a mistake if I met him somewhere in town."

"Did that keep you from making a mistake then?" Molly asked.

"Once I did. It was the second year I was here an' I weren't expecting him yet," Ida told Molly, her voice lowering. "I was surprised an' excited to see him. I looked up from the sewing I was working on an' seen him come in an' I called him by his name. I called him Jackson."

"Was he angry?"

Ida reflected on that. "He didn't seem angry then. He jest said serious like, 'What is my name?' an' I said, 'Mr. Crowden' an' he said that was better," Ida hesitated then went on. "But he was quiet that evening an' brought out the whiskey bottle an' had some. He weren't drunk, but at first I thought he was relaxed. Then when we got ready for . . . ." Ida looked up at Molly and stopped.

"When you went to bed, what did he do?" Molly prompted.

"He spanked me," Ida almost whispered. "He put me over his knee like my pa did when I was little an' he spanked me. That time he hurt me. Not like Mr. Baker hurt me, no broken nose or bones, but my bottom hurt for days. He spanked me hard an told me I had been a bad girl. He told me never to be naughty again an' I knew to be more careful after that. That were the only time he made me cry. That were the only time he were rough with me," Ida finished lamely.

Molly looked away, ashamed to hear this and remembering the one time Jackson was rough with her. She remembered that night, the night Grace was conceived. Molly had hoped that the passion of that night would rekindle their failing marriage. Instead, it was the death knell, only she didn't know it then. That was when her love began to die until it withered away to nothing but anger and hate. She couldn't mourn Jackson's death. She had mourned for him little by little for the past four years until she had no more grief to give.

"The ranch is going to go under," Molly looked back at Ida. "I don't know if the land will pay off all the debts. I won't know until after the spring round-up. I am not asking you to leave." Molly rose to go, walking slowly to the door. "I will get back to you on what will happen. I have a lot to think about right now." Molly reached for the door and went out. Ida sat blankly in her chair, trying to process this shocking turn of events and what it might mean for her future.

Jake followed Molly, feeling a twinge of guilt at his actions. Whatever Molly was up to, it was her business, not his. He always held by the belief that unless asked, he shouldn't meddle in the business of others. But this was his kid sister. He had watched over her for most of her growing-up years. Less than two months ago, she had fought her way back from a breakdown. Jake wasn't interested in her business, but he knew Molly was still fragile. He didn't want anything to throw her back into the dark days. And, by the conversation with the lawyer, Jake had a pretty good idea of what was bothering Molly. Jackson had a house on Bleeker Street. He kept a woman there. Jake did not doubt that the woman was getting paid for more than keeping the house in order.

Molly never stopped nor looked back after she left Mr. Raile's office. The block before the end of the street, she crossed to the other side and approached the last cottage. Jake slowed and watched as Molly marched onto the porch and knocked on the door. The woman who came to the door was young and carried a baby. Her smile faded when she saw Molly. After a few moments, the woman backed up and Molly went into the house, door closing behind her.

A little closer to the little house, a buckboard sat along the road, unhitched and empty. Jake went to it, pulling himself into it, and sat and watched the cottage. He had the time to wait.

It was almost an hour before Molly emerged. Jake watched her closely. He could see that Molly was deep in thought. She walked stiffly, not looking around at her surroundings. She would have walked right by the wagon without seeing Jake if he hadn't spoken up.

"This is what was between you and Jackson?" he asked softly as Molly came alongside the wagon.

Startled, Molly jerked to a stop, looking up at Jake. Her eyes filled with tears, but they didn't fall. She nodded, then looked away.

"Sis, how long have you known?" Jake asked.

"I found out last fall when Jack left for school," she said dully. "But she has been in that house since before Grace was born. What kind of woman am I who cannot keep her husband from wandering?"

Jake jumped off the wagon and drew Molly into an embrace. "Honey, it isn't a reflection on you. Jackson had his reasons, I am sure, but I know you tried. I know some men just can't be satisfied with one woman."

"You'd never do that to Anna, would you?"

"Never have, never will. I gave Anna my promise, you know that, but Jackson came from a different place. I'm sorry, Sis, but I can't explain it more than that. We won't ever know what went through Jackson's mind." Jake thought for a minute then said, "That is Jackson's baby, isn't it?"

Molly pushed away from Jake and nodded. Turning toward town, she began to walk. Jake fell into step beside her.

"Are you all right?" Jake asked softly.

"I wanted to kill her," Molly answered dully, "in the beginning. But it isn't her that I am angry at. And Jackson is dead. I have to get over being angry with him. He used us both for different reasons." Molly hesitated and looked at Jake. "If I look around my anger, I know Jackson wasn't a bad man. But he wasn't the husband I wanted; it took me all this time to know that. He was selfish and arrogant enough to think he could have a wife and a mistress. That girl in there was in a bad place when he," Molly tossed about for the right word, "hired her. He gave her more than she ever had before. I can't blame her. She was desperate, and Jackson offered her security and a home.

"I confronted Jackson last fall when he came to get me at Twin Peaks. He tried to justify his actions, and he threatened to take the children away if I fought him," Molly went on. "I truly think Jackson thought with time, I would come around and, if not forgive him, at least accept the way things were. He had no intention of giving Ida up. I was living with a stranger, and I didn't like him or his rules. When the blizzard hit, all I could think was maybe this would be how I got free."

"You've been down that road before, Molly. It is time to let that go." Jake decided it was time to change the subject. "So, what will become of the woman now?"

"When I went there," Molly said slowly, "I wanted to tell her to get her things and get out. But after talking to her . . ." Molly took a breath. "This is going to sound strange, but I would like to give her that house. It might be tough for her, but she has saved some money and has some chickens and a cow. She could take in sewing or laundry to supplement her income. She'd be better off than she was before Jackson found her. There are women who have had less and made it."

Jake nodded and put his arm around Molly, giving her a squeeze. "I think that would be a good thing then.

Maybe it will help you pick up the pieces of your life to do something good for another person."

Molly nodded. "I thought that too. I think I need to talk to Mr. Raile again."

CHAPTER **11**

Going for Jack -
Spring 1887

Molly wrote a letter to the Englishman she knew and posted it while they were in Laramie. She told the gentleman about the Burtons and that they would be looking for new positions soon. She explained their skills and why she wouldn't be taking them with her when she returned to Twin Peaks. She gave instructions on how she could be reached if they were interested in hiring the couple. With this task done, there was little else to be done before arriving at the train station.

Neither Jake nor Molly had ever been on a train. They booked seats in a first-class Pullman car. Giving their valises to the Black porter, they climbed the stairs onto the train. The car was about half full, and all conversation quieted as Molly and Jake made their way to the seats assigned to them. Before they reached them, a white porter hurried down the aisle toward them.

"Excuse me," the man said brusquely, "but I think you are in the wrong car." The porter looked severely at Jake.

Jake looked at his ticket calmly before looking directly at the porter. "No, these are our seats." He shouldered past the man.

"But we don't allow Indians to ride here," the porter was becoming angry.

"Excuse me," Molly was livid. "This is my brother, and he will accompany me to St. Louis. I don't think you want to oppose us on this."

The porter looked at her in confusion. She was obviously a well-bred, wealthy woman by her clothes and demeanor. That she claimed this mixed-blood man was her brother was hard to believe, even though Jake was as well dressed as Molly.

"Mrs. Crowden and I have shares in this railroad," Jake said amiably. "If you value your job, I'd just turn around right now and move away."

The porter wavered for a moment, then turned on his heel and left. Molly looked at Jake as she found her seat and settled into it.

"That was good," she smiled. "Very convincing lie."

"It wasn't exactly a lie," Jake grinned. When Pa and Sarah came home from St. Louis in '82, he thought it might not be a bad idea to invest a little of Twin Peak's profits in something entirely different. He bought shares in this railroad."

Molly was surprised. "I had no idea. Pa thought of that?"

"You'd be surprised what our old mountain man father comes up with sometimes," Jake said. "He always said the free-range ranchers would someday regret their methods of letting cattle try to survive the winters on their own. I think we are seeing that come to pass now Pa also said we needed more than one income source. Look at Twin Peaks, Molly," Jake went on. "It was built on the trading business that Old Tom and Pa had with emigrants on the Oregon Trail. He brought in Matthew Jorgensen and Jim Bates as partners. Now, Matthew heads up the haying and the garden produce with Army, Jeremiah, and Will's help. When Matthew turned that small flock of sheep over to Will, it turned out that Will had a talent with those critters. Now Will has a large flock and his sheepherders. Noah, with Emmett's help, pretty much handles the hog operation. I run the horse enterprise, Thomas heads up the cattle, and now Pa has a trading post. The cattle prices took a real hit last year, falling to half what they had brought in the past. But Twin Peaks will survive and even thrive because our other assets will carry us through the low cattle prices, and Matthew's hay carries the cattle, the sheep, the hogs, and horses through the winter. Pa was the one who had the vision, and when he shared it with Matthew and Jim almost forty years ago, he got the best partners he could hope for. Now the Jorgensen and Bates children are grown, and like Thomas and me, they all have a place with Twin Peaks. Look at Jeremiah with his lumber mill. He's getting settlers and ranchers sending wagons for his products. All these enterprises were started with Twin Peaks' capital. All of us kids have grown up to take our place on the ranch. Twin Peaks is a bigger operation than the Anchor J or most ranches out on the plains. But it is because we are diversified that we will get through this winter and these low cattle prices."

Molly thought about that. Twin Peaks, with its assortments of small cabins that ranged along the river and up into the surrounding valleys, was a place she always took for granted. But that Twin Peaks was a more extensive operation than the Anchor J with its thousands of cattle never occurred to her. Jackson, with his mansion of a ranch house and his wealthy family in England, hadn't achieved the success her fur trapper father had amassed. That was something to think about. It was at supper that evening in the elegant dining car that Jake brought up another subject.

"When are you planning on burying Jackson?" he asked softly, intent on cutting up his steak.

"As soon as the hands can get graves dug after Jack gets home," Molly replied nonchalantly.

"You plan on burying him at the Anchor J?"

"Why not?" Molly asked. "It saves hauling the bodies."

"Molly, think about this," Jake said. "You have to get Jackson and those other cowboys in the ground before it gets too warm, but it is still plenty cold enough that you can pack the bodies with ice from the icehouse or snow from drifts that are still in sheltered places. If you transport them overnight, they will stay cold. You don't have a burying ground at the Anchor J, and we do at Twin Peaks."

"I don't want Jackson at Twin Peaks," Molly said stubbornly.

Jake fixed a severe eye on his sister. "Molly, I know you are angry at Jackson. I know you can't forgive him. But you have two children who loved their father. It would be different if you planned on living at the Anchor J, but you don't. Someday, your children will start to ask why their father is buried at the ranch you didn't want to keep. Your children deserve to have their father's grave in the family burial plot."

Molly didn't reply. Thoughtfully, she chewed her food and avoided looking at Jake.

"Molly," Jake said softly, "you know I am right."

Molly nodded. "I know. I want to punish Jackson still, but he's dead. Maybe all I am doing is punishing the children." Molly put her fork down and looked up at Jake. "When we get home, maybe you could get some men to dig graves at Twin Peaks. We can pack the bodies with ice and bring them in a few days. We might as well bring them all. I don't even know who to notify about the dead cowboys."

The rest of the trip was uneventful, and when they disembarked at St. Louis, they were met at the station by their Uncle Joe and Aunt Katie. Uncle Joe was Kade's younger brother and a lawyer in St. Louis. Jake and Molly met them at Thomas' wedding years earlier. Uncle Joe resembled their father in a more sophisticated way. At the wedding in Laramie, Joe had been in the thick of a bar brawl, and while out of practice, he held his own fighting alongside the Twin Peaks men. Jake had an instant liking for his aunt and uncle on that visit. They had befriended Jake's mother when Jake was a baby and knew of his Native heritage. They accepted him as a valued nephew then and now. It was with pleasure that Jake greeted them.

"You two haven't aged a bit," Jake said, shaking Joe's hand.

"Has it been eleven years?" Joe replied, smiling. "I probably wouldn't even remember the year except that it was the year of the Custer massacre. We still keep hearing about that."

Joe turned his attention to Molly. "Molly darling, I am so sorry about your husband. You have our sincere condolences."

Molly nodded, then said neutrally, "It was a shock. But now all I want is to get Jack and bring him home. I want both of the children with me now."

"I am sure that will help," Katie said. "You can take our buggy and team tomorrow and go for him. The school is about fifteen miles from the city, so you can easily be there by noon." She took Molly's arm. "But now you must come home and rest from your train ride. And we have eleven years to catch up on."

The evening was a pleasant one. Joe and Katie's children, grown with their own children, came over for supper. These were cousins who Jake and Molly had never met but had heard so much about in letters back and forth between their parents. The evening was full of memories and stories.

Katie insisted they eat before they left in the morning, even though Molly wanted to leave very early. Molly wanted to be at the school right after the boys had lunch. She wanted Jack fed before he heard the news of his father. He might not want to eat after the news, and it was a long buggy ride back. Katie packed a picnic lunch for Molly and Jake.

Molly blinked in surprise when Jake walked into the dining room for breakfast. Jake was dressed all in buckskins. Anna must have made him a new set of clothes as they were soft and clean, decorated with beads and long fringes down the sleeves. Jake wore a bear tooth necklace with a leather belt around his waist. Attached to the belt was his big skinning knife. Today, he wore moccasins on his feet, and his shaggy hair was pulled back and tied with a thong. It had been years since Molly had seen Jake in full Indian dress. He wore buckskin shirts often, but not usually trousers. All that was missing was warpaint and feathers.

"Whoa," Uncle Joe said, "you aren't going to war, are you?" But he was smiling.

Jake laughed. "I hope not. I'm not packing iron. I won't get a lot done with only a knife."

Jake turned to Molly. "I never had a chance to tell you that we got two letters from Jack last fall before we couldn't get out to get more mail. He wrote that bullies in the upper grades picked on the new boys. One day, Jack had enough and pulled the little boot knife I gave him and poked it in the neck of a big boy. Jack said the bullying stopped then and stayed stopped." Jake hesitated but decided against telling Molly that Jack threatened to cut the boy's throat and scalp him if he or his friends were bothered again.

"Anyway, one of the older boys asked Jack where he learned to use a knife, and Jack told him he had an Indian uncle," Jake grinned, "and I reckon that would be me. The boys didn't believe him. They started calling him 'Injun Jack,' to tease him. Jack wrote that the name calling didn't bother him, but he didn't like the boys not believing him. I thought I'd arrive today and prove them all wrong."

"So here we go to pick up Jack," Molly laughed. "The Indian and the lady."

The trip was uneventful other than the stares from people they passed. The school came into sight shortly after the sun reached its zenith in the sky. They were in Joe's single-seat buggy, and as the horse trotted up the school drive, they could see boys in the athletic fields behind the main building. Jake guided the horse to the main building, and tying the horse to the hitching post, he helped Molly out of the buggy. Together, they walked up the steps to the front door.

To say they made quite a spectacle would be an understatement. Classroom faculty turned to watch the lady and the Indian walk down the hall to the office. Many walked out into the hall to gaze after them.

"You'd think they'd never seen an Indian before," Jake murmured to Molly.

"Probably not in the halls of wisdom," Molly whispered back. "Bet there aren't a lot of students here from the wild western mountains."

The headmaster greeted them cordially after he got over his surprise.

"I am Jack Crowden's mother," Molly began. "I have come to take him home."

She pulled a paper from her handbag and handed it to the administrator. She had notified the Laramie Daily News of Jackson's death, and an obituary ran the next day. Molly brought the paper with her to prove her words. She also brought a letter from the solicitor introducing her to the headmaster. There was no question that Molly was Jack's mother and had the right to take him from the school.

They sat visiting quietly for a few minutes, the headmaster offering his condolences to Molly. Jake sat quietly next to Molly. This was her business, and she didn't need his help. But finally, the headmaster turned to Jake.

"I heard a rumor that Jack told the boys that he had an Indian uncle," he said neutrally. "Am I to understand he told the truth?"

"That is what most people call me, although I am only part Indian. My father was Ute, but Molly and I have the same mother," Jake answered smoothly. "I grew up with my mother's people but had a half-brother with the tribe. I spent a lot of time with him when I was old enough. My adopted father, Molly's father, was an old mountain man. He was just about as Indian as my Ute relatives. Don't let

Molly's fine clothes fool you; she can drop a deer with a rifle and ride the fleetest horses."

The headmaster studied Molly and smiled. "I think I believe you on that. It would explain a lot about how well Jack handles the horses here. Let's go and find Jack."

"We don't want to tell him about his father until we leave," Molly cautioned. "We want to be alone with him, so please do not say anything."

The headmaster nodded, and they left the office, heading for the outside athletic fields.

As Jake and Molly accompanied the headmaster across the field, the boys began to notice the visitors. Slowly, activity stopped, and the boys turned to stare. It wasn't long before a small figure emerged from the group.

"Mother! Uncle Jake!" Jack ran to them, throwing himself in his mother's arms. After hugging his mother, Jack turned to his uncle. "Uncle, it is good you are here," he said proudly.

The rest of the boys approached, silently watching the strange Indian man that Jack was embracing.

"You do have an Indian uncle, then?" one boy asked.

Jack turned to the boys. "This is my uncle. He is a Ute warrior."

"Did you fight in Custer's Massacre?" asked a boy, his tone accusatory.

"The Sioux and Cheyenne went to war with Custer, not the Utes," Jake answered gravely. "But when some of the Cheyenne warriors found our ranch later that same month, our ranch had to fight them. We lost two of our best men that day."

That silenced the boys for a moment before another boy asked, "Did you fight against the other Indians then?"

Jake looked at the boy, remembering that day. "I fought for my family, my land, and my children that day,"

Jake replied seriously. "When you live in the West, you do what has to be done for survival."

"The Utes were who massacred Nathanial Meeker and kidnapped his wife and daughter," another boy spoke up belligerently. "Did you do that?"

"No," Jake replied shortly, "I had a brother in the Battle of Milk Creek. He was killed. The Utes were within their rights in that battle, but the Meeker killings and kidnappings were unfortunate. I wasn't there for either of those things, but I went when I heard, and I searched for the kidnapped women and helped get them back to safety. It was the best I could do for the whites and the Utes."

The boys stood silent, digesting that. Finally, one little boy about Jack's age asked, "Can you throw a knife as good as Jack says you can?"

Jake grinned. "I'm not sure how good Jack says I am. Want me to throw a knife at something?"

The little boy looked around and saw the boundary posts surrounding their playing field. "That?" he pointed at a nearby one.

Jake looked at Jack. "Do you have your boot knife with you?"

Jack nodded, leaning down to retrieve it. He handed it to his uncle. Jake eyed the post. It wasn't very far away and an easy target. He threw the little knife, and it stuck in the post. He heard the boys murmur their approval.

"That is too easy," Jake said. "How about I try for one four or five posts down?" With that, Jake pulled his big knife and let it fly. The satisfying thunk of the blade hitting the farther post was followed by the surprised comments of the boys.

"Get them for me, will you, Jack?" Jake asked.

"If you are going to fight, you have to have the skills," Jake told the boys.

"Can you shoot just as well?" a boy asked.

"I can with a rifle," Jake answered. "But a pistol is only good for close shots, and I am not as good with that. Few men are. The rifle and knife are my chosen weapons. But peace is my desire. Remember never to pick a fight but have the skills so you don't have to back down if a fight comes your way."

"Have you ever killed anyone?" a boy in the back asked.

Jake grew serious. "Yes. But it isn't something a man wants to do," Jake remembered circumstances where he was so angry that he wanted to kill, but he decided this was not something to say to young boys. Jake turned to Molly and nodded. It was time they left.

Jack fairly bubbled with excitement when he brought out his packed valise and joined Molly and Jake at the buggy. He was excited about going home and proud he proved to the boys that he had not lied about his uncle's Indian background. They were almost a mile from the school when Jack thought about asking about his father. Molly was expecting the question.

"Has spring round up started?" Jack asked. "Is that why Father isn't here?"

Molly looked away, trying to appear calm. "Let's wait a minute to talk," she said, indicating a small stream they were approaching. "The horse needs a drink, and we can stop there and visit while Jake takes care of him."

When they stopped, Molly drew Jack away and saw an old fallen tree. She went to it and sat, pulling Jack in front of her.

"Honey, there was a bad blizzard in January. Your father was out in it and lost his way," Molly said seriously. "Your father didn't make it home."

Jack stood silent, watching her. Molly wasn't sure he understood the gravity of her words.

"Jack, your father died."

The boy stood rigidly. After a moment, he simply turned and walked away. Molly rose to go after him.

"Let the boy alone, Molly," Jake said softly. "Give him time to be alone before you go to him."

Molly nodded, knowing that there was nothing she could do to ease Jack's grief. A mother hates to see her child hurting, but this was a hurt she could not kiss away.

Jake, Molly, and Jack descended the train at Laramie three days later. Jack was quiet, nursing his grief, but glad to be back in Wyoming. Jake and Molly left the child to his sadness, knowing he had to work through this on his own. There were no words that would bring Jackson back, and Molly was reluctant to talk about Jackson anyway.

"I need to talk to Mr. Raile," Molly said when they stood outside on the train platform. "Would you take my valise and Jack back to the hotel?"

"I'll get us rooms, and then Jack and I can go to the mercantile," Jake replied. "He must have grown two inches since he left. I bet none of his ranch clothes will fit him. I'll get him some work clothes."

Molly nodded absently. She had business to take care of before leaving town and wanted to get on with it. She wanted to ride out in the morning heading for the Anchor J.

◆

Before leaving Laramie for St. Louis, Molly had again visited the lawyer and left instructions. When Molly returned, she was pleased to find out he had taken care of her requests. With papers in hand, she made her way again down Bleeker Street to the cottage at the end. Ida Baker was not surprised to find Molly again on her front porch, but the worry lines on her face showed her concern. She stood back and allowed Molly to enter the house, closing the door behind her.

"Can you support yourself and the boy if you have this house to live in?" Molly asked abruptly as she settled in a chair.

Ida was surprised. That was not what she expected Molly to say to her. "I reckon so iffen I kin keep the chickens an' the cow," she thought about that. "I kin take in laundry or mending. Might depend on what you want for rent."

Molly studied the woman, then leaned forward and held out one of the papers she carried. Ida took it and opened it, slowly reading what was written. Then she raised surprised eyes to Molly.

"This says I own this house?" Ida asked.

"That paper says that the house is yours," Molly confirmed. "As soon as the ranch is sold, there will be no more credit at the store. You will have to make out. I don't want the chickens or the cow, so they are yours too."

Ida looked down, studying the paper, then asked softly, "Why are you doing this?"

"I admit it was not what I originally thought I would do," Molly replied. "But it seems the right thing to do.

You were a victim of your circumstances. Circumstances caused by men and the rigid expectations that we women must live in order to endure. I don't want the ranch, and I don't want this house. You might as well have your home."

"Missus, I don't know what to say," Ida was at a loss.

"Maybe someday life won't be so hard for women," Molly said, "but until that happens, maybe women have to stick together to help each other. I hope this helps you and your boy." Molly stood up. "I have something else for you. You can use it, burn it, or save it for later, but the boy should have a right to his father's name." Molly handed the woman another paper.

Ida took the paper and read it. She looked up at Molly, clearly stunned. "You had the doctor do this?"

"I did," Molly answered. "You go by Ida Baker, and if you want your boy to be called Dick Baker, that is just fine. But someday, he might want to know about his father, his birth father. If he does, then you will have this. Your boy has a right to his name. This is the proof if you ever need it."

And with that, Molly let herself out of the little house, leaving a stunned Ida Baker sitting in her chair, holding the deed to her cottage in one hand and a birth certificate for her son in the other. A birth certificate for a boy named Dick Crowden.

CHAPTER 12

New Lives in Old Places – May to July 1887

T rue to his word, Jake completed both tasks Molly asked of him. Before leaving Laramie, Jake found a freighter who had moved large buildings. Bear Turner was, just as his name implied, a big bear of a man. He had been freighting most of his life, starting near St. Louis in his early years and migrating west as needed. Middle-aged and confident, Bear told Jake he had the teams and manpower to move anything. He would arrive at the Anchor J by the third week of May.

Leaving Molly and Jack at the Anchor J, Jake rode home and got a burial crew ready. Molly and Jack would come a week later with most of the Anchor J hands, as well as Buster and Catherine. A couple of men would drive the wagon and travel by night, if needed, with the bodies packed in ice. The burial would take place immediately, with Matthew presiding.

The burial was a solemn affair, as most funerals are. Molly stood, rigid and dry-eyed, with Jack on one side and Grace in her arms. Jack, with tears streaming down his face, had the hardest time. But when the family returned to the schoolhouse, where a meal was ready, Jake took Jack off for a while. When Jack joined the gathering, he had gained his composure and even went off with the other boys his age.

The day after the funeral, the Anchor J hands returned to the ranch. It was time to go out to the range and start the spring round-up. Molly returned the next day with her father. Kade offered to help with the house moving. Kade might not be a carpenter, but he had enough practical sense about everything to be good counsel for Molly.

With Kade's help, Molly decided to move the wing of the house that was used for guests. Three bedrooms were in a line on the first floor with a storeroom behind them. Molly planned to remove the walls to leave one bedroom on the first floor and the other two rooms as sitting rooms. The storeroom would be converted into a kitchen. Upstairs were three smaller bedrooms, a small sitting room, and a bedroom combination that the Burtons had used. There was room enough to leave the bedrooms for the children, and Lydia could have the tiny two-room apartment. Molly was satisfied with taking the guest addition. There were few memories of Jackson in that part of the house. An added benefit was that Molly, Lydia, and the children could live in their current rooms until the other part of the house was pulled to Twin Peaks and remodeled.

It was an impressive sight to see Bear Turner with his crew and his horses arrive at the ranch. Since they had many miles to move the two-story house, Bear brought all his teams with him. If needed, he could hook a forty-horse team to the house, and there would be some places, like a river crossing, where he would need them all. He also brought two carpenters who helped with the skilled labor of detaching the addition from the main ranch house and securing the house for its trip. The house was eventually jacked up, and a platform and wheels were rolled underneath the structure.

Bear Turner had thirty-six horses and ten mules, many of draft horse breeding. Because there were no formal roads between Twin Peaks and the Anchor J, Turner used no less than eighteen horses at a time but often hitched more teams when the ground got particularly rough. The house had to be dragged over the river one time. Kade had scouted for the best crossing for the house, and extra logs were added to help float the structure across. Molly felt it was too nerve-wracking to watch her future home make the move and opted to stay home and begin packing her things.

It was three weeks before the Turner crew returned on their way to Laramie and told Molly that the house was secure on its new foundation. The two carpenters were busy tearing out walls, and Kade was installing a stove in the kitchen. It was time to pack wagons and follow the house. To Molly, she was going home, and her heart soared.

There was so much to do when Molly, Lydia, and the children arrived at their home at Twin Peaks. Molly had chosen a plot of land not too distant from Kade and Sarah's home, and Kade's trading post. Men from Twin Peaks had already been to her homestead and erected a lean-to barn and corral for horses. Kade and the carpenters were just finished with the remodeling of the downstairs rooms.

Molly's bedroom was downstairs and much smaller than hers in the addition she left behind at the Anchor J. That suited Molly just fine. She was done with the elegance and expansiveness of her previous home. She wanted to live more simply. This two-story home was still far bigger than any other home at Twin Peaks. But Molly was satisfied with it for many reasons. It was familiar to the children, and it was finished. For Molly, there were no lingering memories of Jackson in this section of her house. This had been the guest wing, not a family space. Finally, the children were settled into their new upstairs rooms next to Lydia's tiny apartment. It was similar to the sleeping arrangement they had at the Anchor J.

It took a week of sorting and putting items away, and finally, Molly was settled. When she looked out her parlor window, she could see the river in the valley bubbling over rocks. Her kitchen window faced Twin Peaks, and her back door faced her barn and corrals. The porch had been rebuilt, and in the evenings, she, Lydia, and the children could sit on the porch, hear the distant river, and enjoy the air as it cooled. Molly was content. She was home, and she never wanted to leave Twin Peaks again.

The Englishman Molly wrote to about the Burtons was indeed interested in hiring them. He wanted them to start as soon as possible, giving instructions on how the Burtons could catch a stage a day's ride north of the Anchor J, and it would take them right by his ranch. So, not more than two weeks after Molly's return from the funeral, a cowhand was sent with the surrey to catch the stage, and the Burtons were on their way to their new employment. Molly was not sorry to see them go. They were a nice couple, but stuffy. They had been Jackson's people, not hers.

One other Anchor J employee went to Twin Peaks with Molly. This was Punch, the crippled cook and handyman. While Kade was at the Anchor J helping with the house moving, Punch approached him asking about a job. Punch couldn't cowboy anymore, but he was good help on the ground and could cook a good meal. Kade hired Punch to feed the hands in the Twin Peaks' bunkhouse. Until then, different women in the community would feed whatever men were there. Usually, it was just Luke, but now Noah and the young schoolteacher joined Luke as occupants of the bunkhouse. When extra men were hired for haying or assorted building jobs, it began to be a burden on the families to feed so many extra mouths. Kade hired Punch to do the cooking and any odd jobs needed around the ranch. Good with carpentry, Punch joined the two carpenters who remodeled Molly's house.

When Punch took his pay from Molly when he left the Anchor J, he had a somewhat unusual request.

"Mrs. Crowden," Punch said when he came for his money, "I don't hardly ever get to town to spend much. I get plenty tired of having to wait for a wagon to catch a ride to wherever I want to go. I have some money saved too. Might you want to sell one of those run-about buggies Mr. Jackson has and a single-driving horse? Be right nice iffen I could come and go myself whenever I want."

Molly could certainly understand that. Not able to ride comfortably for more than a short time, Punch ended up walking beside a saddle horse when traveling by horseback. For this reason, Punch seldom left the ranch.

"Take the little roadster with the folding top," Molly suggested. The roadster was a single-seat buggy with four wheels. It was light and could easily be pulled by a single horse. "Go out to the corrals and pick through the driving horses and take whatever one you want. I think I'll keep the buckboard, but if I need anything else, Twin Peaks has several conveyances I can always use."

The Anchor J, Molly found, was not difficult to sell. Since she didn't want to keep the ranch, she asked her solicitor to decide a fair price and advertise it. Molly didn't have to wait until after the spring round-up to sell. Almost all the proceeds from the sale of the ranch and the few cattle remaining on the range would be needed to pay off Jackson's investors. Molly was hopeful that when the dust all settled, the investors had their money. Molly intended to keep a buggy, a small sleigh, and a dozen head of the imported cows Jackson had kept at the headquarters over the winter. These would be added to the Twin Peaks herd if the sale of the Anchor J brought in cash to pay off the rest of the debts. However, Molly's solicitor was confident the sale of the ranch, along with the three quarters of land that Jackson had purchased on the plains from homesteaders, would bring enough to cover debts and perhaps have a little left over.

Molly hadn't returned to the Anchor J from Laramie more than two weeks when Jake's cousin Will rode in one late afternoon. Tall, silent Will stood wringing his hat as she ushered him into the parlor.

"Your pa says you are selling this place?" Will inquired.

"I am," Molly answered. "I want to move home to Twin Peaks, and I need to pay Jackson's stockholders."

"Reckon, I'd be interested, if you can name me a price," Will still wrung his hat, looking to the floor.

"Really?" Molly asked, surprised. "You'd want to live here?"

"Expanding my flock," Will answered. "Need more space."

Typical of Will, he hardly answered in complete sentences, but Molly understood. She was also not surprised. Will was such a solitary man. What difference would it make to him if he was across the river from Twin Peaks in his small shanty or a half day's ride away at the Anchor J. He just liked to be alone.

"Will, I will send you to my lawyer in town with a letter," Molly answered. "He will set the price depending on what the market is now. But I will tell him in the letter that I wish you get the ranch. I will tell him that if the investors are taken care of, to let you have the ranch at the lowest possible price."

"I talked with your pa," Will added. "This will be part of Twin Peaks; only I will run the sheep operation out of these headquarters. I ain't interested in the homesteader land Jackson bought up out on the plains, just this main parcel. I can run the sheep up into the mountains from here in the summer and cut hay along the river for the winter." That was a long speech for Will Bates.

And so it was, with backing from Kade, Twin Peaks and the Anchor J merged. Forever after, the Anchor J would be known as the Twin Peaks Anchor J Unit.

Kade watched for his boys to stop at the trading post. He saw Jake that morning and asked him to round up his brother, Thomas, and stop in when they had a chance. Kade had made some decisions about Twin Peaks, and his sons, grown men now, were taking leadership roles in the ranch operation. He wanted to fill them in on new developments. He had been to visit Matthew Jorgensen already. Matthew, the late Jim Bates, and Kade were the three principal owners of Twin Peaks, but soon, the next generation would be taking over. For the day-to-day running of the ranch, it was pretty much the younger generation that handled everything. Both Matthew and Kade had pulled back, giving more rein to their sons and the sons of Jim Bates. However, while Kade still handled most of the finances, he felt discussing these matters with his sons was important.

Kade heard Jake and Thomas ride up and stomp up the steps to the trading post. Kade was playing a game of solitaire and looked up, smiling, when his sons walked in.

"I'm getting lazy playing cards during the day," Kade smiled. "Feather is napping, but when she wakes up, I promised to take her for a ride."

"You deserve to be lazy," Thomas grinned. "So, what is on your mind that you needed us to stop by?"

"Well, boys, I made a decision regarding Twin Peaks' finances without consulting you, and I feel you need to know," Kade replied. "You know your sister is selling the Anchor J?"

"That isn't new," Jake answered.

"Well, Will stopped by a week ago with an idea. He wants to expand the sheep. He has a line on about two thousand more head."

Thomas and Jake exchanged looks. "Pa, I know that sheep are a good investment right now," Jake began, "and I know the sheep go into the mountains in the summer, but do we really want that many sheep around here all winter?"

"Oh, God," Thomas groaned, "that would make near four thousand sheep to shear. That is not my favorite job on the ranch."

Kade laughed at that. "I hear you, but Will has the money to buy the sheep. He wants to expand. But what Will came to me about was the Anchor J. He wants backing to buy the headquarters and move the sheep operation there. Twin Peaks will back him to purchase the land. He can move the sheep from the Anchor J to the mountains in the summer and leave his place here at Twin Peaks across the river for the hog operation. He thinks young Noah, with his brother Emmet's help, can run the hog operation. And there is plenty of river bottom around the Anchor J to put up winter hay for the sheep."

Thomas brightened at that. "I think that sounds pretty good." He thought a minute then added, "Are we going to have to take a crew up there for the shearing every June? For that many sheep, it could take a bit of time, and we have enough spring work here to do."

"Will has a plan for that," Kade answered. "He'll get a professional shearing crew each year to handle that chore. We'd be out of the shearing completely."

"We are for it," Jake grinned, looking at Thomas.

"How soon will this happen?" Thomas asked hopefully. "Does Will have a crew coming this year?"

"Sorry, boys. It's too late this year to line up a shearing crew. We will help Will with the shearing one more time before he moves his flock to the Anchor J. He has his sheepherders arriving next week, and we will shear before Will sends them to the mountains. Then Will is off to buy more."

"Well, guess we can handle one more year," Thomas said grudgingly. "Knowing it will be our last shearing helps."

"Poor year for me to decide to remain at Twin Peaks over the summer," Jake grinned. "I should be in the high mountains by now riding broncs and get out of the shearing."

"It will be good for you to stay, brother," Thomas said, slapping Jake on the shoulder. "Live like the rest of us blokes down here."

The shearing occurred in mid-June, the week before Molly was expected to return to Twin Peaks. Her house was almost ready for her, and the two carpenters from Laramie could finish the rest of the remodeling. That freed up the rest of the men so they could help shear.

Swift Hawk and Lathe Jorgensen had already taken their families to the high mountains, but the rest of the Twin Peaks men were involved in the shearing. Matthew was the experienced shearer, but Will, Jeremiah, and Army had learned from him. The three younger men took the brunt of the work since Matthew was getting up there in years.

The shearing took place across the river where the hogs were kept. Will had one big corral where he could hold all the sheep. From there, groups were pushed into a smaller adjoining corral. Attached to this small corral were four pens that could hold ten head of sheep. The men herding the sheep would load ten sheep in each small pen. Here the shearers would go to work until all ten sheep were sheared. When the forty sheep were done, they were turned loose onto the meadow to graze and forty more were loaded. Kade kept a tally as each pen of sheep was sheared and turned out. When the shearing was over, Will had an accurate headcount of the animals.

As the sheep were sheared, the sheep's fleece was laid out flat, rolled up, and tied with a soft string. It was then placed in a large sack. This sack was hoisted to the top of a frame that looked like four ladders tilted together. The sack, at least seven feet long, would hang from this frame, and the "tramper" would climb the ladder-like outside of the frame and lower himself into the sack of fleece, tramping it down. More fleece could be added, and more tramping took place until the sack was filled. Then a new sack was hung, and it started all over again. Noah and Emmett got the honors of tramping the fleece down in the sack. One would tramp until coughing and sneezing, the next boy would take over, giving the first boy time to catch his breath and breathe in some fresh air. It was hard, dirty, dusty, and smelly work.

It wasn't much better in the corrals for the men working with a thousand sheep, but like all the ranch work where most of the men were involved, the joshing and joking made even the worst of jobs fun. The camaraderie of the people of Twin Peaks Ranch was unique, perhaps, but also cherished. It is what made the ranch more than a community. It was a home.

Will broke out of the trees and viewed the homestead in the expansive meadow. There was a small garden, a small barn, a corral, and two cabins, one large and one small. He found he was nervous. He had a request, or maybe an offer, and he had no idea how it would be received. He saw Marcus come out of the barn at the dog's bark and turned, scanning the pasture. Marcus recognized Will and waved, waiting for him by the corral.

"You're early," Marcus remarked. "We didn't expect you so soon. Weren't you shearing?"

"Finished yesterday," Will retorted. "Sent them with herders this morning."

Marcus nodded. "Rosie is in with Susan. Supper is almost ready. Want to stop and get a bite, or do you want me to send her out? We can keep Billy with us for a while."

"Ah, I'll put this horse away first. I kin eat a bite. Want to talk to you all." Will didn't look at Marcus as he loosened the cinch and pulled the saddle off. Will's usual appetite didn't include food when he first visited Rosie. Marcus watched him a minute, then turned away.

"We'll wait for you then," Marcus commented, walking toward the larger of the two cabins.

Little Billy was walking and starting to talk, and his little face lit up when he saw his father enter the cabin.

"Daddy," the child cried, holding up his fat little arms.

Will scooped the toddler up and swung him in the air, delightful laughter coming from the child. Then settling the little boy on his shoulders, Will approached the table. Rosie looked up and smiled, but only held up her arms to take the toddler and settle him in a chair beside her. Will slid in beside them both.

Will was silent as he ate. This was not unusual. Rosie, Marcus, and Susan were used to Will's quiet ways. Marcus had told the others that Will wanted to talk to them, but they all knew that words only came out of Will's mouth when Will felt the time was right. The women and Marcus usually carried on conversations around their supper table, and this night was no different. When

Will finished his plate, he pushed it away, took out cigarette paper and tobacco, and rolled himself a smoke.

"Twin Peaks bought the Anchor J," Will spoke, his gaze on his cigarette.

"That's news," Susan replied. "What does the ranch want with a place a half day's ride away?"

"I'm gonna run my sheep out of there."

"You keeping them there year 'round?" Marcus inquired.

"Reckon I'll still send them to the mountains in the summer, but we will herd them back and forth from the Anchor J," Will answered. "Plenty of hay there to put up and it will give me room to expand the flock."

"Pretty big fancy house you got there," Marcus commented. He had been by the Anchor J when he went for supplies. While he had never stopped there, he could see the size of the place from a distance.

"Molly moved one wing of the house to Twin Peaks," Will continued. "But reckon the house is still big. But the bunkhouse suits me better. Can't abide all that room."

"You are just going to let that big house set empty?" Susan asked.

"Wal, that's what I wanted to talk about," Will started hesitantly. "Be a good place for you all to move in to. Be easier in the winter to be lower in the mountains. Closer to Twin Peaks for supplies."

"You want us to come to the Anchor J? All of us?" Susan asked quietly.

"Reckon so. Don't think Rosie would come without you, and don't think you'd come without Rosie and Billy," Will observed.

Rosie got up, cleared the table, and busied herself at the dry sink, pouring warm water into a basin and beginning to wash dishes.

"What exactly do you have in mind, Will?" Susan inquired. "You want us to pay you rent or..." her voice trailed off.

"No, I don't mean that. I jest figured you'd be better there. I could buy your land here or lease it, and you could stay at the Anchor J. I'd be obliged if I could take meals with you. Like I do here." Will looked away, glancing between Rosie and the couple.

"And you'd live in the bunkhouse," Susan stated it as a fact.

"Reckon, mostly," Will reddened. "Maybe I'd hire you to feed a haying crew if you wanted, but that's not part of the deal. I just got this big house, and it needs to have..." Will's voice stopped as he groped for the right words. "It needs people in it . . . like a family."

"Lot to think about," Marcus inserted seriously, "but it does have some merit. It would be easier to get through the winters down there."

"I'm done," Rosie interrupted. "I'm heading back to my cabin." She abruptly turned and went out the door.

Will stared after her a moment. "What's wrong with her?" he said, looking at Marcus.

"She's scared," Marcus replied.

"Scared?" Will had used up his supply of words. He looked questioningly at Marcus and Susan.

"She goes to the Anchor J, and there will be people who will come by," Susan spoke slowly. "Some of them people may stop."

"Hell, she used to live in Laramie," Will exclaimed. "She's seen plenty of people."

"She's lived here more than four years as a woman, not a whore," Susan answered quietly. "She's been pretending you and her and little Billy are a family, but she knows the truth. At the Anchor J, she'd be the whore living in the big house with her former madam and her man."

"I don't think of her as a whore."

"Don't matter what you think," Susan went on. "It's what she thinks. And she's scared. She don't want to be a whore."

Will looked between the former madam and her Black barman and protector. Abruptly, he got up and followed Rosie out the door.

Rosie was beside the heating stove, when Will entered. She was starting a fire. The nights still got chilly this time of year in the mountains. Will watched her. Rosie did not turn around or acknowledge that he was there, but he knew she was aware he had come in. He kicked off his boots by the door. Going toward Rosie, he touched her shoulder.

"Yer upset," Will said softly. "Tell me."

"Ain't upset," Rosie didn't turn to him.

"You don't want to go to the Anchor J."

"I didn't say that."

"Yer body tells me that," Will whispered, running his fingers through her hair. "It's like you don't want to go there."

Rosie turned to him then. "We go there, who will I be? Jest Rosie, that whore from Laramie." Her eyes were wide with fright at the thought, and she pulled away from Will.

"I reckon you will be Mrs. Will Bates."

Rosie stopped, her gaze turning back to Will. "You don't mean that. What would your people say?"

"Don't matter what any people say. You're the mother of my son. Maybe we have more young 'uns too, someday. Don't you want to marry me?"

"I dreamed," Rosie stopped. "Dreams don't come true for gals like me."

"Well, this one will. Let's get you moved to the Anchor J, and then I'll get Matthew to marry us. Lessen you refuse me." Will reached out, his hand tenderly moving to her neck, pulling her toward him. "Tell me it was me you dreamed of," he whispered.

By the end of June, Will was living at the Anchor J, and Molly was home at Twin Peaks. The transition went smoothly for both of them. Will had bought another two thousand head of sheep and had them in the mountains with his herders. He had been to Laramie, hiring hands to put up hay during the summer at the Anchor J. He hadn't returned to Twin Peaks since he rode out after shearing.

Molly wiped her brow and opened the corral gate, letting the mares and foals out to pasture. July was well on the way, and the July sun could be hot. It was time for lunch, and Molly realized she was famished. Where had the morning gone? When she worked with the young horses and the foals, she was like her mother, lost in a world of hooves, soft muzzles, and the big gentle eyes of her horses. Thank goodness Lydia wanted to stay on as Grace's nurse and Molly's general housekeeper. Molly had the freedom to work with the horses and ride with abandon. When she first settled back on Twin Peaks, she wanted to be useful and part of the ranch. Molly asked Jake what she could do to help him.

"Molly, Ma has been gone seven years," he said seriously. "At first, I never realized how much she made my job breaking horses easier by gentling the foals. You helped her do that for years before you got married. I'd love for you to work with the foals and yearlings so they are not so wild."

Molly was overjoyed. There was nothing she loved more than working with horses. Every week, Jake and one of the hands would drive a small package of horses to her corrals. Sometimes it was mares and foals, sometimes yearlings. For a week, Molly would work with the youngsters, haltering, brushing, and leading them around in the cool mornings before turning them loose in her pasture for the afternoon and evenings. At the end of the week, the horses were exchanged with another small group and Molly's work began all over again. If the larger colts had never been touched, Jake and sometimes Luke or James would help her the first day to halter and tie up the young animals. For the rest of the week, Molly was on her own with them. It didn't take the young horses long to enjoy the brush and learn that Molly meant them no harm. By the week's end, most youngsters crowded around her for attention.

In the afternoons, she often saddled a seasoned horse and rode out, enjoying a quiet ride or maybe coming upon the cowhands working cattle and lending a hand. Sometimes, Jack rode with her; sometimes, she took Grace with her and visited Sarah and her father. Grace loved to play with Feather, which allowed the adults to visit. Sometimes, she met up with Jake, riding out with him like she used to do as a young girl. Jake and Anna had not gone to Jacob's cabin in the mountains this summer. Anna lost a baby in 1882, five years previously. Since then, she had only become pregnant once and had lost that baby early. This summer, Anna was pregnant and expecting a fall baby, so she was well into her pregnancy as summer came on. Jake didn't want to take any chances by traveling with her, so he sent Lathe, Hawk, and their families to the high mountains without him this year. Molly knew her brother looked wistfully toward the distant peaks, but if Anna could bring this child into the world alive and healthy, a summer in the lower elevations would be worth it to Jake. As for Molly, she loved having her favorite brother home this first summer she was back at Twin Peaks.

Molly walked to the house, studying it as she walked. When Jackson built the additions to the Anchor J ranch house, she hadn't thought they needed so much room. But today, as she went up the stairs to the porch, she was glad for this wing that had been dragged across the river valley to Twin Peaks. After Jackson's funeral, Molly picked out this place along the river, which was an easy ride from the main headquarters, the schoolhouse, and her father's store.

Not too long after Molly was settled in her new home at Twin Peaks, Punch began showing up every few days, always with a reason for coming. Two nights ago, he had stopped with the excuse that he was trying to bake a pie and needed Lydia's opinion. But watching the middle-aged Punch with Lydia made Molly suspect that another interest other than cooking brought Punch to their porch. Molly had a sneaking suspicion that Lydia was just as interested in Punch. Two nights ago, with Punch's buggy tied up to the hitching post, Luke had also ridden by and stopped. The four sat until late that night on the porch after the children went to bed. That had happened several times over the past month, sometimes with Luke and Punch, sometimes with Thomas or Jake or any of the other community members, men and women alike. It was a part of being back at Twin Peaks that Molly loved the most. She could interact with her friends, laughing, joking, and being at ease. As she thought about it, there wasn't anything from the Anchor J that she missed. Yes, she thought, she was home and loved it here.

On this hot July day, Molly was startled to see a rider coming from the east. She paused on the porch to watch. At first, she thought it was Luke, who had been hunting some strays that way a few days ago. But as the rider came closer, she knew she was wrong. It was a tall man like Luke, but it wasn't Luke. The rider stayed close to the river, not coming close to the house, so it was almost when the man was adjacent to her home that she recognized Will. She raised a hand in greeting, and Will returned it, but didn't stop to visit. Molly smiled, that was so like Will. He seldom had anything to say, so a hand raised in greeting was almost a whole conversation with him.

It was almost noon when Kade left the trading post, heading to the house for lunch. Kade noticed Will ride by the store and Sarah's house and continue on to Matthew's. He thought it strange that Will didn't stop by first to see his mother, but maybe Will needed to ask Matthew something about the sheep. Will hadn't been home since the ranch took possession of the Anchor J, and Will went there to live. Kade shrugged. He was sure Will would stop later.

Sarah and Kade were almost done eating when Will filled the doorway. Sarah smiled and got up for another plate while Will hung his hat on a hook by the door and took a place beside Kade at the table.

"What brings you home?" Sarah asked as she set a loaded plate of beef steaks and potatoes before Will.

"Passing through," was Will's response as he began eating.

Sarah raised eyebrows to Kade. Where in the world was Will passing through from to stop here? But neither Kade nor Sarah asked. Will was intent on his food and they both knew it was hard enough to talk to Will without him focused on eating.

"Have you got your sheep moved to the mountains?" Kade asked eventually.

Will nodded.

Kade filled the gap, visiting with Sarah about community happenings he heard about in the store while Will ate. Finally, when Will was almost finished, Sarah addressed him again.

"How do you like living in that big house?" Sarah asked. "Do you find yourself rambling around in it?" That was something she wondered about. At Twin Peaks, Will had a small one-room cabin across the river where the hog operation was located. He had been content in that tiny cabin for years, but now he had the Anchor J ranch house with its multitude of bedrooms in which to live. She wondered if the house was basically shuttered, and if Will lived in one room.

Will finished his meal, not answering, and took out tobacco and paper and began rolling a cigarette. Sarah and Kade waited, knowing that an answer in the shortest number of words would come at some point.

"I don't live in the main house," Will answered finally, lighting his cigarette.

Sarah was surprised. "Where do you live?" she asked.

"Bunkhouse," Will offered no explanation.

"My goodness," Sarah exclaimed. "Is that big, beautiful home just sitting empty?"

Will cleared his throat before saying, "I got a couple people living in the old part, and a woman and child live in the west wing." He hesitated before adding, "I take my meals at the big house."

Sarah just stared, thinking about this. "Where did you find people to live at the ranch with you?" she asked. "Do they work for you?"

Will had always lived at Twin Peaks, seldom going to town. It seemed sudden to Sarah that Will knew people outside of their own community. And she knew no one from Twin Peaks was living at the Anchor J. Even Buster and Catherine moved their modest house closer to Twin Peaks in June, where Buster could pick up some day work at Twin Peaks while raising a small herd of cattle of his own.

Will pushed away from the table and went to the door, looking out. "The couple have a parcel of land up in the mountains. I visited them when I took my sheep up," Will glanced over his shoulder toward Kade. "Don't reckon you got a shot, do you?" Will asked.

Kade nodded and got to his feet. In a small cupboard, he got out a seldom-used whiskey bottle and poured Will two fingers. Kade knew Will was having trouble with something he wanted to say. Kade could see Will was having more difficulty talking than usual. Will had never asked for whiskey before. Kade glanced toward Sarah, and they exchanged looks. Will was working up to some more news. Will took the whiskey in one quick gulp, holding his glass out for seconds. Finally, he spoke, but his words took the breath out of Sarah.

"The woman has my son."

Silence settled on the three of them briefly before Sarah found words. "You have a son? You have a woman, and she has a son, and the son is yours?" Sarah knew she was babbling, but she was trying to make sense of Will's news.

Will nodded, looking back out the door.

"How old is the boy?" Sarah asked, her voice hardly a whisper.

"Two years, there 'bout."

"You have a two-year-old son, and you are just telling me now?" Sarah was not only incredulous, but also beginning to be angry.

Will nodded. Then he turned from the door and walked back into the room.

"I came to see Matthew," Will said. "He's coming day after next to the Anchor J to marry us. James will come too."

"You are getting married in two days and just thought you'd tell me? Am I even invited?" Sarah's voice rose with frustration at this silent son.

"Ma, I won't ask you to come. I can't shame you that way." Will gave his mother a steady look before turning his gaze to Kade and adding, "She's been a working girl."

"Well, I'll be," Sarah began impatiently, irritated. "I have nothing against a woman working. I know there aren't good jobs for women, but . . ."

"Sarah," Kade cut her off in mid-sentence, "Will means the woman is a soiled dove . . . uh, a painted lady."

Sarah looked at Kade blankly, not registering his meaning. She had lived too long away from civilization, and this was out of her realm of expectations. Kade tried again, "Sarah, Will's sayin' the girl worked in a . . ." he tossed around in his mind how to put it, "a house of ill repute."

Sarah's eyes got big, and her mouth formed an "Oh" without any sound coming out. She seemed to deflate in her chair. She stared at Will.

"That's why I'm having Matthew come to us," Will said simply.

Sarah rallied, anger filling her, "You are marrying a prostitute?"

Will nodded.

"My son is marrying a . . ." Sarah couldn't repeat it.

Will turned around and went to the door again, looking out.

"Do you even know if the child is yours?" Sarah asked angrily.

Will turned back to his mother, his face set. "The child is mine. The woman is mine. I'm getting married. I'm not asking you to come, but if you ever see my son—" Will paused an instant, ice in his tone. "I expect you to treat him good." With that, Will snatched his hat off the peg and left the house, leaving a stunned Sarah listening to his footsteps go down the stairs and out to his horse.

Sarah's eyes filled with tears, and she looked up at Kade. "How could Will do this to me?" she asked.

"Sarah," Kade said soothingly, "I don't reckon Will did anything to you. He's found a woman and been with her. They have a child, and he wants to do the right thing."

"He's with a . . ." Sarah couldn't go on. "I didn't raise my boys to frequent prostitutes!"

"Honey, I think you forget how old Will is. He's the same age as Thomas. He's thirty-four years old. Do you really think Will hasn't bedded a woman yet?" Kade wasn't careful with his words.

Sarah looked around wildly. "Well, I know he wrote to that one woman once, but he came home alone after meeting with her. I just never thought he'd frequent a . . ." She stopped abruptly. "I'm ashamed he'd go to a place like that," she said decisively. "Thank goodness James got married early. At least I have one godly son."

That struck Kade funny. "Godly? Woman, listen to yourself. What you are talking about has nothing to do with God an' a lot to do with a man's needs. 'An I don't think you better set yer youngest too high on a pedestal lest he break a leg when you push him off."

"James wouldn't!" Sarah sputtered.

"Did you hear Will say that James would go with Matthew when he married them? Maybe you better ask James what he does an' doesn't know 'bout that."

When Jake rode through later that day, changing horses, Kade asked him to ride up to James and ask him to come and visit his mother. Kade had a sneaking suspicion that James knew more about his brother and his brother's business than any of them.

It turned out that James, indeed, knew about Will's woman. When confronted by Sarah, James had none of Will's tendencies to be silent.

"How on earth did you know?" Sarah asked. "Did Will tell you he had a woman?"

"Oh, Ma, you know better than that," James smiled at that. "Will doesn't come out and tell anyone what is on his mind. I went looking for Susan and Marcus five years ago after Miss Tillie's had been closed down in Laramie. I heard they were living somewhere east of here in the mountains."

"Who are Susan and Marcus?"

James looked levelly at his mother before answering. "Those are the real names for Miss Tillie and her barman. They didn't use real names in the business."

Sarah breathed deeply, trying to calm herself. "Why would you know them and want to look for them?"

"Ma, do you really want to know everything?" James asked patiently. "Let's just leave it that I met them and liked them. They did me a good turn when I was courting Mary. I visit them every once in a while. Two years ago, when Mary and I took the kids camping in the mountains around the Fourth of July, we went there to see them."

Sarah's eyes got big. "You took children to a brothel?"

"Oh, for God's sake, Ma!" James was losing his patience. "They lived on a farm in a mountain meadow. Other than the quite gaudy furniture, they are fine people."

"So, are this Marcus and Susan a married couple then?" Sarah pushed.

For the first time, James got a little uncomfortable. He thought about his answer before he spoke. "Marcus is a Black man and Susan is white. They have worked together for most of their life." He left it at that.

Kade watched James and knew his lie. James was protecting his friends. This, Kade was certain about, but it made no difference to him. It was Sarah who found this situation hard to bear. She thought she raised two upstanding sons. And she did. She didn't know that even upstanding sons had more on their minds than work and a cold beer. Sarah had been too sheltered out here at Twin Peaks. The real world was creeping into her secluded one.

Will walked up to the front porch of the ranch house. He watched the river bottom for the buggy that would bring Matthew and James. Matthew would marry him and Rosie, and James would be the best man. James was the only one who understood. What James and Matthew told the rest of the family, he didn't care. It was time to marry Rosie and give his son his name.

Rosie and Susan were sitting on the porch, already dressed for the wedding in new frocks. Will studied Rosie. He had bought her a pale blue dress with lace around the collar. She had been overjoyed at his gift. She had been a pretty woman before her face was scarred. Seen from the side, she was still pretty. Will had gotten used to the scars. Susan wore a modest dress she had sent for from Laramie. In upper middle age and with the loss of so much weight, Susan was a handsome woman. Her laugh was still raucous, and sometimes her language was too, but otherwise, she didn't resemble the obese madam of Miss Tillie's.

"Where's Marcus?" Will asked, climbing the steps to the porch.

"Out back checking on the lamb on the spit," Susan replied. "You sure Matthew and James will eat lamb? A lot of cowboys on the plains won't touch that meat."

"Remember, I'm part of Twin Peaks, and I raise mutton too," Will replied. "It was Matthew that first wanted some sheep. Don't think it will be a problem. They should be coming just about any time now." For some reason, Will found talking to Susan and Marcus far easier than talking to his family. Maybe it was because their past occupation was to entertain people. Perhaps it was because Will knew they wouldn't judge. In any case, he could almost carry on a conversation with the couple.

"They are coming now," Susan said, pointing. She had just seen a carriage come around the bend of the river. She pointed to the west.

Will turned, looking for what she saw. There in the distance was a buggy, but as they watched, there appeared another behind it, and then another, and another.

Beside the buggies and buckboards were mounted riders. As they kept coming, it seemed as if the whole community of Twin Peaks was coming. Will raised surprised eyes to Susan.

"I jest told Ma and Kade," Will said. "I didn't think anyone would . . ." He didn't finish and instead turned, looking at the approaching people.

Marcus came from the back of the house and went to join Will and Susan. "I don't figure your family meant to let you go off and get hitched without them," Marcus said softly.

"Maybe since you are getting so many guests, Marcus and I better go inside and make ourselves scarce," Susan suggested tactfully. "Might be best we don't stay out here."

Will looked at her, understanding her meaning. Susan was giving Will the chance to be more respectable without a former madam attending his wedding. "No, I done told Ma how it is," he said firmly. "If they come, they come to meet everyone. I ain't hiding anymore who I am or who I am with. Not hiding any of you. They take me and you all or none of us."

Will looked down at Rosie as he said this. She turned worried eyes to him. It had been years since Rosie had fallen from grace. She wasn't sure how to act with these people and Will's people at that. But there was no changing it. The line of horse-drawn vehicles approached.

"Don't reckon we got enough food," Will murmured.

"Somehow, I don't think it will be a problem," Susan laughed. "I remember country gatherings from way back. I reckon every woman there will have her favorite dish wrapped up in the wagons."

And indeed, food was not a problem. James, Mary, and their brood were driving a buckboard first in the line.

Behind them came Kade and Matthew in the carriage, and Sarah and Mattie were in the back seat. Kade drove to the end of the yard and pulled up, handing the reins to Matthew. A wagon driven by Jeremiah carried planks and sawhorses, and after makeshift tables had been set up, food began to appear from each arriving wagon.

The men were busy unhitching horses, and the women fussed about the food. Kade descended the buggy and reached up to help Sarah down.

"Why don't we go up there and meet Will and his friends," he said. "Matthew will take the team."

Sarah turned a grim face to Kade. "I don't know if I can do this, knowing what that woman was."

Kade's face got hard. "Sarah, we have talked about this. You shun Will now; he won't forgive you ever. It is his choice, not yours. I'm stayin', but if you want to turn back, Matthew will give you the reins. Go or stay but understand that it is your son over there. I am stayin' for this wedding. You will go home alone."

Sarah was surprised at Kade's angry tone. Kade seldom got angry. She turned questioning eyes to Matthew, who had remained silent.

"Sarah," he said softly, "even our Lord accepted the fallen woman. Are you going to sit in judgment when Christ did not?"

Sarah thought about that. "It just doesn't seem right," she said uncertainly.

"Sarah, it is written in Romans, 'Who are you to judge someone else's servants?' We will all stand before our Lord. It is for him to judge, not you." Matthew spoke softly. "And our Lord himself said to the chief priests in the Book of Matthew, 'Truly I tell you, the tax collectors and the prostitutes are going into the kingdom of God ahead of you.' So, Sarah, it is for you to forgive and act as a Christian. Can you do that for Will?"

Sarah looked at Matthew and then at Kade. Her eyes filled with tears, but they did not overflow. Finally, she nodded. She leaned forward out of the carriage, reaching for Kade's hand to help her. Kade and Matthew were right. Will was her son. Somehow, she had to get by this.

Standing with Rosie, Will watched his mother's hesitation getting out of the buggy. Slowly, Sarah and Kade walked across the lawn as the rest of the arriving guests put out food, unhitched horses from wagons, and secretly watched Sarah greet her son and his bride. Sarah was reserved, holding onto Kade's arm for support.

"Congratulations, Will," Kade said, smiling and reaching his hand out to shake. Will grasped his hand and shook it, smiling gratefully into Kade's eyes.

"Mother, Kade," Will said slowly, "this is my intended, Roselyn, and our," he hesitated on what to call them, "friends, Susan and Marcus."

Sarah looked at Will and then at Rosie. Rosie stood beside Will, and her eyes were wide with anxiety. Sarah took in the girl's pretty, but modest dress, and her heart melted a little. Sarah reached out a shaking hand toward the young woman.

"Pleased to meet you," Sarah said softly.

"Thank you, Ma'am," Rosie said quietly, taking Sarah's outstretched hand and looking down. "I don't reckon you imagined Will would marry the likes of me."

Sarah was taken aback for a moment at the girl's honesty. Sarah studied her. Rosie was pretty unless she turned her head where the scars were so evident on her face.

"You are my grandson's mother, I hear," Sarah said brusquely. "I would expect no less of my son than to marry you." Sarah looked around. "Can I see my grandson?"

Rosie turned to Susan. Behind Susan's skirt, a little boy peeked out, shy before all these strangers. A smile broke out on Sarah's face.

"Oh, my, but you are quite the little gentleman, aren't you?" Sarah said, kneeling to the little boy's level. She reached in her pocket and pulled out a candy. "This is for you. Come get it."

The child's eyes widened at the treat, and looking up at his mother for permission, he darted forward and snatched the candy before retreating to Susan's skirts. Sarah looked up at the white woman and the Black man who stood off to one side of Will and Rosie.

"And you must be the other grandparents?" Sarah asked politely.

"We certainly try to be," Susan answered. "Can't say I've ever been this content in my whole life than here with this child."

"Well, then," Sarah said gently, "I don't think a child can have too many people love him." Sarah looked to Kade, and he nodded approvingly. Sarah was trying.

"I think we will go and get our things out of the buggy then," Kade said looking at Will. "Matthew will be along any minute to speak to you before the service."

The service was short and pleasant. Will introduced Rosie as Roselyn, the name that Matthew used at the marriage ceremony. Like Tillie and Charlie, Rosie was no more, and in her place stood Roselyn. There was plenty of food to eat after the ceremony, and everyone laid down blankets in the yard and ate in small groups, close enough to participate in many conversations. After the meal, the men went for a tour of the ranch headquarters with Will, and the women retreated to the covered porch to enjoy the shade. Will had made few changes to the Anchor J since his arrival. The cookshack stood vacant, waiting for Will's sheepherders to return to the headquarters in the fall. At least one or two of his men would stay the winter. In addition, he had four Mexican men hired this year for the summer.

The bunkhouse was where Will lived. He didn't go into detail, but he had his bed and his books there. When Kade followed the group behind Will, looking into the outbuildings and barn, Kade remembered Will bringing up the obituary Will had read once in the newspaper about a man and woman who had children, but lived in two establishments. Silent, solitary Will had his escape from the big house where he took his meals. Kade wondered how often Will crossed the lawn after dark and stayed the night with Rosie. Smiling inwardly, Kade chastised himself. It was none of his business.

A beef haunch was fitted on the spit for the evening meal, and the day was a pleasant one of conversation and companionship. After the evening meal, a jug of whiskey was uncorked. Matthew pulled out his fiddle and Army his harmonica, and the dancing began. As the little children got tired, they were put to sleep on the floor of the parlor of the main house. The gaudy greens and reds of the furniture and the carpet were startling to see among the fine, dark woods of the ranch house, but no one commented on it.

As was typical of country dances, the merriment went late into the night. It was well past midnight when most of the older couples had begged off to bed in either a bedroom in the main house, bunkhouse, or cookshack. The younger couples pitched tents with no intention of going to them until the wee hours of the morning. Pregnant with Jake's and her fourth child, Anna had finally taken herself to her tent, and Jake went to sit on the ground next to Thomas.

"Today turned out better'n I thought it would," Thomas said by way of greeting. "I was some worried about Sarah's reaction. Pa said she was taking this union hard."

Jake nodded, watching the few couples still dancing to Army's harmonica. Matthew had long since taken his fiddle and gone off to his bed. "Sarah's a good woman. Just took her some time to come around," Jake said. Changing the subject, he nodded toward the dancers. "What you think of that?" he asked. Molly was dancing to a slow melody with Luke. Jake had noticed them together quite a bit that evening.

Thomas looked at his sister, laughing at something the tall cowboy said. Thomas nodded his head slowly. "I kind of like it."

"Me too," Jake agreed. "Molly is starting to be her old self again, and I can't think of anyone who would be more fitting in her life than Luke. Luke is a good man. It was our good fortune that he stayed with us when Pa offered him a job."

Thomas gave Jake a knowing look before adding, "It was the good fortune of all of us that day," he said softly, "for a lot more than gaining another hired man."

CHAPTER 13

Between Anger and Love – August 1887

Molly finished with the four yearlings that Jake brought her earlier in the week and let them out to pasture. She had worked with these colts before, and they remembered her, so the morning work was easy. Here she was with three-fourths of the day ahead of her, and she was all alone. It wasn't often that happened.

Lydia went off after breakfast with Punch in his buggy, ostensibly to pick berries for pies. Punch wanted Lydia to help him make some pies. Molly just smiled at the ruse. They were two middle-aged people who neither wanted marriage but wanted each other's company. Then Grace, with the insistence of a four year old, demanded to go with them. Lydia packed a picnic lunch and said she would be home before suppertime if Molly could get along without her.

Jack had come flying downstairs just at dawn and surprised Molly in the kitchen while she was starting coffee. Grabbing a biscuit from the table, he headed toward the door without a word.

"One moment, young man," Molly spoke sternly. "Where are you off to so early today?"

Jack often went to Thomas's to see if the men had any-thing he could help with or to ride along with them. Jack was only two years younger than Martha and Sam's first son, TJ, and the same age as their second son, John Henry. If nothing was happening at the corrals, he wandered over to Sam's to see what TJ and John Henry were up to. Any day now, Lathe and his family should be home from the high country, and that would add their boys, Slade and Jesse, to the mix. And finally, Jake and Anna's son, Kade Brown, was only a year younger than Jack. Molly thought that the boys sometimes ran in packs.

"Uncle Thomas is taking us boys with him to the mountain cabin. He is taking Noah some supplies," Jack answered. "I gotta go."

"Well, you could say good morning and give me a hug," Molly retorted.

"Mother, I am in a hurry," Jack said bluntly. "I gotta go." He pulled open the door and was gone before Molly could get another word out.

Molly sighed. This was as good as it got between them lately. Jack wasn't taking his father's death well. Not that Molly expected Jack to be his usual sweet self, but he had become increasingly more belligerent and con-frontational as the summer went on. When Molly first brought Jack home, he had looked to Molly for comfort. He kept asking his mother to tell him stories about his father. Jack wanted to know what his father had done while he was away at school. Jack wanted to know sto-ries about his father from earlier days. Molly shut down quickly, claiming to be unable to talk about those times. In reality, she still harbored a deep anger toward Jackson and wanted to protect Jack. She didn't want to talk about her husband for fear that she would make a slip and say something that she didn't want Jack to hear. Give him time, Molly thought, and he would find his way. It was good he had two uncles who spent time with him, filling the gap left by his father's death.

Molly sliced bread and spread jam on it, then, eating quickly, she went out to her horse. She had half of the morning left and all afternoon. She was going to go for a longer ride. She hadn't had the opportunity to ride other than short rides between working with the young stock, trying to give Grace her time, and the household chores she helped Lydia with. Molly decided the day wasn't to be wasted.

She set off toward the ranch headquarters but didn't stop there. She wanted to ride along the river, exploring the favorite hills and meadows of the river bottom she rode as a young girl. It was a beautiful day, bright with sun, but not too hot to enjoy. She was over an hour west of the ranch headquarters when she came upon a rider driving a small herd of cattle away from the ranch headquarters. Molly spurred her horse into a rolling lope, catching up. As she approached, she saw Luke driving steers and taking them farther away from the hay fields. Luke had been at the mountain line shack for the last couple of weeks, so Molly hadn't seen him since Will's wedding. She smiled, happy to see him, and waved when he turned in the saddle to see who was approaching.

"'Bout time I got some help around here," Luke called as she approached.

"Too hard for you, cowboy?" Molly laughed.

"These steers seem to think the short grass coming up from where Matthew has cut hay is pretty sweet. They keep moseying back every few days."

"How far do you push them away?" Molly asked.

"Maybe another mile or so," Luke said. "That should keep them off the hay ground for a week. But they will wander back. They seem to know the grass is short and sweet where we cut," Luke swung his rope at a lagging steer before continuing. "Won't be long, and Thomas will want to take these steers off to sell. Thank goodness Kade got a government contract, or we'd be taking the terrible prices the rest of the ranchers are getting in Laramie. When Kade first signed a five-year contract, I think some people thought he was crazy. At the time, he could have gotten more going to the cattle buyers. But your pa is a crafty old man. He told me then that he might not make a killing, but if the price drops, he would be glad for the security of the government contract. And he was right about that."

"Pa is pretty steady about things like that," Molly replied. "Jackson was always trying to get him to invest in more cattle and run more on free range. But last winter ruined the Anchor J. Pa was right about the winter blizzards, and last summer was such a terrible drought. Between that and the crash in the cattle markets, there are a lot of ranches that went under."

They rode in companionable silence, pushing the straggling steers ahead of them. After a mile and a half, Luke called a halt.

"I think this is far enough today. It will take these steers a bit to wander back now."

They turned their horses and headed back. They had ridden about a half mile when Molly looked around, seeing places she remembered from her teen years. She turned to Luke.

"Have you ever been up there?" she indicated, a tree-covered hill rising from the river bottom scarred by an old landslide.

"Up that hill? What's up there? That's a pretty steep grade."

"Come on," Molly said, spurring her horse away from Luke and moving toward the slope. "Catch me if you can."

Molly hit the trees, ducking under some branches and reining around others. As her horse climbed, she followed a faint old trail. She could hear Luke and his horse crashing along behind her. Her horse dug into the steep slope, straining as he went. Suddenly, they reached the top, coming out on a small flat, open area. The landslide, decades earlier, had taken any trees with it, leaving a rock-strewn cliff where a person could look down upon the valley with no obstructions. The small open area was grass-covered, and trees lined along the back and side before the mountain rose again.

"How the hell did you find this place?" Luke laughed, pulling up beside her.

"I didn't," Molly said, dismounting and tying her horse to a sapling. "Come look at the view."

The two of them stood on the cliff's edge and could see a mile up and down the river valley. Below, the river glistened in the midday sun, and far to the west, they could see the straggling steers they had been driving.

"I was ten the first time I saw this," Molly said. "Jake and I were out riding with Ma and Pa. I don't know where Thomas was that day, but it was just the four of us. We were down there," Molly indicated the valley they had just come from. "Pa told Jake to take me and check a little switchback along the river for strays. He said he and Ma were going up to the lookout. Jake was ten years older than me, and looking back, I'm sure he knew the folks just wanted us out of the way. But I was ten, and ten-year-olds don't have a clue." Molly laughed at that, remembering. "Jake starts riding off, and I see Ma and Pa climbing that hill. I wanted to see what the lookout was, so I just turned and followed. When Jake saw I wasn't with him, it was too late for him to catch me.

"I'm sure the folks heard me coming," Molly smiled. "You can't climb that slope with all those trees and branches without making some noise. Ma was standing on the edge here like we are now, and Pa was tying up the horses. I remember Pa said something like, 'I thought I told you, daughter, to check a switchback' but he didn't sound mad. Jake came crashing up then, and he said, 'Sorry, Pa,' but I couldn't figure out what he was sorry about."

Molly turned and looked at the little clearing. "I mean, I was a kid. I had no idea why they wanted to dismount and tie up their horses. But Jake told me to come with him, and since I had seen the lookout, as they called it, I left. But a couple days later, I was out riding this way with Thomas. I told Thomas I was going to check for cattle, and I rode up here again. I could see where the horses had been tied. The grass was grazed down short all around the saplings, so I knew they had been tied there for some time. I could see at the back of the clearing under the trees where the grass was all mashed down, like when deer lie down in the meadows. But I knew it wasn't any deer that mashed that grass down. I couldn't figure out why Ma and Pa would want to lie down and nap on such a fine day with work to do. It took me a few more years to put it together in my mind that they weren't napping," Molly grinned at Luke. "Of course, by the time I figured it out, I also understood why Ma and Pa turned up missing so often. It got to be a little joke at times when they just wandered off together."

"I remember your folks together," Luke smiled. "They were something else. There was no doubt that they loved each other. People laughed about it, but it was cute too."

Molly turned back to look up at Luke, suddenly serious. "I just wanted what they had," she whispered. Tears filled her eyes, but didn't overflow. "I just wanted that kind of love."

Luke regarded her, seeing the hurt in her eyes. Without thought, he reached out and touched her cheek, pushing a stray hair off her face. His fingers lingered, feeling her softness. "You deserve that kind of love," he said simply. Then he bent to her level and kissed her.

The kiss took Molly by surprise, but it was not unwanted. After a brief hesitation, she returned the kiss, moving into Luke's embrace. Had she been blind, she thought? Is this where her budding friendship with Luke was supposed to go? Is this why she was glad to meet him on the river valley? She wasn't sure of anything except one thing. She wanted the kiss. She wanted it with Luke, and one kiss wasn't enough.

If you had asked Luke later what had happened after that first kiss, he would have been hard-pressed to answer. He wasn't sure what happened next. But eventually, they made it to the shade of the trees. Clothes came off in no particular order, and all thought was gone except the overpowering wanting in each for the other.

Luke wasn't surprised at himself. He had watched Molly since he first saw her, visiting Twin Peaks at Christmas time with her husband the first year Luke worked for Kade. She was the most beautiful woman he had seen. Wearing the finery that Jackson always dressed Molly in, she looked no less than a princess to Luke. After that, Luke would see her on her occasional visits, sometimes out riding with Jake in her split skirts. She was like a nymph on a horse, graceful and competent. Yes, Luke had watched her, but she had belonged to someone else.

Then, last fall, she had come to stay at Twin Peaks for over a month, going on the fall gather with them. She still belonged to someone else, but she looked broken and sad. Luke couldn't help but watch her. She ruined every other woman he saw. No other measured up to Molly.

Now here she was in his arms, and he was only a bit owner of this big ranch, little more than a ranch hand. But there was no stopping after that first kiss. Luke didn't want to stop, and it was apparent that Molly didn't either. All thought left Luke except possessing this woman and loving her. They moved together, finding delight, then pleasure, and finally ecstasy. When Luke rolled off Molly, they were both breathing heavily, satiated.

With his arm under Molly's neck, he pulled her gently to him, her head resting on his bare chest. His fingers played in her hair as they lay, their bodies calming. He wanted to say something but was suddenly tongue-tied. What should he say to a woman he just bedded? A woman he knew he loved. He wasn't sure of her feelings, only her desire. Finally, he spoke softly, wanting to get out the words before the moment was lost. Wanting to tell her how he felt about her.

"I reckon," Luke started slowly, "this wasn't exactly the proper way to go about . . ."

Luke's words were cut short by Molly. She stiffened and then abruptly pushed away from him and sat up. "Don't!" she exclaimed angrily. "Don't ever say that to me!"

She looked around wildly for her chemise and blouse. Finding the chemise, she pulled it over her head, but the blouse was inside out, and in her angst, she couldn't get the sleeves right. She worked that blouse savagely, trying to untangle it. Luke watched in bewilderment and shock. What had he said?

Luke grasped Molly's shoulders, turning her toward him. "Molly, stop! Tell me what I said. What is upsetting you?" He took the blouse from her, shaking it out, finding the slccvcs, and pulling them right.

Molly's eyes were wide, with what? Anger? Fright? Luke helped her into her blouse, then looked for her pantaloons and skirt. Molly took the clothes and stood, pulling them on viciously. Luke got up, pulling his trousers on, and faced her, hoping she was calmer.

"What are you upset about?" he asked, trying to sound calm. "What did I say? Or is it you regret what just happened? That we...," he let that thought drift off.

"You said this wasn't proper!" Molly spoke vehemently. "Every time he said that word, I lost some of the things I loved. I lost my riding clothes, my saddle, my children, my horses, my freedom! I don't want to be proper!" She turned away from Luke, muttering, "I don't, I don't."

Luke stared at her. Going to her, he turned her toward him and pulled her close. She resisted briefly, then gave in, letting him hold her.

"Molly, if that is the problem, I don't want you to be proper," Luke whispered. "I want to take you again and again. I want to see you riding your horse with your hair streaming out behind you in the sunlight. You can go without clothes for all I care." Luke heard a small giggle from Molly on this. "But honey, I want you. I have wanted you for years, but you weren't free. Molly, I don't want this day to end, but it will. And since it must, I want to know you will be mine."

Luke thrust Molly away from him then, holding her at arm's length where he could see her face. "Molly, I am not a rich man. I'm only a small partner in this ranch. I have little to offer you. But I want you. I want to marry you if you will have me. And I promise I will never ask you to be proper."

Molly smiled faintly at this. Looking at Luke, she realized she didn't want this day to end either. She had never looked at Luke with desire before, never thought of him as a suitor. But he had visited several times with Punch, and she had looked forward to those evenings on the porch. Suddenly, she knew why she looked for Luke when she was out riding. Since that night at the fall gather when Luke had almost stumbled on Grace and her, Molly had felt a connection to this tall, lanky cowboy. Molly nodded up at Luke.

"Yes," Molly whispered. "I'll marry you. But I won't be ordered around. You have to agree to that."

Luke nodded. "I like the way you are right now," Luke whispered. "I don't want any changes."

Molly and Luke were about a mile from the ranch headquarters when Luke turned to Molly with a thought.

"I need to go and speak with your father."

Molly returned his gaze. "No, you don't," she said firmly. "I have been a married woman for ten years and have two children and my own home. I don't need my father's permission to marry. Much as I love him, I can make my own decisions."

Luke regarded her thoughtfully. "You're right about that, but I wouldn't speak to Kade to ask for your hand," Luke hesitated, looking forward toward the ranch. "Molly, I have such respect for Kade. Hell, when he hired me on, he could just as well put a bullet in me and tossed me in the ground with the rest. But instead, he trusted me, gave me a job. I want your father's blessing, but either way, we'll marry."

Molly thought about Luke's words. She had no idea what he was talking about. She studied him before asking, "Put a bullet in you? Put you in the ground with the rest? I don't understand. Why would Pa put a bullet in you?"

"You don't know how I came to work here?" Luke asked cautiously.

"Jake always said he met you riding along the river, and when Pa met you later, he hired you," Molly answered. "Isn't that true?"

Luke took a big breath. "Well, partially, but there's a lot left out," Luke hesitated. "I thought maybe you were told." Luke looked away and then back at Molly, his face serious. "I was in a cavalry unit. I was the only new recruit. The rest had ridden together for a long time. The other men were pretty much of the same mind. Our orders were to make a presence on the plains, restoring order. It was the summer after the Custer massacre. But my captain and the rest were out for revenge. They knew men killed with Custer. When we came on small bands of Indians, we just killed them," Luke looked uncomfortable. "We came upon Jake about a half day from a camping spot upriver that had a big tree. Captain decided instead of just killing Jake outright, he would bring him back to that spot and hang him. Jake was able to pull the bridle off his horse. It was a stud and spoiled at the time. The stud wanted to go home, so it high-tailed it. Cap had Jake tied up and made him run all afternoon behind us. It was pretty rough on him.

"We tied Jake to a tree, and one of the men hung a hanging noose on a branch. Jake saw that all night. I tried to speak up for Jake, but only got my nose broken for my trouble. Jake had just been cut loose from the tree the next morning when your pa and the rest of the men came loping up. There were some words spoke, and then one of the soldiers made the mistake of pulling a trigger. Twin Peaks men were ready. Your pa got winged, but there were no other casualties. All the soldiers were killed. I pulled Jake down and cut his hands loose, but we just stayed down until the shooting was over. Jake spoke up for me, and your pa offered me my freedom or to ride with them."

"Why didn't I ever know this?" Molly asked. "Why wouldn't someone tell me?"

"Molly, think about it," Luke answered. "Yes, my captain was in the wrong, but Twin Peaks made war on the United States that day. And I was a witness to it. At first, I wasn't sure I'd make it out of there alive, even after the shooting stopped. I took Kade's offer, and here I am. But if you think about it, I am a deserter. My name was Luke Brode then. That is why I go by Luke Brooks now. Just so no one would recognize my name and put it together with the missing cavalry troop. And from that day to now, even on the ranch, I have never heard anyone refer to that day. It was decided on the way home that it would be forgotten from that day forward. No one has ever breathed a word of it. I don't even know if any of the wives were told. I'm sure many were, but it was never brought up again."

They rode on for a few minutes before Luke spoke again. "Do you see why I want to talk to your father? He trusted me many years ago, and I respect that. I want to tell him our plans and ask for his blessing."

Molly rode silently for a few minutes, thinking about the story Luke told. After a bit, she looked at Luke and

nodded. She understood Luke's need to get Kade's blessing, and she was fine with that.

It turned out it wasn't hard to get Kade's blessing. The
couple stopped at the trading post and found him alone,
going over accounts. When Luke told Kade their plans,
Kade's grin said it all. Clapping Luke on the shoulder, he
pulled Molly into an embrace.

"Daughter," he said in her ear, "I couldn't ask for a better man to make you happy."

They decided not to say anything for a day because
Molly wanted to talk to Jack and he most likely wouldn't
be home until late that night. Morning would be a better
time to visit with the boy.

"I'll tell you how Jack takes the news," Molly told Kade
and Luke. "Then we can make some plans."

Molly was in the kitchen making breakfast when Jack finally got up. Grace too, was sleeping late, and Lydia was
in the garden. Molly enjoyed making breakfast, but on
this day, she wanted to be alone in the kitchen to talk to
Jack. At four years old, Grace would not find it difficult
to adjust to another person in her life, but Jack might be
a different story.

Jack took a seat at the table, and Molly put a plate of
eggs and bacon in front of him. She watched him eat.

"Did you have a nice day yesterday going up to the line
shack?" she asked.

Jack just nodded.

"Who all went with you and Uncle Thomas?" she
persisted.

Jack shrugged, then between bites, he mumbled, "A bunch of us."

Molly sighed. She had hoped a conversation with Jack would help ease into her news, but that wasn't going to happen. Might as well jump in with both feet, she thought.

"Jack, you know Luke has visited us some lately," she started.

Jack nodded.

"You like him, right?"

Jack nodded, then relented enough to remark, "He's good at checkers."

"Yes, I think I noticed that," Molly agreed, smiling. "Well," Molly began again slowly. "I was out riding yesterday and ran across Luke. He's such a nice man, and we got to talking and decided to get married."

Molly watched Jack for his reaction. At first, Jack just kept chewing then suddenly, he stopped and looked up at his mother. As if the words suddenly sank in, Jack stood pushing his chair back so violently that it tipped over, crashing to the floor. His face darkened, and his fists clenched.

"You can't do that!" his voice was tinged with anger.

"Jack, it's been seven months since your father passed."

"You can't marry anyone!" Now Jack was spitting mad. "You are married! You can't marry anyone else."

Molly stared at Jack. He was shaking with anger.

"Jack, your father is dead," she tried to speak calmly.

"I know that!" Jack was screaming now. "I know he's dead, but you are still married to him! You haven't grieved for him! You act like he never was here! You don't visit his grave. He gave you everything! He did everything for you! You can't marry anyone!"

Screaming these words at her, Jack turned and ran from the kitchen, the back door slamming behind him. Molly set her frying pan down, intending to chase after Jack, when she heard Grace cry from upstairs. Grace must have heard Jack screaming. Reluctantly, Molly let Jack go and went to comfort Grace.

It was a beautiful morning, and Jake was enjoying his ride. He was riding a nice five-year-old gelding. Having turned toward home, the horse had dropped into a nice running walk, head swinging from side to side. This was going to be a hard horse to let go, Jake thought. But then, most of the good ones were. Selling horses was Jake's business, and he was used to it. Now and then, he kept one back, like his stud, Savior, but most were sold as five- and six-year-olds.

Like most men of the mountains, Jake rode surveying his surroundings. These mountains didn't have the danger that used to lurk here, but they weren't safe either. It was a while since a wolf pack had invaded their land, but there was always a chance some roaming outlaw or disgruntled Indian might ride through. It never hurt to keep a watchful eye. He had been schooled in watching his surroundings, first by his mountain man stepfather, Kade, and second by his half-brother Brown Otter.

He saw the horse and rider coming at him when they were not much more than a speck. They were coming fast too. Jake thought maybe something had happened at the ranch and someone was coming for him. He pushed his horse into a rolling lope, trying to discern who was the rider. It wasn't long before he recognized Jack, riding as if his life depended on it and using the reins to whip the horse as it ran. Jake spurred his horse into a gallop to meet Jack, calling to him. But as Jack neared Jake, he didn't slow the horse or acknowledge Jake at all; he just whipped his horse on.

"Jack, stop!" Jake called after the boy, but there was no slackening of the speed.

Jack's horse was lathered, and Jake saw it stumble slightly as it went by. Jake recognized the signs. The horse was about at the end of its endurance. It could soon stumble and fall, hurting itself or the boy. Jake turned his horse, and in four strides, he was upon Jack. Reaching over he grabbed the boy by the waist, dragging him off the horse. The poor animal was so tired it struggled to stay upright, coming to a stumbling halt. Jack was kicking and screaming at Jake, and Jake dropped him abruptly to the ground. Then, stepping off his horse, Jake faced the boy.

"What the hell are you doing?" Jake demanded anger in his voice. "You are going to kill that horse."

Jack was shaking with fury. "I don't care!" he screamed. "I don't care! I don't care!" He was clearly out of control.

Jake tried to curb the anger he felt. He didn't know what was wrong, but treating a horse like Jack was doing was unacceptable. However, this was his nephew. Jake tried to speak more calmly.

"You better care. We don't treat horses like that at Twin Peaks. There is no reason to run a horse to death."

Jack's fists were clenched, and he faced Jake. "You don't know anything, you fucking half-breed!" he fairly screamed the words, his whole body rigid.

There was no conscious thought to Jake's reaction, swift as it was. He strode forward and reached for the boy. Kneeling on one knee, he thrust the boy over his other. Grasping the waistband of Jack's trousers, he gave a savage pull, popping the buttons and pulling the trousers down, revealing the boy's white rump. Surprised, Jack fell momentarily silent until the first hard slap. Then he began struggling, screaming his anger, frustration, and humiliation.

"You can't do this! Let me go! Let me go!" Jack screamed.

Jake kept spanking. He had never been this angry at anyone from the family before. In all his life, no one from the community, not family nor friend, had ever attacked him, verbally or physically. Jack's insult came out of nowhere. As Jake held down the struggling boy, the thought came to him that maybe Jack had heard those hateful words from his father. That hurt Jake even more. In all the years Jake had known Jackson, his brother-in-law had never shown Jake anything but friendship and respect. That Jackson may have used these insults about Jake behind his back, hurt more than a knife to the heart.

The child's milky rear turned pink, then red before Jack suddenly collapsed over Jake's knee, great wracking sobs coming from him. Jake stilled, hand held aloft, ready to spank again. Then, taking a breath, Jake rolled the boy off his leg onto the ground. Standing up, Jake watched as the boy curled, sobbing into a fetal position.

Turning, Jake went to Jack's horse. The animal was not far, standing, head down, sides heaving, front legs spread for balance. Loosening the cinch, Jake took the saddle off the animal. Then fashioning a halter from a rope on his saddle, Jake slowly led the horse to stand beside his own saddle horse. By the time he had finished, Jack's sobs had lessoned to hiccups. Jake went back to stand over the boy.

"Pull your trousers up," Jake commanded brusquely, poking Jack with the toe of his moccasin. When the boy made no move, Jake gruffly repeated, "Pull your pants up and sit up, or I'll tan you again."

Jack moved then, pulling his pants up to his waist and sitting up.

"How did you know to say those words to me?" Jake questioned.

Jack just shrugged.

"Jack, answer me," Jake said angrily, "or I swear I'll take you over my knee again. Did your father call me that?"

Jack shook his head, not looking at Jake.

"Look at me, Jack. Who did you learn to say that from?"

"The man who came to do the accounts last summer."

"Who did he say them to?" Jake persisted.

"To Father, but Father told him never to say that to him ever. Father was angry about it."

"So, you thought it was all right to say them to me?" Jake asked bluntly. He felt relief that Jackson had not taught Jack the words.

"I was angry," Jack mumbled.

"There is no anger that justifies what you did to that horse or to talk to me like that," Jake said, his words cutting. "What made you so angry?"

"Mother said she is going to marry Luke," Jack spat, anger returning.

That was good news for Jake. He liked Luke and thought Luke would be a good match for his sister.

"I thought you liked Luke?"

"Luke's all right," Jack admitted, "But Mother can't marry anyone. She's already married."

Jake regarded the boy. Was Jack daft? "Jack, you know your father is dead."

"Why does everyone keep saying that?" Jack's voice rose. "I know he's dead! I know it! But Mother doesn't even cry for Father. She doesn't talk about him, visit his grave, or keep his picture in the house. I know he's dead, but she is still Mrs. Crowden!" Jack was warming to his subject, and his voice rose. "Father gave her everything! He did everything for Mother! And Mother doesn't even grieve for him! She has no right to marry anyone. She has no right!"

"Jack, you have a half-brother in Laramie." The words came out before Jake thought about them. But Jack's unwarranted attacks on Molly set an already angry Jake off even more.

Jack looked stupidly at Jake. "How could I have a brother there?"

"You have a brother in Laramie, and your mother knows. The boy has a different mother than you. Your father gave your mother many things, but maybe you better ask yourself if the things he gave her were things she wanted."

Jake turned and went to his horse, mounting it. Jack watched him blankly, the wind taken away from him. When Jake urged his horse forward, leading Jack's horse too, it finally registered on Jack that he was getting left.

"Where are you taking my horse?" he cried, struggling to his feet while holding his trousers up.

"I'm taking this horse back to my corrals. This is a Twin Peaks horse. You don't deserve to ride this horse."

"How will I get home?" Jack was beginning to panic.

"You have two feet, don't you?" Jake asked. "Time you use them." He looked up at the sky before adding grimly, "It might rain tonight. You better not leave your saddle out here." With that, Jake put gentle heels to his horse and leading the spare animal, they moved toward the ranch headquarters, leaving the boy staring miserably after him.

⚬

Molly was a half mile beyond the trading post when she saw the distant horseman. As they got closer to each other, she recognized Jake leading Jack's horse. Fear rising in her, she spurred her horse forward to reach him.

"Where is Jack?" she asked breathlessly.

"Walking," Jake answered bluntly. "He doesn't deserve a horse."

"Jake, whatever happened?" Molly asked, perplexed at Jake's cross tone.

"He was angry enough to try to run this horse to death," Jake's face was grim, his tone still angry. "If I hadn't pulled him off, he would have."

"Oh, God," Molly murmured. "He told you why he was angry?"

Jake nodded. "Not an excuse, Sis. That boy needs to learn to control his anger. And for now, I won't let him have another Twin Peaks horse. If he needs something to take him back and forth, stop at Matthew's and get a mule. A mule won't let him mistreat it." Jake was silent for a moment before adding, "I told him about the woman and boy in Laramie."

"Oh, my heavens, no," Molly whispered. "You didn't."

"I did," Jake answered. "Wasn't my place to do that, but he was attacking you and other words were said. Reckon he needed to know."

"What words were said?"

"You can ask him," Jake answered bluntly, picking up his reins. With that, Jake urged his horse forward and left Molly.

Molly turned to watch him go. There was no question that Jake was angry. She had never seen him this way.

She touched her heels to her horse and rode on. Somewhere ahead of her, her son was walking home.

Molly wasn't prepared for what she saw when she approached Jack. His dirt-strewn face was streaked with tears. He was struggling to carry his saddle, bridle, and blanket while holding up his pants. As she approached, he looked up at her, and his eyes filled with tears. He didn't say a word. Molly dismounted.

"Let's throw your saddle on top of mine," she said. "It isn't that far of a walk, so I'll walk with you."

She helped Jack get the saddle over hers, noticing how he had to keep a grasp on his trousers.

"How did you pop the buttons on your pants?" she asked softly.

"Uncle Jake did it," Jack's words came out low, almost muffled.

"Uncle Jake? He was pretty mad at you when I saw him. He doesn't like to see an animal abused. From the looks of your horse, he had been ridden hard." Molly took out her knife and went to Jack's saddle, cutting off one of the saddle strings. "Here, let me tie it together with this."

After Molly got Jack's trousers trussed together enough so they wouldn't fall off of him, the two turned and started walking home.

"Uncle Jake said he told you about the boy in Laramie." Molly wasn't sure how to put it, but Jack knew what she was trying to say. He asked his own question.

"Why didn't you tell me Father has a son in Laramie?" Jack asked softly.

"I didn't want you to be angry with your father," Molly answered simply. "I thought I could be angry with him for all of us."

Jack thought about that. "Were you ever going to tell me?"

"I don't know, Jack. That is one hurdle I didn't want to cross right now. I didn't want to hurt you."

They walked on in silence for a while. Then, remembering Jake's words to her, Molly asked, "Uncle Jake said you had words. He wouldn't tell me what it was about. I'm guessing it was about how you treated your horse. But how did that pop the buttons on your britches? Did that happen when Jake pulled you off your horse?"

Jack looked away, ashamed to look at his mother. "Um, I was mad and said some things that made Uncle Jake angry. He, um, spanked me."

"Oh," Molly murmured. "What did you say?" She asked slowly.

Jack looked away and cleared his throat. Molly could see he was uncomfortable before the words came out of his mouth. "I called him a fucking half-breed."

"Oh, Jack, you didn't!" Molly's gasp of horror was enough to scare Jack even more than his uncle's anger.

"Mother, I don't even know what those words mean!" he exclaimed. "I just heard them last summer, and they just came out. Why are they so bad? What do they mean?"

Molly looked at her son gravely. "Oh, Jack, what have you done?" she asked, shaking her head. They walked on silently for a moment while Molly gathered her thoughts. Finally, she stopped walking and faced her son. "The word that starts with an 'f' is a disgusting word, a terrible word that I will not even say. You will have to ask some man to tell you what it means. All I'll say about that is it is an ugly word that speaks to something that should be beautiful."

"The word half-breed means a person of mixed heritage. You know your uncle is part Indian. When you call him a half-breed in the angry tone you most probably used along with that terrible word, it is an insult of the highest form."

"I didn't know," Jack said sadly, ashamed of himself. "I didn't mean it. I was just angry, and the words came out."

"Oh, Jack, you are learning a terrible lesson today, I'm afraid," Molly started walking again. "Once the words come out of your mouth, they can't be stuffed back in again."

"Will Uncle Jake forgive me?"

"Sometimes forgiveness comes, but it takes a long time to rebuild the trust you break when you attack someone you love. Somewhere between your anger and your love for your uncle, you said terrible, hurtful things to him," Molly said sorrowfully. "I know your uncle has had to fight for his name many times. People think it is all right to insult a person of mixed heritage. But here at Twin Peaks, your uncle is respected. I am sure he never thought someone from the ranch would call him that. I can only hope Jake can forgive you. Just as important, I hope you can earn his trust again."

Jake saw his father and brother lounging on the trading post porch, so he reined his horse in that direction. Reaching the store, he didn't dismount, just sat his horse, and looked at his father and brother.

"That horse you are leading looks pretty spent," Thomas remarked casually.

Jake gave Thomas and his father a hard look. "Jack thought he'd run him to death. I left Jack out there to walk home. Going to put this horse out to pasture for a while. Jack is not allowed another Twin Peaks horse," Jake spoke, his face a mask and his tone emotionless.

"Reckon that is a good lesson for the boy," Kade re-marked. "Why was he so hard on the animal?"

"He was mad," Jake said shortly.

"About what?" Thomas asked.

Jake glanced at his father. "Apparently, Molly told him this morning that she and Luke are getting married."

"I wondered about that when you said Jack was mad," Kade said. "They told me that news yesterday afternoon. Molly wanted to wait until morning to talk to Jack."

"Well, I'll be," Thomas remarked, smiling. "I take that as good news. Have they been courting, and I missed it?"

"I don't reckon they been courting as such," Kade said grinning. "I know Luke has dropped by Molly's with Punch some. An' they sure were a dancin' up a storm at Will's wedding. Don't think either of them really thought much 'bout marryin',"

"Something must have transpired yesterday to trigger that decision," Thomas speculated.

"Well, now, I can't be real sure," Kade smiled at Thom-as, "But I'd swear that Molly's blouse was buttoned some wrong when they stopped by, but then I might have mis-understood that."

Thomas grinned widely at that. "You think maybe? Well, hell, good for them. Anyone else, and I'd break his damn neck for messing with Molly, but I think Luke will be good for her."

Grinning, Kade and Thomas looked back at Jake and found him sitting stonily on his horse, making no comment. When Jake saw the men's attention was back on him, he reined his horse back a step and began to turn away.

"I just wanted you to know that Jack isn't getting an-other Twin Peaks horse anytime soon." Jake's tone was flat. He urged his horse forward and trotted away.

"What the hell bit him?" Thomas asked, bewildered. "I'd think he'd be happy about Molly and Luke getting hitched."

Kade pondered the question, watching his retreating son. "Don't think it was the news that upset Jake. Maybe it was just Jack's misuse of the horse."

"Yeah, could be. Jake's mighty particular about the horses," Thomas watched Jake riding away. "But he usually doesn't take something like that out on us, and he was positively unsociable. That is not like him."

"Reckon what's botherin' him will pass over or come out in time," Kade speculated. "We'll jest have to wait an' see."

CHAPTER 14

Honeymoon on
the Mountain –
Early September 1887

M olly and Luke decided to have their wedding in two weeks, just as September began. They wanted a simple gathering with just the friends and family from Twin Peaks. They chose mid-morning to be married, followed by a noon meal. Then, they would go to the line shack in the mountains to be alone for a week. Noah, who had been at the line shack, was due to be home any day now. Luke and Molly would take his place, riding the mountain slopes to watch the cattle. Of course, being alone there was the main draw for both of them. Now that Luke had updated the line shack, it would make a nice honeymoon retreat for the couple.

Jack was accepting of the arrangement. He wasn't happy about the changes, but after his disastrous day, he was watching his temper and his mouth. He started to protest about having to ride a mule, but Molly's stern look shut him up. For a couple of days, Jack stayed close to home, but then restlessness finally forced him to go to the ranch. The story of why he was riding a mule had circulated, though, and the men left it alone. The other boys ribbed Jack some about the mule, but eventually, even that stopped.

It was evident to everyone that Jake ignored the boy. If Jack tried to talk to Jake, Jake nodded or grunted or answered with monosyllables. For that matter, Jake had become more morose than Will. Even with the rest of the men, Jake had little to say.

"Jake's downright moody," Thomas complained to his father.

"Leave it alone," Kade replied. "He's working something out in his mind."

Two days before the wedding, Kade had enough. When he saw Jake go by with his last horse of the day, he called to him to visit with him. Jake came, but his face was set. There was no smile of greeting.

"Son," Kade began. "You got something weighin' you down? I think it has somethin' to do with that nephew of yours. Thomas tells me you been ignorin' the boy lately."

"Don't reckon I really want to talk about it, Pa," Jake said evenly.

"That's apparent," Kade agreed, "but it's not good. Your bad mood's been weighin' on everyone. Your sister is getting married in two days. Luke asked you to stand with him. Don't think a scowling brother is going to make your sister happy."

Jake thought about that. Coming to a decision, Jake relented and dismounted, tying his horse. Mounting the stairs, he and his father went inside the store and sat at the table.

"Pa," Jake started, taking a big breath. "That day I caught Jack running that horse to death, we had us some words. He was pretty much hysterical, and I should be able to understand that and get over it, but I can't." Jake relayed the events of that confrontation to Kade. Kade sat quietly, letting his son speak.

"Remember when I killed the Ute brave when the Utes were moved out?" Jake asked. "That was the first and only time I ever felt prejudice from my Ute people. I'm used to it when I go into white man territory. But that shook me with the Utes. Now, here I am in my own community. This ranch is my safe place. I never have to fight for my life, my name, or my dignity here. And then those words come out of Jack's mouth, and this isn't a safe place anymore."

"He's barely ten years old," Kade said softly.

"I know. I keep telling myself that. And Molly told me he didn't even know what the words meant. But I keep hearing them. The only thing I am grateful for is that he didn't learn them from Jackson. Jackson might have been a bad husband to Molly, but I always thought of him as a friend."

"Jake, you are thirty-eight years old. You have fought fer your name fer most of your life an' I have respected you fer how you handle yourself both here an' in the outside world." Kade thought for a minute before going on. "You're right, this is your safe place. No one here, little Jack included, has anything but love an' respect fer you. Your nephew said words he didn't understand. It was wrong, but you got to understand that." Kade hesitated, letting Jake think about this. "Your sister is getting married in two days. The best wedding present you can give her is to make peace with yourself an' her son. Think 'bout that."

Jake nodded, his eyes fixed on the distant wall. "I'll try, Pa."

Lathe and Hawk and their families came home the day before the wedding. Buster and Catherine and their children rode up the morning of the wedding. Molly had asked Catherine to stand with her. Molly wore a new riding skirt she had made herself and a pretty soft blue blouse. This was going to be a wedding that suited her. The tables were loaded with food, and after eating, Army brought out his harmonica so the bride could dance with her new husband and her father. Jake also took a turn with his sister, holding her tight and whispering his congratulations in her ear. Jake was relaxed at the wedding, smiling at the happy couple and back to his easy ways. It was a toss-up whether people were more pleased with the wedding couple or having Jake back in a good mood.

There was little else planned for festivities. It took nearly a half day to reach the line shack, and the bridal couple wanted to make the mountain meadow before they lost the light. So it was that they rode off just as the sun was reaching its zenith, leading a pack mule with supplies, and waving merrily to their friends and family.

Molly woke with the sun streaming in the window. Luke was up already, and she was alone in the line shack. Molly stretched luxuriously, warm under her quilts. From her nose peeking out of the covers, she knew the cabin was chilly. It gets cold at night the higher up in the mountains that one went, and they were much higher in the line shack than the mountain valley.

She had enjoyed the ride up to the line shack the day before. With the trail widened to wagon width, she and Luke could ride side by side the whole way. They found they had much to visit about. They each went through their childhoods, likes and dislikes, and present happiness.

Luke was the youngest child of a family of seven, with three older brothers. The eldest two brothers got the family farm. The third brother apprenticed to a storekeeper and went to live in town. When his parents both died in his eighteenth year, Luke knew it was time to leave. He started west, stopping at farms as he went, working day labor or through a harvest to pay his way. He joined the Army at twenty and was sent to Ft. Laramie. Here, Luke became the only new recruit in an established cavalry platoon. It was on the disastrous mission with this platoon that Luke had first met Jake and, ultimately, Kade and the Twin Peaks men. From that horrible beginning, Luke and Jake established a firm friendship, and Luke became a valued member of Twin Peaks.

The ride to the cabin had been an afternoon of getting to know each other better for both Molly and Luke. The evening was an extension of that. The couple unloaded the supplies, slid the two single beds together, and proceeded to learn a lot more about each other. As Molly lay, snuggled in her blankets the next morning, she smiled, remembering just how well they had learned about each other.

Molly heard the cabin door open, so she gathered her quilts around her and went to the door adjoining the sitting room. A fire was started, and as she entered the room, she could feel the beginnings of the warmth radiating from the stove. Luke stood shirtless in front of the fire. He saw her enter and turned to smile at her.

"I forget how cold it is running to the privy outside. Have to remember a shirt next time," Luke grinned. "Come here and let me share your blanket."

Molly went to him, opening the quilt to let him in. She looked up at him. "What do you have planned to do today?" she asked.

"Well, I wanted to suggest we just spend the day here," he bent down, nuzzling her ear. "I mean, four times last night wasn't quite enough. I'd be up for more rest too, of course." He grew serious then before continuing. "Did you notice there weren't any cows in this meadow when we came in last night?"

Molly nodded. "Is that unusual?"

"At this time of year, it is," Luke returned. "Noah said he had to drive cows back to Crystal Lake about every other day. He did that before he came down, but that was three days ago. I would have thought that some of them would have drifted back by now."

Molly understood what Luke was saying. This meadow by the line shack was where they gathered cattle and held them during fall gather before pushing them down the trail to the ranch. As the number of livestock increased over the years, this meadow couldn't support them all, so now, every few days, as they gathered cattle in the fall, the accumulated herd had to be sent down the trail to keep the grass from being depleted. The old cows knew the routine. As the nights got colder in the early fall, cattle began their trek toward the lower altitudes and congregated in this meadow. One of the line shack rider's jobs, along with watching for predators and injured animals, was to push the cattle off this meadow, conserving its grass.

"I'd like to ride over to the lake and check out that meadow. It just seems strange there aren't cows here," Luke finished. "You want to take a ride?"

Molly smiled at that. "I am always ready for a ride. Tell you what, you gather the horses, and I'll get dressed and pack a lunch for us. We can have a picnic at the lake. It is such a pretty place."

Luke nodded, going for a shirt and jacket. Just before he went out the door, Molly called to him from the adjoining room. "Why don't you tie on a blanket too? We might want that for our picnic," she said, smiling wickedly.

"Oh, woman," he answered, grinning, "you read my mind."

Crystal Lake was just that, a body of sparkling water high in a mountain meadow that reflected the sunlight like a crystal chandelier. Molly and Luke reached the lake a little over an hour after leaving the line shack. They pulled up as they left the sheltering trees and surveyed the lake and its surrounding mountain meadow. It was a beautiful sight, with green grass and a lake, all bordered by aspen and pine trees. But on this day, no cow or calf was in sight.

"This is not good," Luke said quietly. "Not a cow to be seen but look at the pasture here. It is dotted with cow pies."

"There has been a passel of cattle here recently, but where did they go?" Molly asked. "Are you thinking what I am thinking?"

Luke gave her a hard look. "I'm thinking the rustlers Kade has been worried about for the last several years finally found our mountain range."

"If that is true," Molly said, "then there will be a trail. There were a lot of cattle on this ground not long ago, and they will make a lot of tracks."

Luke surveyed the area. "They won't drive the cattle towards the ranch. I'd guess they would push them toward the plains to the north. I've gone out that way with Jake many times when he has taken horses out that direction to sell."

Molly and Luke rode toward the north of the meadow, watching the ground. There was a trail of sorts that Luke and Jake had followed to ride out to the prairie. As the couple crossed the meadow, suddenly, they came upon a shape hidden in the grass around some brush trees. Luke put up his hand to stop Molly and pointed.

"There's a calf there," he said. "See it in the brush?"

Molly looked, spotting what he saw. A little calf lay curled up, motionless on the ground, partially hidden by foliage. He didn't move a muscle or his head, but his eyes rolled in his head, watching the people on horseback.

"His mama put him to bed this morning and told him to stay put," Luke remarked slowly. "Usually, you find a half dozen calves together with one old cow nearby watching over them. But the rest must have been lying more in the open. When the herd was pushed out, the rest were in the path and were gathered up, but this little baby stayed put. He's a young one too, probably less than a month old. A summer calf, not a spring calf like most of the others."

"He's defenseless here alone," Molly remarked. "I hate to leave him, but to take him to the cabin will only put us farther behind. I can only hope it will survive until we get back. Let's find that trail."

They rode farther, and Luke found where the trail to the north began. The tracks told the story. As the cattle bunched up to go down a ravine, hooves churned up the ground. Luke dismounted to study them.

"Here," he said, pointing. "Shod hooves."

Molly rode a short distance away and found another set. "So, there are at least two men," she said.

"Yeah, at least, but I'm going to reckon there are three or four," Luke contemplated the situation. "They started gathering cattle on the closer slopes as soon as they saw Noah head down. They probably have been watching up here for a while or know us. Maybe they come to trade at Kade's store and know a bit about our routine. They knew they had a couple of days to gather whatever was close and then skedaddle before the next cowboy comes up to check on the cattle."

"Where would they take these cattle once they hit the plains?" Molly asked.

"No telling," Luke answered. "Might be some cattle buyers nearby they can sell fast. Might break the cattle up and mix in with a herd heading to the railroad. Might even have some hiding place they can take them to. Once they get to the plains, they can mix other cattle prints over these and lose anyone following, and if there is rain, the tracks are lost forever. They probably think they have a week or more before any cattle are even missed. Might even take fall gather with a hundred head short before we would even suspect."

Luke looked down the trail and then back the way they came, thinking of their options.

"Molly, I want you to ride back to the ranch. You can get there by evening and alert Jake and Thomas. I'll trail these and see if I can get ahead and hold them up."

"Luke, I'm not going back and let you go after them alone," Molly's voice was firm. "Any help would be two days behind you. Jake once said he could ride out of the mountains this way to the north in a day. That's with horses. Pushing cattle, they may not get out of the mountains by tonight, but they will by early tomorrow. That puts help too far behind you. I'm going with you."

"Molly, it is too dangerous," Luke began, but Molly cut him off.

"Luke, you promised me. You told me you wouldn't tell me what to do, how to act," Molly wasn't angry; she was resolved. "I know how to shoot. I can ride as good as anyone. And these are my cattle too. I'm not letting my husband of one day ride away without me."

Luke regarded her and then slowly nodded. "Promise me one thing," he said softly. "Promise me you won't get hurt. Promise me you will listen to me if things go south."

"That is two things," Molly retorted, side-passing her horse to his and leaning toward him for a kiss. "But I'll agree to that. Now let's ride."

The trail down the mountain to the plains began by following a gentle depression formed by a trickle of a stream. This trickle was joined by other mountain brooks and became a larger creek, rushing and tumbling over rocks. The trail followed the water as it went down into a ravine. Sometimes, the ravine would widen into open areas, and sometimes, the trail became single file along the edge of the creek bank. They could see tracks here and there of shod horses following the cattle, but when the slopes became gentle along the creek, they found at least one more set of horse tracks.

"They probably have one rider in the lead to pull off and seal up some gulches the cattle could cut back toward home on," Luke commented when the trail widened, and they could ride side by side. "Then, when there is room, one or more of the men will get ahead of the cattle again. They probably had this scouted out early and knew when to get ahead of the cattle and when they didn't have to worry. I've seen a couple of places where the cattle have spread out in open areas, and a rider has ridden almost into the trees to turn them toward the trail again. I'm thinking they have a cow with them that is hell-bent on returning to her calf."

Molly nodded, understanding what Luke meant. Many of these cows had been in the mountains during the summer for years. They were now getting pushed away from their homeland. They'd want to return to what is familiar to them, and that one mother cow would want to go back to her baby. Maybe there were more calves left behind that Molly and Luke hadn't seen.

They rode on, making good time. Their horses were fresh and could move faster than a herd of cows. It was shortly after noon when they heard the bawling. At least one mother cow was wanting to go home.

"Why wouldn't they just turn that cow loose?" Molly asked.

"Greed, maybe," Luke answered shortly. "Or maybe the cow didn't start bawling right away, thinking her baby was safe. If they cut her out to turn her back, they risk losing some of the other cows wanting to go with her. There's not a lot of room to maneuver down this trail. And when a bunch of these damn half-wild cows get a notion, it's harder to keep them together. Safer to keep after the old girl and hope she quits."

They rode, knowing by the noise of the bawling cow how close they were coming. Finally, from the nearness of the mother cow's mournful call, it seemed that any curve might bring them on top of the herd. Luke stopped and searched the land.

"I think the trail makes a sharp curve up ahead," he said, motioning with his arm. "This is a tolerable steep ridge the trail is going around, but after a wide turn, it travels north again. A small creek comes in from the right, maybe a quarter mile ahead. The cows will want to go that way. One or more of the men will have to be up there to stop them." He looked again at the slope he was considering. "I think our horses can make it up there," he said pointing up. "We can split up then. I can go ahead and see if I can pick off the lead men, and you should be able to get up on the ridge and look down on the middle of the bunch. With the trail almost single file, they will be spread apart quite a long way. This might be our best bet to hit them when they are busy with the cattle and the riders are a far piece apart."

Molly nodded. Putting spurs to their animals, they began to climb to the top of the ridge. The climb was steep and rocky, but the horses were sure-footed and in good shape. At timcs, they went straight up, and when the slope was particularly steep, they wove back and forth, gaining altitude at each turn. Finally, they made the top, their horses' sides heaving from the effort.

"Now, it gets tricky," Luke said. "We are above them on this ridge. I'm going to head straight north. I hope I am right that this is the place where the trail makes a big turn. I want you to go over toward the west some. You will have to tie your horse and walk. You can't ride your horse right to the edge of the ridge and look down at them because you will be too visible. But there should be trees or boulders you can hide behind. Find the riders in the middle of the herd or at the back and be ready. Wait to hear my shots when I get to the front. If I am wrong and can't get in front of the leaders, I will come back for you, and we will trail them farther to find a better place."

"When I hear you shoot, I do too?" Molly asked.

Luke nodded, but then he turned to her. "Molly, all them cows together aren't worth you. Don't take any chances."

"I could say the same about you," Molly answered simply. "So be careful."

Molly found a sapling to tie her gelding and crept forward carefully to the edge of the ridge. It was a steep drop to the creek bed. She could see the cattle moving, single file below her, but at the moment, no riders. She waited, knowing Luke had a farther distance to ride to get in front of the leaders. Suddenly, below her, a rider came into view. The rider rode in a single file with cattle in front of him and cattle behind him. Luke was right; the rustlers probably took turns moving forward as the lead rider fell off to block possible paths where cattle could veer off into a gulch leading toward their home range. Molly felt it was an eternity waiting to hear a shot from Luke, but she kept her gun sights on the rider as he wound his way along the creek bed with the cattle. Just as the rider Molly had her sights on almost disappeared around the bend, she saw the rider on drag come into view. He had no cattle behind him. That was when she heard Luke's shot.

Molly still had her sights on the first rider and squeezed the trigger. She saw him double over, and then he was out of sight. She didn't wait; she swung her rifle toward the rear and sighted on the rustler at the back. Alerted by the shots, he spurred his horse toward the trees on the other side of the creek. Molly swung her rifle toward him, trying to get him in her gunsights. As his horse scrambled up the bank, Molly squeezed her trigger again. The rider fell like a rock, the horse struggling to reach higher ground, then stopping, reins dragging.

The cattle below whirled, stampeded by the shots. Cattle came from Luke's direction, frightened by the shots in front of them, and in their panic, the animals wanted to return to their familiar home range. Molly had no doubt that one of the cows leading was the mama cow, missing her baby. Molly waited for a couple of minutes, just in case another rider emerged, but when she saw no one, she ran back to her horse. There was still gunfire coming from Luke's direction. From the sound of it, he had at least two rustlers that he was fighting.

Molly had yet to get far after mounting when the gunfire ceased. Not wanting to run into an ambush, she rode cautiously in the direction Luke had gone. She came to another outcropping, and looking down, she saw one body lying on the bottom by the creek, a horse standing ground tied nearby. Where was Luke? She could see no one farther on, so she rode her horse along the edge of the cliff, looking for any movement below. She saw another ground-tied horse beside a body. Luke had gotten two of them. But she couldn't see Luke. Molly backtracked along the edge, searching the bottom. That was when she saw Luke's horse. The animal was down at the bottom of the steep incline, struggling.

The slope from the ridge down to the creek was steep, but she thought her horse could handle it. Urging it forward, the horse dug in, almost sliding toward the creek on its hindquarters. Rocks and gravel came rattling loose, but the horse stayed upright. Reaching the bottom, Molly leaped from her horse, rifle in hand. Where was Luke?

When Molly reached Luke's horse, her heart sank. In one glance, she could see a bullet hole in the animal's flank, and the front leg of the animal was clearly broken. There was no coming back from an injury like that. The animal was suffering. Without thought, Molly drew

an invisible line between the horse's eye and the opposite ear, then doing it again with the other eye and ear.
Where the lines intersected, she sighted with her rifle
and pulled the trigger. The horse collapsed and lay still.
Damn, damn, damn, she thought. Even humanely shooting a suffering horse was a horrible task.

Molly surveyed the trail along the creek. Not finding
Luke lying among the rocks, brush, or water, she looked
up the cliff wall. That was when she saw him. Halfway
up the steep slope, Molly saw a boot sticking out from
behind a boulder, but she instantly knew it was Luke.
Heart in throat, she began to climb, clawing her way up
to him.

Luke was unconscious, but breathing. He had a gash
alongside his head and was bleeding on his side. Molly
tore his shirt and saw the slice along his side, a bullet, in
and out. She put pressure on the wound, trying to stop
the bleeding. Taking off her neck scarf and Luke's, she
tied them together and wrapped them around his torso,
pulling it tight over the wound.

"Luke! Luke!" she cried, over and over, trying to wake
him. It was no use. He lay silent and limp among the
rocks.

Molly had to get him down to the horses. Carefully,
she pulled him around so his head was on the downslope
side. Cushioning his head in her lap, she pulled him
down the slope, sitting on her knees and backing slowly
downward. Gravity was her friend. She would back up a
foot or two on her knees and pull him with her. Finally,
carefully, she made the bottom. She sat there panting,
looking at her horse. She had to get Luke back to their
own range and get help. A plan was forming in her head.

Two of the rustlers' horses were standing ground tied
nearby. She went to them, tying one to the other. She

passed the dead rustler she had killed and saw his rifle on the ground nearby. She picked it up and put it in the scabbard. The second man she had shot was nowhere to be seen. Molly hoped he was either farther down the trail dead or hightailing it to the plains alone. Next, she went forward and found the horse and rifles of the second man Luke had killed. Leaving the men, Molly gathered the rifles and their horses. None of these men would come back from the dead and find a weapon or horse to use, she thought grimly.

Coming back to Luke, she checked him. He still breathed, and there was almost no bleeding from his side wound. His face was a mess of blood, but it was all dried. The gash was deep but not bleeding any longer.

Molly went to Luke's horse and untied the blanket he had on the back of his saddle. She was thirteen when Jake showed her how the Indians moved their belongings using travois. She had been fascinated with Jake's stories then, and on this day, the knowledge of making a travois would help her. There was no way she could get Luke on a horse, but she could roll him onto a travois.

It took her some time to find downed timber that would work, but with her hunting knife, she was able to break or cut off branches that would get in the way. With the blanket and a rope she took off Luke's dead horse, she was able to lash the blanket on the poles. She chose her own horse to pull the contraption. She didn't think her gelding would like the travois dragging behind it, but Molly knew the horse. As well-trained as it was, she thought she could keep the animal under control.

When she had the travois strapped onto her gelding, she led him around, getting him used to it following him. The big bay horse threw his head from side to side, prancing a little, but Molly spoke to him softly, and it didn't take him long to know the travois wouldn't hurt him. Molly led the horse near Luke. It took all she could do to get Luke onto the blanket, trying not to touch his wounds. She almost wished that by pulling and dragging him, he would wake up, but her hopes were dashed. Luke lay, breathing, but silent.

Molly started out leading the horse. She had a long rope attached to the extra horses of the rustlers, and they followed along obediently behind the travois, the lead horse eyeing it fearfully, but coming. Right after Molly took her first steps, while she was watching behind her to make sure all was well, she stumbled over a rock in the path. Her ankle twisted, and she went down in front of the horse. Her gelding stopped, startled to find her almost underneath him. Molly rolled, tried to stand, and gasped at the pain in her ankle.

Using her horse's front leg to pull herself up, she staggered as she moved toward the saddle. Grasping a stirrup, Molly steadied herself and surveyed her leg. She hoped it was only a sprain, but the pain was extreme, and she couldn't put her weight on it. She hopped to the side of her horse, glad the injured foot was her right one. Reaching for the saddle horn, Molly pushed off with her good foot and reached the stirrup with her left. *I intended to ride anyway, as soon as I was sure the horse wouldn't panic,* she thought. This was as good a time as any to find out.

The going was slow, and Molly was losing the light when she made it to Crystal Lake. She knew she couldn't make the cabin. The trail through the gorge to the cabin was too narrow to pull the travois safely in the dark, and the drop was too steep. She would have to make camp here before getting help.

Without dismounting, Molly picketed the extra horses to trees. Finding a good camping spot near the lake,

Molly dismounted. Using her horse as a support, she untied the straps for the travois and lowered it carefully to the ground. Molly knew she couldn't pull Luke off without using both feet. But having a blanket beneath him would give him some warmth. She pulled a slicker from the back of her saddle and covered him with it. She guided her horse to a tree, holding on to its mane for support, and tied it. With the help of a long stick as a crutch, she hobbled to find wood and start a fire. By the time she got a fire going, it was completely dark, and she was tired. But she couldn't rest. She still had much to do.

Molly had to take the risk of leaving Luke. She needed help, but help was a long way away. She found two thick logs nearby and dragged them to the fire, having to crawl backward, pulling them behind her. Putting one end of each in the fire, she hoped they would burn for several hours. Luke was defenseless here, but hopefully fire would keep predators away.

When Molly had done all she could for Luke, she limped to her horse and mounted. Riding to the picket line, she chose one horse and untied it. Leading the extra horse, she headed toward the line shack and the trail to home. There was a half-circle of the moon that gave her some light, and her eyes adjusted to the darkness, but it was still frightening to ride through the narrows in the dark. Molly hoped the horses could see their footing better than she. She breathed easier when the ravine opened up, and she came out onto the line shack meadow.

She rode directly to the trail in the trees that led down to the ranch. She rode a quarter mile down the trail until it was surrounded by trees, the brushy foliage dense on each side of the trail. Here, she dismounted and took the bridle off her gelding. Holding the rustler's horse firmly, she mounted it, then lashed her own bridleless horse, driving him down the trail toward home. At first, the horse hesitated, not understanding, until Molly cried out at him and whipped him again. He shied away and headed down the trail at a lope. Molly lost sight of the horse but could still hear it. She could hear the four-beat sound of the animal as it dropped to a trot. He would be home in the horse herd in the morning when Thomas and Jake gathered horses. They wouldn't miss her saddled horse. They would know there was trouble.

Molly made tracks back to the line shack on the rustler's horse. She rode right up to the front door. Not wanting to risk the horse getting loose, she tied him securely to the porch rail and went in. It didn't take her long to pull quilts off the bed along with the sheet underneath. She also took one cook pan and some bread. With her hands full, Molly returned to the horse, tying the blankets on the back of the saddle. Holding the pan and bread, she clambered back on the horse, wincing when her ankle touched the ground. Then, turning the horse, she returned to trace her steps back to Luke.

It was probably well after midnight when Molly returned to the campsite at the edge of the lake. She had eaten a little of the bread. It was tasteless to her, but she felt she had to keep her strength up. She had forgotten the packed picnic lunch. It was still on her horse, trotting toward Twin Peaks.

The campsite was as she left it. The fire was only coals, burning red in the gloom, but still alive. She added more wood and was glad for the light of the flames. Luke was as she left him, breathing but unresponsive.

Molly stripped the horse's tack off and turned it loose. The other horses would just have to live through the night with whatever they could reach where they were tied. Her ankle pained her, and she did not want to deal with the horses that night.

Molly crawled to the lake with the pan and filled it with water. Creeping back to the fire with the pan, she spilled some water on herself. It was cold, and with the chill of the mountain air, Molly shook with cold. She put the pan in the fire to heat, then went to the saddle she'd dropped on the ground and untied the blankets. Luke, still unconscious, was shivering under the thin slicker, and she wanted to warm him.

When the water was hot, she tore a length of sheet and, using it as a washcloth, washed the blood off Luke's face. The fire helped her see the torn skin and the purple-blue of the skin around the head wound. Next, she used her knife to cut off the neck scarves she had used to bandage his side. The blood had dried, and she pulled a scab off, causing the wound to begin to bleed again. There was no response from Luke. If he had been awake, it would have hurt him. But even with the pain, there was no response. She washed this wound too, and covered it with the cleanest part of the sheet, pulling it tight around him to stop the bleeding.

By the time Molly got both wounds cleaned and re-bandaged, she saw the barest hint of light in the eastern sky. It would be light in another hour or two. She was spent. The adrenaline that had fueled her to this point was wearing off. She sat down beside Luke, and as gently as possible, she pulled off the boot from her sore foot, almost crying out in pain. Then burrowing under the quilts with Luke, she gave way to her fatigue. She curled up to his good side, her arm over him, her head on his shoulder, and fell asleep, even as she silently prayed. *Don't take him, Lord. Don't take him away from me.*

.♦.

Jake shrugged on a coat and went out into the early morning chill. The sun was brimming the mountain ridges to the east. He stretched and surveyed the meadow, looking for the horse herd. It wasn't far out this morning. Jake was turning to walk to his corral for his saddle horse when something caught his eye. He turned back to the horse herd, studying it. There, mixed in with the remuda, was a saddled horse, contentedly grazing. He recognized it immediately. That was Molly's horse.

Jake sprinted to his corral and quickly saddled the horse left in to gather the herd. Once mounted, he spurred his horse out and rounded up the horse herd. They were used to coming in every morning, and this was no exception, except that Jake pushed them harder and faster than normal. He had just shut the gate when Thomas joined him, walking up the hill from his cabin.

"Shit, Jake. What's your hurry this morning?" Thomas called, grinning. "You have an appointment somewhere?"

"Thomas, Molly's horse is here!" Jake called over his shoulder. He dismounted and waded through the herd to catch Molly's gelding. Putting a rope around the animal's neck, he led it to the fence. Thomas had come inside the corral, worry stamped on his face.

"There is old, dried blood on the saddle horn," Jake muttered. "There is trouble on the mountain. I'm going up to find them."

"I'm coming too," Thomas said, catching a horse.

By the time the two brothers had their horses saddled and ready, Hawk, Sam, and Lathe had joined them, ready for a day of work. Jake told them about Molly's horse and where they were going.

"Sam, I'm thinking there might be one of them hurt. Can you get a wagon and bring Martha?" Jake asked. He turned to Lathe. "Tell Pa. He has to know."

Sam simply nodded and turned, riding to his cabin to alert his wife. Lathe nodded, spurring his horse toward the trading post.

"I will go with you," Hawk said. The two brothers nodded at Hawk as they mounted their horses. Then the three of them started across the meadow. They would not spare the horses going to the line shack today.

When Jake, Thomas, and Hawk reached the mountain meadow, they first checked out the line shack. They could see only the one pack mule grazing in the small, fenced pasture behind the shack. Still, they needed to check the cabin.

Inside the cabin, they saw the beds, bare of blankets and sheets. Clothing and cooking gear were strewn around, but the shack was empty of Molly and Luke. They went back outside and surveyed the meadow.

"There are about five ways they could leave from here," Thomas commented,

"Let's spread out and look for tracks," Jake answered. "That horse was sent to us as a message. Something is wrong. I'm sure of it."

The men spread out, surveying the trails leading away from the line shack. It wasn't long before Hawk called Jake and Thomas.

"Here, they went this way."

Jake and Thomas joined Hawk, seeing what Hawk saw laying on the ground. "That is a piece of Molly's clothing," Jake said. "She's telling us which way she went. At least, I hope it is Molly leaving the sign."

They rode farther and found more clothes or pieces of cloth. They were sure of it now. Either Molly or Luke left a trail that was easy for them to follow. By the time they got to the narrow gorge, they knew they were headed for Crystal Lake.

When the men broke out of the narrows, they put heels to their horses and loped through the tree-covered slope until they came out on the large meadow surrounding the lake. Jake pulled his horse to a stop, Thomas and Hawk pulling up beside him.

"There," Thomas said, pointing, but Jake had already seen it.

In the distance, near the shore of the lake, they could see the rough campsite. There was no smoke coming from a fire or movement at the camp. Two saddled horses stood tied to trees near the camp, and one horse was loose, grazing nearby. A saddle lay close to the camp, laying haphazardly on the ground. There looked to be a pile of blankets that possibly covered bodies.

"No sign of Luke's horse and those animals aren't ours," Jake spoke softly. "Best keep an eye out. Hawk, stay up here in the trees until we see what is there. I don't want to be caught in an ambush."

The brothers pulled rifles from scabbards and approached slowly. There was no movement from the blankets, but as they came closer, they saw that two bodies were under the blankets, covers pulled high over their faces. As they neared, the brothers saw Molly's long hair flowing from under the warm wraps. Jake touched his horse's sides, and it leaped forward. As he reached the camp, Jake dismounted on the run, Thomas behind him.

"Molly," Jake called softly. "Molly, wake up!"

Molly stirred, pushing away from Luke's side where she was sleeping. Seeing her brothers, she struggled to sit up, grimacing in pain.

"Jake, Thomas!" she cried. "Thank God!" Then she turned suddenly to Luke. "Is he still breathing? I can't wake him!" Her voice rose in desperation.

Thomas went to Luke's side and pulling back the blanket, he studied the man. "Yes, he's breathing. Why can't you wake him?"

"I don't know. He has a gash on his head. I don't know what to do!"

Molly clutched at Jake and tried not to cry. Until now, she hadn't cried at all, but now, with help arriving, she felt the tears welling. She looked at her brothers, and Jake knelt to her.

"What happened, Molly? Where is Luke's horse?" Jake asked gently.

Molly took a big breath. "Rustlers. These are their horses."

Hawk rode up, confident that no lurking enemies were waiting to confront them. Seeing Hawk, Molly suddenly had a thought. "Those two horses have been tied up all night." She looked at the sky. "It must be closing in on noon. Those poor horses haven't had feed or water since probably this time yesterday."

"Take care of them, will you, Hawk?" Jake asked. "And gather that grazing animal and saddle it. Molly will need it." Jake looked back at Molly. "Now tell us what happened."

Molly started at the beginning, how they had seen the signs and knew that rustlers had gone off with Twin Peaks cattle and that she and Luke had gone after them.

"When we caught up with them, they were strung out quite a long way. When I heard Luke open fire, I got one of the men and winged another. There were two dead men up ahead when I went to find Luke. I wasn't there to see what happened to Luke, but his horse had a bullet wound and a broken leg. I think the outlaws shot Luke's horse, and when it fell, it went over a steep rock-strewn slope. Luke had a bad gash on his head, and he just lay there. He has a bullet wound on his side, but I don't think that is serious. What scares me is I can't wake him." Molly looked hopelessly at her brothers.

"Luke shouldn't have let you go with him," Thomas began angrily, but Molly cut him off.

"Thomas, don't you start," she said severely. "I am part of this ranch and refuse to be treated like a China doll. Not by Luke or you or anybody."

"Did you get hurt?" Jake asked gently.

"I got some rock chips in my face, but nothing serious. Then when I was bringing Luke out, I tripped and twisted my ankle pretty bad." Molly pulled the blanket off her legs and the men saw her one ankle, twice its normal size and badly bruised.

"How the hell did you get Luke back here?" Thomas asked.

"I made a travois with some blankets we had with us and pulled him here," Molly said. Then, looking at Jake, she smiled a small smile. "You taught me how to do that, remember? I must have been about thirteen or fourteen. I never thought I'd have to use that skill, but it sure came in handy."

Getting Luke through the narrows was no easy task. It took all three men to hoist Luke onto a horse with Jake sitting on the horse behind him to hold him steady. Luke was deadweight and taller than any of them. Jake had to keep Luke upright as they rode through the narrow section of the trail above the ravine. It would not have been the time for Luke to come awake and struggle. The granite trail had a rock overhang that Jake had to duck a little under, holding tight to Luke in front of him. But Luke didn't stir, and Jake held him tightly. Sam was waiting for them when they came out on the other side.

"I heard your horses on the stones," Sam said, smiling. "Didn't think I wanted to try to share the trail with you." He sobered when he saw Luke.

"Where's Martha and the wagon?" Thomas asked.

"They are almost here. Kade insisted on coming, so I made better time than them," Sam answered. "Kade is driving Martha up here."

The wagon pulled into sight within minutes, and the men dismounted and lifted Luke carefully from the horse. Martha had thrown a featherbed into the buckboard, and the men carefully laid Luke on it. Helping Molly off her horse, Thomas carried her to the wagon, where she got on with Luke. Martha did a cursory evaluation of Luke and Molly's injuries, and then the wagon took off toward the ranch.

"Hawk, Sam, and I are going to stay over a day or two up here," Jake told Kade before they pulled out. "We will clean up Molly's campsite, and we want to ride the trail tomorrow and see if we recognize the dead men. We'll get shovels from the shack and get some dirt over them. I use that trail enough. I don't want to ride by some stinking outlaw bones every time I go that way."

The wagon pulled out, and Thomas rode along behind it. Molly watched Jake, Sam, and Hawk recede as she lay in the wagon with Luke. The sun was shining through the trees, and it was a beautiful early fall day. As the wagon went through the meadow by the mountain shack and descended into the wagon track down the mountain, Molly lay her head on Luke's chest. Her eyes brimmed with tears, remembering her one night with Luke. *Sadly,* she thought, *our honeymoon is over.*

Working Things Out –
September-October 1887

It was a cloudy, damp day outside, which didn't lighten Molly's mood. She had been home three days, and Luke still lay motionless as if dead. Molly watched his chest rise and fall with his breathing to prove to herself that he was still alive. But the question was, how long could he live this way? She and Lydia had tried to rouse him to drink, but it had been no use. They knew that without water, Luke would not survive much longer. Molly had no medical training, and Martha only knew what she had learned from her now-deceased mother-in-law and one medical book she had ordered years before. There wasn't much on head wounds and little encouragement when the patient was unresponsive. Still, Molly sat beside Luke, constantly talking or reading to him, moving his arms and legs, and massaging him. She had to try. Until the breath went out of Luke, she had to do something, or she would go mad.

She heard the back door open and voices coming from the kitchen. Footsteps sounded in the hall, and Jake walked in. Lydia had told her that Punch had delivered the news that Jake, Hawk, and Sam had returned from the line shack the night before. She wasn't surprised that Jake was here, checking on Luke.

"Any change?" Jake asked softly from the door.

Molly met her brother's gaze, but her lips trembled, "No."

"Don't give up," Jake said. "It has only been three days."

"How long can he live without food or water?" Molly questioned.

Jake shook his head, not knowing the answer to that. Then, he crossed over to his sister and gathered her in his embrace. "Honey, this is out of our hands. It is between Luke and God now. You just have to be strong."

"I am so tired of being strong!"

Jake chuckled sadly at that. "I reckon you are, Sis," he said. "Everyone is here for you. Lean on us when you need."

Molly nodded her head. After a few minutes, they parted, taking seats by Luke's bed.

"We found the bodies," Jake said, changing the subject. "One of them was a former hand from the Anchor J, one of the cowboys that came up the trail last summer. He probably couldn't find a job after you sold the Anchor J. We didn't recognize the others. Three of them. The wounded one must have made it out to the lowlands."

"I hope he dies from his wound," Molly said heatedly. "I suppose that is another reason I'll go to hell."

Jake laughed at that. "Honey, I think the Good Lord will forgive you this time too. I'm sure he knows how worried you are now."

Jake stayed an hour, talking quietly with his sister. He offered to stay with Luke while she went out and got some rest, but Molly would hear none of that.

"I have a cot I pull out when I want to sleep," Molly said firmly. "I don't want to be very far from him in case he needs something."

Jake nodded and got up to leave. He walked to the door and then turned back to talk to Molly once more.

"Molly, you are going to have to get out some soon, so you don't get sick yourself."

"I know," Molly said softly, "but this ankle still pains me. I don't think resting here is hurting me any."

"Well, just take care—" Jake stopped speaking abruptly, his gaze on Luke, studying him.

Molly caught his intense scrutiny and turned to look at Luke, then back to Jake, "What?" she asked anxiously.

Jake walked back close to the bed. "Watch his eyes."

"They are closed," Molly said.

"I know, but just watch them," Jake insisted.

There was movement on Luke's face: little twitches or fluttering of the eyelids. There would be a little movement and then nothing. But after a minute, another little twitch.

"What do you think it means?" Molly asked, hope in her voice.

"I have no idea," Jake admitted. "But I'm going to guess that his mind is coming alive. That is more action than he has shown since he was hurt, so let's hope it is a good sign."

Jake hated to leave Molly, but he knew he could not help. He had work to do. He went out to the back porch where his horse was tied. Jack sat on the steps, his head in his hands. When Jack heard the door open, he rose and backed down the steps beside Jake's horse.

"Uncle, can I talk to you?" the boy asked fearfully.

"Jack, you can always talk to me," Jake answered levelly. He had not interacted much with his nephew since the incident, but he had come to terms with it after talking with Kade.

"Uncle Jake, I sure am sorry for what I said to you that day," Jack started. "Mother told me how bad my words were. I didn't know. I was angry and remembered those words, and they came out."

"Reckon it can happen that way," Jake said noncommittally.

"Mother told me what half-breed meant. And why it is an insult when said in anger and with the other word too." Jack struggled not to cry. "I was wrong to say it."

Jake just nodded. He thought the boy was doing fine without his helping him.

Jack took a breath then. "Mother wouldn't tell me what the other word meant. She said it was a disgusting word for something that should be beautiful. She told me I'd have to ask some man what it meant because she wouldn't say it."

Jake laughed at that, breaking the tension between them. "Your ma is a pretty smart woman," Jake said. "Take her advice, and don't use that word."

"Have you ever used that word, Uncle Jake?"

Jake chuckled at that. "I reckon most all men and even some women get around to using that word at some point. It isn't something I'd say in polite company, that's for sure. But there have been times," he thought about that. "There have been times of anger or stress where it slips out. Not too much different to how it did with you."

"Is it really as bad a word as Mother says it is?" Jack inquired.

Jake grinned at the boy. "Tell you what, when you start thinking that girls are pretty and interesting, you ask me again what it means, and we can talk about it then. You are too young."

"I am not ever going to think girls are interesting!" Jack exclaimed.

"You are ten years old. That will change," Jake laughed. "For now, just don't use that word, or I'll help your mother wash your mouth out with soap." Jake turned to his horse, untying it.

"Uncle Jake?" Jack said softly. "Will you ever love me again?"

Jake stepped into the stirrup, mounting easily. He looked down on the boy. "I never quit loving you, Jack. I was angry, but I'll always love you."

"I love you too, Uncle Jake," the boy said softly.

Jake nodded, then reined his horse around, and started for home. He had two more horses to ride that day. Time was getting away from him.

Molly watched Luke like a hawk the rest of the day. Sometimes, there was no movement in Luke's face, and then there were periods when his eyelids fluttered, and once, his eyes opened for a brief moment. Molly called out to Luke then, but there was no response. But hope was alive. She had to believe that these were good signs.

Just before dawn the next day, she was awakened from her cot by the thrashing coming from Luke's bed. She was at his side in an instant, trying to calm him as he struggled, arms and legs jerking.

"Luke! Wake up," she called to him.

Suddenly, he quieted, then slowly turned his head towards her, his eyes open. "Water," he whispered.

Molly had a glass nearby and helped lift Luke just enough that she could put the glass to his lips. He drank greedily, water running down his chin. Then, as if that was all the strength he had, he went slack again, falling back into a stupor. But Molly knew, and in her heart, she rejoiced. Luke was coming back. The journey might be longer than she wanted, but she was a patient woman. Luke was coming back to her.

Molly ate breakfast in her room, keeping a close vigil on Luke. She heard the kitchen door slam and running feet coming her way. Jack burst into the room, excitement brimming in his features.

"Mother, the mule is gone!" he shouted excitedly.

"Did you leave a gate open last night?" Molly asked distractedly.

"No, it was latched," Jack said. "But there is a Twin Peaks horse in the corral with your horse."

Molly smiled fondly at her son. "Guess your Uncle Jake decided to trust you again," she said softly. "You better live up to his expectations this time."

"I will, Mother. I will for sure!" Jack responded happily. "Can I ride over and thank him?"

Molly nodded, looking fondly at her son. She had known that, eventually, Jake would forgive the boy. It was a great day for Jack to be taken into his uncle's fold again. As she sat thinking about this, she heard Luke whisper behind her.

"Things seem to be working out," he murmured.

Molly whirled around to face him. Luke's eyes were open, and he had a slight smile on his lips.

"They are now," Molly replied, her smile wide. "Things arc definitely working out now."

Luke's recovery was not instant. At times, he despaired at how weak he was, but Molly kept his spirits up, working with him as much as he could stand. At first, he was exhausted, hardly able to stay awake to eat a meal. When he first sat up in bed, swinging his feet over the side, he was struck by a sudden dizziness that left him weaving until he laid back down and almost instantly fell back asleep. However, each day, he got better, and almost a week later, Luke was able to stand and walk to the parlor. Collapsing in a chair, he fell instantly asleep.

But once he gained some strength, his condition improved dramatically until, after two weeks, he was awake most of the day, even helping out a little. With Jack's help, he dragged a stool out by the woodpile. There he stood or sat, chopping small branches into kindling. When the dizziness struck him, he would stagger to the stool and sit, head in hands until it passed. He persevered, and gained strength each day, and the dizzy spells became farther apart.

The ranch was readying for the fall gather, and Luke wanted to go. Five days before the crew was going to leave, Luke saddled a horse and mounted. Instantly, he became so light-headed that he had to grab the saddle horn to avoid falling off. Molly, who was with him, grabbed his leg to help support him.

"Help me off, Molly," Luke whispered, dragging himself down. He stood next to the animal, leaning into it for support. After a pause, Luke said softly, "Well, reckon I'm not going to fall gather."

Two days later, Thomas rode up to Molly's big house. He tied his horse to the rail and stomped up the stairs. Lydia heard him coming and let him in.

"The missus and Luke are in the kitchen," she said.

Thomas found the two of them at the kitchen table, nursing cups of coffee. They looked up and smiled at their visitor.

"Come to see when the invalid is going to work again?" Luke smiled, not entirely joking.

"Actually, Jake and I thought I should see if the two of you want to come to fall gather with us?" Thomas smiled.

"Nothing we would like better," Luke said wistfully, "but I have tried for three days to ride a horse. When my feet leave this earth, it gets to spinning away from me."

"So, I have heard," Thomas replied, accepting a cup of coffee from Lydia and sitting at the table. "I had in mind for you both to ride up with Punch in the wagon. He's cooking this year, but he could use some help."

Luke looked at Molly, who nodded. "We could probably do that," Luke said. "Might be nice to be up in the high country when we don't have to chase rustlers."

"Well, it's settled then. You two and Punch can cook, and there are always other chores around to do," Thomas said. "And here's another thing. We got some of the kids going with us. The boys have been pestering me for a couple of years to go with us, but I haven't wanted to have a passel of kids with us unless there was a woman to help with them."

Molly smiled at that. "We always went as kids, didn't we?" she said. "I can't remember when I didn't go. I think Ma took me in a cradleboard. How many boys are you taking?"

"I put my foot down on those younger than nine," Thomas said. "So those going would be Sam's TJ, Lathe's Slade and John Henry, and Jack if you are fine with that." Thomas grinned before continuing, "Jenny is too young this year, but Jake's Kestrel and James and Mary's Alice are going."

Molly smiled back at her brother. "Jack can go, and I'll leave Grace with Lydia. So that's four boys and two girls. Should be fun for them."

"Then there is Noah and Emmett too, but they have both been to fall gather for many years. I don't think of them as kids anymore," Thomas added.

"How old are Mary's stepsons?" Molly inquired.

"Noah is nineteen now. He turned into such a good man," Thomas answered. "And Emmett is fifteen and hounding James to move to the bunkhouse with his brother. He will turn sixteen this winter, and I think James will let him. They are good additions to our ranch. I've always been glad James brought that family home."

"I know the story," Molly observed, "but I haven't gotten to know James's family that well. But I will. That is on my list of things to do. It just takes time."

So, it was decided that Luke and Molly would ride the supply wagon to the mountain shack and help Punch. Jack would be riding his new horse, and a second horse was cut out for him in the remuda. The boys might go with them, but they were expected to work while they were there.

As Thomas finished his coffee and stood to leave, he paused at the door, looking back at his sister and brother-in-law. "Hell, maybe you two can have a second honeymoon up there. Punch is bringing a tent, and all the kids are excited to camp out. You'll have the shack to yourself," he said, grinning wickedly at the couple. Thomas turned and left, leaving Molly and Luke smiling. They liked that thought.

CHAPTER 16

Second Honeymoon – October 1887

It was a brilliant, warm fall day when the crew started up the mountain and headed to the shack to start the fall gathering. While everyone knew that mountain weather could be unpredictable anytime, extra care had to be taken during the fall. For that reason, the wagon was loaded with supplies and piled high with tarps, sleeping gear, and winter wear. It might be warm this day, but there was no guarantee that would last. Even on warm fall days, the nights were cold. Extra blankets were a necessity.

Molly enjoyed the ride up the mountain. Wedged between Punch and Luke on the wagon seat, she enjoyed their stories. Before he had a crippling accident, Punch was a top cowpuncher. He had worked on several spreads over the years breaking horses. It wasn't an easy job. Most ranches other than Twin Peaks started their horses as four- or five-year-olds. Most of the horses had never even been halter broke. These horses were big, wild, and just plain broncs. This was one reason Jake wanted Molly to work with the young horses. It made the young animals easier to start under saddle, and it made them better horses in the end.

"I recollect one big five-year-old I was starting," Punch said. "He was stout and a real spook. I rode him for almost a month before I could get him used to me swinging a rope on him. So, one day, I figured it was time to latch onto something. I see a pretty good log with a broken branch, so I took aim and roped it." Punch stopped talking long enough to spit a stream of tobacco off the side of the wagon. "I stopped this colt and had him face that log and I jest tugged the rope a little to make the log move. That colt's head like to near come off, he raised it so high. But he stood his ground, so I jest thought I'd give it a little jerk agin. The colt jumped, but he kept facing that log. Now, I should have jest called it a day and let the log go, but I figured I'd do it one more time. I give that log a big jerk, and that colt come unglued.

"He whirled and ran. But when he whirled, he turned into the rope. That shortened the distance between the log and the backside of the colt. That doggone log comes flying at us, nipping at the horse's hind legs." Punch paused to spit. "I was trying to take my dally off, but when the colt whirled, the rope not only was around the colt's chest, but it jammed my dally. We were in a wooded area, an' I was a watchin' fer branches coming at me an' the log swinging behind us an' it was a wild ride for sure.

"Suddenly, I missed duckin', an' I took a branch in my gut. Off I went. I had the foresight to hold onto the reins like my life depended on it, but it was some dicey as the horse dragged me an' the log for longer than I wanted. I finally got the horse stopped an' in the melee the rope comes lose lettin' that log go. I was scratched up, sore all over, an' sportin' a big black eye an' cut lip. I rode that colt back an' told the boss, 'I don't reckon' this horse will make a cow horse.' I don't know what happened to the animal, but I never rode him again."

Luke chuckled at the picture that came to mind of Punch's wild ride. "That is why I like to ride the horses Jake, Lathe, and Hawk have well started," Luke said. "I surely love a talented horse and don't mind working with a horse to teach him, but I leave the bronc riding to others if I can."

The trip to the mountain shack was pleasant, and Molly was almost sorry it ended. Listening to Punch and Luke talk about their past life and stories of the West made the trip go by quickly, but eventually, the wagon came out on the upland meadow with the shack in the distance. Fall gather was indeed starting.

All the men and kids got busy pitching tents when the wagon pulled up to the shack, and they unloaded their gear. Molly, Luke, and Punch unloaded the food supplies into the cabin and left the bedrolls of the riders for them to sort out when the tents were secured. Molly and Luke were the only ones using the cabin for sleeping, which, with the second honeymoon idea, suited them just fine.

Punch started a campfire, and the three cooks got a meal prepared. The weather was so nice the whole contingent sat around the campfire after eating. This was what Molly enjoyed the most about fall gather. When the work was done, everyone sat around the campfire, reminiscing about days gone by, telling stories, and planning the next day's activities. The young'uns were sent to their tents first, and then the group broke up soon after. Morning would come early, and there were many miles to cover to gather cattle.

Molly had coffee ready early in the cabin while Punch and Luke started breakfast over the campfire. Horses were caught up and saddled, breakfast eaten hastily, and crews were divided up to go out in different directions looking for cattle. It was a beautiful morning, crisp but sunny. It was a perfect day to ride in the mountains. But that was to change very quickly.

A pall came over the cabin before ten that morning. Molly looked up from where she was peeling potatoes and glanced out the window. The sky was darkening, big threatening clouds coming over the treetops. She got up and went outside to the porch, Luke and Punch following behind.

"This isn't good," Luke said quietly. They all knew how treacherous storms could be in the mountains.

"And the temperature has dropped," Molly said. "I am glad I made the kids take heavy coats."

"If I remember right, they argued about that," Luke grinned.

"They did, and maybe if I weren't here, no one would have given it a thought," Molly answered.

"Every man that rode out has a slicker and heavy coat," Luke commented.

"I know, but they are grown men and know what the mountains are like," Molly continued. "Kids think they are invincible to whatever is thrown at them until it happens. When they come home, I bet they will tell me they are glad I insisted on coats."

As they stood, watching the darkening sky, the first fat snowflakes began to fall. The snow was wet and came straight down, silent in the stillness of the meadow.

"I hope this doesn't last," Molly murmured. "I don't like the idea of anyone out on snow-covered mountain slopes, especially children."

"Jake divided up the kids between the men," Punch injected. "They will take care of the kids." But both men knew that Molly had reason to be worried.

The snow did last, coming down harder and harder as the day went on. By noon, the heavy, wet snow was caving in the tents. Punch and Luke went out and brought in all the bedrolls and packs to keep them dry. Luke went out for hours chopping wood as the temperature continued to plummet. Molly and Punch had a big pot of soup simmering on the cookstove and dough rising for bread. When the men came in, they would want something warm to eat.

By dusk, Molly was pacing the cabin, unable to control her concern for Jack and the rest of the men and children. Luke and Punch attempted to comfort her, but it was no use. It was a great relief when they heard the catcalls and war hoops of a group bringing in the first of the cattle. Pulling on coats, the three rushed outside.

Sam and James led the first crew in, and they had the young boys with them. Luke and Punch collected the horses from the boys and sent them right inside to warm up. Before they even got the horses unsaddled and turned out, Army, Thomas, Emmett, and Noah came in, Alice and Kestrel with them. That only left Jake, Lathe, and Swift Hawk still out.

"We hadn't split up when the clouds began to roll in," Thomas said. "Jake figured he'd better go as far as possible today and bring back what he could in case it snowed. So, those three may be late." Thomas could see his sister, while relieved the children were accounted for, was still concerned. "Don't worry, Sis. Those three are as comfortable in the mountains as the rest of us are in our beds. They will be in directly."

But Jake, Lathe, and Hawk weren't in directly. The rest of the hands had been fed and found space to sit on the floor of the shack and eat. The cabin smelled of wet clothes and food, intermingled with wood smoke and pipe tobacco. The children had all gone to the bedroom to find places to sit on the floor and beds. The adults could hear them laughing and giggling about their day.

Even without Jake, Lathe, and Hawk, it was wall-to-wall bodies in the little cabin. The men told stories and reminisced quietly, but all ears were tuned to outside, hoping to hear the whoops and yells of men pushing cattle. It was three hours past dark when they heard them, and as one body, they rose and went out to greet the incoming men and take care of their horses. Jake, Hawk, and Lathe stumbled into the cabin, snow-crusted and cold, but otherwise unharmed. Shrugging out of their coats, they found hot food and a place to sit and warm up on the floor.

"This came up too fast to predict," Jake said, shaking his head. "We got out to the northwest, and I think we got everything in from there. We left half of what we had gathered at Crystal Lake. We will have to send a crew to check there tomorrow. It was dark by the time we got to the lake, and I wasn't too keen on pushing cattle through the narrows, but some of those old cows came on anyway. We couldn't stop them, so we just tried to thin out the followers."

"We are going to have to start what we have in the meadow down to the ranch tomorrow," Thomas said. "This meadow is already so snow-packed that these cows won't get much feed."

Jake nodded, chewing on a piece of hot bread. "Send the boys back with them," he said. "Pa is going to have to start feeding hay, and he only has Jeremiah and Matthew to help. The boys are old enough to help feed hay."

Thomas nodded agreement, then looked at Noah and Emmett. "You two go with the little boys back to the ranch. Noah, I need you to help with the feeding down there, but Emmett, you ask Kade to find the runners for the buckboard. Pack them on a mule and bring them back tomorrow afternoon. I don't think we will get the wagon back down to the ranch unless we take the wheels off and replace them with the runners." Thomas hesitated momentarily, then added, "You boys, be careful going down that trail. It can get slick with this wet snow. Don't push the cattle too fast either, especially where the side hills are really steep."

No one wanted to stay up late that night. The children were sent to the bedroom to find room on the floor for their bedrolls. The two girls shared Molly's double bed with her, and Luke, Jake, and Thomas put blankets in the bedroom beside the boys. The youngsters were asleep in an instant, the cold and long day taking its toll. Molly climbed into the bed with the two sleeping girls, and Luke bedded down just below the bed. The shack became quiet except for some snores coming from the other room. It was in this stillness that Thomas spoke.

"Hey, Sis," he whispered.

"Hmmm?" Molly replied sleepily.

"How is this second honeymoon working for you?"

Molly had to chuckle softly at that. "I think I am going to give up on honeymoons after this one. They never seem to turn out as I expect."

"At least we aren't getting shot at this time," Luke said from the floor.

"Good point," Jake grinned in the dark. "Always something to be thankful for."

Morning broke, but no sun shown on the new fallen snow. The snow had stopped for now, but the clouds above looked like more could come. The men helped the boys get small groups of cattle started down the trail toward the ranch. Every now and then a rider would follow the cattle down to make sure none would turn around and come back. Most of the old cows knew the routine and that feed waited for them below at the ranch, but some of the young stock might turn, which could be a mess on the narrow wagon trail.

The rest of the men bundled up and headed off in all directions. If the snow began again, getting around on the mountain slopes would be harder and even more dangerous. The men had discussed it the night before and knew that any cattle left behind in the mountains had little chance of living through the winter or coming off the high country on their own. It was crucial to get the livestock home.

It was a long day waiting for the men to return. Molly paced a lot, watching out the shack window. When snow began to fall again in the afternoon, the tension in the cabin was intense. Luke spent a good portion of the day out with the extra remuda, pitching out some of the precious hay to them. He chopped wood and carried it to the shack. He tried to dig out some of the tents and drag the wet canvases to the lean-to, but the snow was wet and heavy, and he quit before he was half-done. The tents would be there when the snow melted in the spring.

Punch and Molly had a stew warming all day, and bread was baked by mid-afternoon. Molly made some cookies, and Punch soaked dried apples and made a pan of apple crisp. There would be plenty of warm food for the men when they returned. It was late afternoon when Emmett came back with runners for the wagon, and Luke bundled up again and went out to take off the wagon wheels and fit the runners to the wagon. Whenever the wagon returned to the ranch, it would need the runners on to get through the snow.

Groups of men began returning just before dark, but it was almost an hour after dark when the last bunch of men came hooting and hollering to the shack. Luke shrugged on his coat and went out to help. He came in soon after with Army supported between himself and Thomas.

"What happened?" Molly exclaimed when she saw Army. Under the crust of snow, she could see Army was pale, his face in a grimace.

"Horse went down on the narrows," Army got out. "I think my leg is broken."

Molly helped Army out of his wraps, and the men took Army in and laid him gently in the bed.

"Let Sam look at that leg when he gets in," Thomas said. "Think he has the most experience with such as that since he is married to Martha."

When Sam got in, he agreed with Army that the leg was broken. "Guess you are going home early, cowboy," Sam said. "I'm going to give you some of our whiskey, and hopefully, it will knock you out. I kin put a half-assed splint on it to keep it still, but Martha will have to look at that leg when you get down. She will know what to do. "

There was no question about trying to transport Army in the wagon down the trail in the dark, so the little girls and Molly joined Luke and the rest on the floor, and they spent a restless night listening to Army, alternating singing a drunken song, or moaning quietly in his sleep. Most of the shack's occupants were waiting for the morning light, wanting to get the next day started and one day closer to going home.

"Molly," Jake said in the morning, "Punch will take Army in the wagon to the ranch today. If there is trouble on the trail, Punch can handle it. Army needs to get some attention before it's too late. We will send Punch and Army off before we start any cattle down. I'll send the girls home too. I don't want the girls riding up here in all this snow. They can help push the cattle down to the ranch and then go to their homes. You can do the cooking, right?"

Molly nodded, "Luke can help." But she turned questioning eyes to Luke. "How will you get home if the wagon is gone?" she asked.

"I'm done with cooking," Luke said quietly. "You don't need me anyway. I will use Army's string of horses and go out with the men to help gather. With Army and Noah gone too, we are getting shorthanded, and frankly, I'm tired of being an invalid."

"Luke," Molly raised worried eyes to his, "what if you get a dizzy spell out there? What if you are on a narrow ridge and that happens?"

"Then I'll do what Jake always tells me to do," Luke answered calmly. "I'll hold on like hell and trust my horse."

"It's not safe," Molly argued.

Luke gave his wife a solemn look before answering. "Honey, when we went after the rustlers, didn't I want you to stay back because it wasn't safe? What did you say to me then?"

Molly shook her head, not wanting to give in.

"You said not to tell me what to do or how to act," Luke said patiently. "I am only asking for the same. I can do this. I have to work through this head injury, and sitting in a cabin cooking is not doing it for me. I'll be careful. Trust me on that. One of these days, maybe we will get a full-fledged honeymoon. I want to be there when we do."

"I'm done with honeymoons," Molly gave a defeated smile, "but you better come home safe so we can start a real life together."

Luke nodded. He gave Molly a brief kiss on her forehead, and taking his winter wraps from a peg on the wall, he turned and left the cabin. Molly watched him go, knowing that she still had a lot to worry about before this fall gather was done.

The gather went on for three more cold, snowy days. The men came in exhausted each night, but there were no more injuries. Cattle have a way of moving down when the weather is stormy, while horses are the opposite. On the plains, in a blizzard, cattle will often move into ravines and gullies looking for shelter, and if the snows are deep, the animals can get covered with snow and freeze or suffocate. A horse will stay on the prairie looking for trees to back up to for protection. Ranchers say that the cattle are dumb then and horses are smart. But in the high country, a loose horse may climb higher into the mountains. They can get into too much snow and get stuck in the high country. A cow, on the other hand, will move toward lower elevations. That tendency of cows to move lower helped the gather. The animals came out of the high meadows and in the new snow, their tracks, once the snow quit falling, were easy to discern and follow.

By the end of three more days, Jake and Thomas were pretty sure they had all of the cattle. With relief, the shack was packed up for the year, supplies loaded on extra horses to haul to ranch headquarters. Molly took one more glance around the cabin and drew on her winter wraps. Luke had her horse saddled and ready when she pulled the door shut and secured it against bears.

"Well, Mrs. Brooks," Luke said, grinning at his wife, "honeymoon two is history. Let's go home."

Molly smiled at Luke and nodded. She reached out a gloved hand to him, and he grasped it. "You are feeling good?" Molly asked.

"Didn't have a dizzy spell all yesterday," Luke said seriously. "I'll probably have to watch for them for a while, but I think whatever was causing them is healing. I think I'm good. Let's go home, honey. Let's start life together."

Molly smiled at that, and they turned their horses away from the shack. Leading the packhorses, they moved across the mountain meadow and started down the trail toward home. The snow was white and glistened in the fall sunshine following the storm. It was a cold, beautiful landscape that bid them farewell for the year.

CHAPTER 17

Freedom - Early December 1887

Molly looked out the kitchen window and saw Jack riding home from the ranch headquarters. The countryside was coated with snow, but there was a good trail to the ranch made by both Jack and Luke on their daily trips to work. It was not even midafternoon, so it was early for Jack to be returning. Usually, he left and returned with Luke, helping the men with the cattle.

Jack was settling in well at the ranch now, helping with chores before going to school with the other boys. Jack also accepted Luke in his mother's life. He called Luke by his name, which was fine with Molly. Jack remembered and loved Jackson as "Father" while Grace had little memory of her late father. Jack wasn't ready for another "father" in his life, but he didn't seem to mind Luke in the family. Jack liked Luke, and his resentment of Luke's taking his dead father's place never surfaced again. That was enough for Molly. For Grace, Luke was her daddy, and she watched for him to walk into the house, little arms raised toward him for a ride on his shoulders.

"Jack's coming home early," Molly spoke to Lydia. "Maybe nothing is going on at the ranch."

Lydia looked up from the counter, peering out the window. "He doesn't look in any sort of hurry. Probably just quitting early."

The two women continued their task together as they watched Jack approach the house. Molly was so grateful for Lydia in her life. Middle-aged, Lydia was a widow with no children. She became Molly's friend as well as helper. She knew just when Molly and Luke needed their time together. Usually, when the children went to bed, Lydia would go up to her little rooms and leave the newlyweds alone. But many nights, Punch would drive up in his buggy, which was now outfitted with runners for the winter. On those nights, the cards came out, and the foursome played some pretty rowdy games.

Molly watched Jack approach and waited. They would know soon enough if he was just quitting early. Jack rode to the porch steps and tied his horse to the railing before coming to the kitchen door.

"Mother," Jack said, poking his head in, "Luke and Uncle Jake want you to come ride with us. The buffalo are out."

"Really?" Molly was excited. She hadn't seen the buffalo for months since early summer when she rode into their valley and skirted them as they grazed. She looked questioningly at Lydia.

"You go," Lydia said. "I'll listen for Grace to wake from her nap. I can clean up the kitchen by myself."

Molly smiled gratefully at the older woman. Lydia was part of the family by now as a nanny, friend, and helper. Molly couldn't imagine what she would do without this calm woman living with them.

"Go gather my horse, Jack," Molly said, "and I will go change and bundle up."

It turned out to be more than just Luke and Jake riding out to see the buffalo. Thomas, Luke, Kade, Swift Hawk, Jake, and Kestrel were waiting at the trading post. Their horses were tied to the hitch rail while they waited for Molly in the store's warmth.

"About time," Thomas teased when Molly rode up.

"Well, let's make tracks then," Molly retorted, smiling. "Is this the first day the buffalo have been out on the river valley?"

The men swung on their horses, and they all headed up the trail to the west. "They were out waiting with the steers this morning when we got there with the hay wagon," Luke answered. "We've been watching for them."

"I've taken bundles of hay up their ravine, trying to lure them out," Jake said. "Leave a bundle a little closer to the river bottom, and finally, out they came."

The little group rode quietly then, each in their thoughts, until they began to see the cattle ahead, strung out in a line, eating the remnants of the morning feeding. Jake led them off to the south, keeping downwind from the cattle. They didn't want to spook the buffalo.

They first saw the same three animals from the winter before, two cows and one yearling bull calf. Now, one of the two cows had a calf at her side. All three of the older buffalo were filled out and looked healthy. They weren't the starved-out animals they first saw last winter.

"They look good," Molly said. "But only one cow must have had a calf."

"They were in pretty poor shape last winter," Kade retorted. "That other cow may not have bred back last year, or maybe she lost the calf. I'm hoping they have both bred back this summer to that young bull. I like the idea of building a herd of them up."

Swift Hawk sat, silent and grave, watching the buffalo eating the wisps of hay. He looked over to Kade before speaking. "I remember buffalo as far as the eye could see," he said softly. "I remember the buffalo hunts. We will never see those days again. I too, want these buffalo to live. Like the Utes, they have been driven off or killed. It is good we protect these."

"Can we go closer?" Kestrel asked.

Jake looked at his daughter and nodded. "I don't want you going off alone. These are still wild animals, and a buffalo cow can be dangerous. Follow me, and we will circle them."

Jake moved off, Swift Hawk and Kestrel following. Jack looked at his mother and then Luke. "You coming too, Luke?" he asked.

Luke grinned and nodded. He glanced at Molly, and she waved her hand at him. Kade was content to sit on the rise and watch, and Molly was content to wait with her father.

"This is a good thing, isn't it, Pa?" she asked. Her father nodded.

"But don't you wonder if the buffalo miss the freedom they used to have?" Molly pressed.

Kade pondered the question. "I don't think these animals really think about freedom in the same terms we do. Reckon they just want enough food an' room to wander. They have room up that ravine an' in the mountain meadow yonder."

"But you have the ravine closed off in the summer, so they can't come out," Molly persisted. "Do you think they wish they were out on the plains with the freedom to go anywhere?"

"Reckon if they want out that bad, they could climb the big slopes and go over the top."

"So, you think they feel free even though they aren't?"

Kade gave his daughter an inquiring look. "Daughter, freedom isn't all about doin' whatever you want or goin' wherever you want," he said gravely. "Take me for instance. In my trappin' days, Old Tom an' I went when an' where we wanted, but we knew places we shouldn't go an' we stayed away. We knew better than to go into the Blackfeet country. Freedom always had borders. When I married yer ma, I had to change. I didn't feel less free 'cause I chose to live with her an' you young'uns. I always felt free, just lived my life differently."

"So, we are all free then?" Molly asked.

"I reckon that depends on what you want."

Molly nodded, thinking. "I guess I want what I have now with Luke. I am happy again."

"Then, honey," Kade smiled at his daughter, "I reckon you are free." He nodded then, watching the bison, thinking. "I reckon we are all free."

ACKNOWLEDGEMENTS

A special thank you to my sister-in-law, Dayna Beckman, for helping me edit this manuscript and get it polished enough to send to my publisher. Without her help, the editors at W. Brand would be finding a lot more errors!

A big thank you to all my friends and followers who encourage me to keep writing my stories. I didn't intend to be a writer, but I had these stories in my head that needed to come out.

Finally, thank you, JuLee Brand and W. Brand Publishing for designing the beautiful covers and helping me see my stories in print. This has certainly been a journey for me and I appreciate all your help in seeing these stories become books.

Johny Weber is a retired assistant professor at Northern State University in Aberdeen, SD. Since childhood, her life has revolved around horses. Marrying a rodeo cowboy, she moved with him to the plains of South Dakota where they both competed in rodeos and then turned to a ranching lifestyle.

Her career in education began by teaching first grade in 1975 and by retirement, she was teaching graduate courses to teachers in a state-funded program. Johny and her late husband raised a son and daughter on the prairies of the Cheyenne River Indian Reservation.

She now enjoys time spent with her children and grandchildren and traveling with her horse and dog to ride the mountains of the west in the summer and the deserts of the southwest in the winter.

Also available by Johny Weber

the Rodeo Road

the *Mountain Series* collection

Book One, *Mountain Refuge* Book Two, *Mountain Grown*

Book Three, *Mountain Ranch*

www.ingramcontent.com/pod-product-compliance
Lightning Source LLC
Chambersburg PA
CBHW020430030726
47495CB00006B/1734